Great Novels
of
Erotic Domination
and Submission

NEW TITLES EVERY MONTH

www.smbooks.co.uk

TO FIND OUT MORE ABOUT OUR READERS' CLUB WRITE TO;
SILVER MOON READER SERVICES;
Suite 7, Mayden House,
Long Bennington Business Park,
Newark NG23 5DJ
Tel; 01400 283488

YOU WILL RECEIVE A FREE MAGAZINE OF EXTRACTS FROM OUR EXTENSIVE RANGE OF EROTIC FICTION ABSOLUTELY FREE. YOU WILL ALSO HAVE THE CHANCE TO PURCHASE BOOKS WHICH ARE EXCLUSIVE TO OUR READERS' CLUB

***

NEW AUTHORS ARE WELCOME
Please send submissions to;
The Editor; Silver Moon books
Suite 7, Long Bennington Business Park
Newark NG23 5DJ

Tel: 01400 283 488

Copyright
This edition published 2011

The right of Holly Cartwright to be identified as the author of this book has been asserted in accordance with Section 77 and 78 of the Copyright and Patents Act 1988. All rights reserved.

ISBN 9781908252098

All characters and events depicted are entirely fictitious; any resemblance to anyone living or dead is entirely coincidental

THIS IS FICTION. IN REAL LIFE ALWAYS PRACTISE SAFE SEX

Marie's Masters

by

Holly Cartwright

CHAPTER 1

Marie stepped from the shower and quickly wrapped a towel around her body and full, pert breasts. Another towel was wrapped around her long brown hair before she slid her rectangular framed glasses on. She unlocked the bathroom door and listened to ensure nobody was out on the landing before exiting briskly and through another door to her boyfriend's bedroom.

Within the bedroom her boyfriend, Martin, was laid on the bed wearing only his boxer shorts. His hands were linked behind his head and his eyes were fixed affectionately and lustfully on the exposed flesh of his girlfriend.

She began to look over the open suitcase and bags that were on the bedroom floor.

"You've packed everything and checked everything so stop worrying," Martin said, admiring the view of her rear as she bent over and sorted through the bags.

"I'm looking for my pyjamas," she replied, a slight hint of sharpness discernible in her voice.

Martin located them beneath the pillow beside him and dutifully threw them to her. Thinking over this cooperative act he realised that he had chosen the wrong course of action. He was making it harder to achieve his goal of naked, passionate sex with her.

Marie began drying herself, removing the towel that was wrapped around her and delicately dabbing over her naked body. Martin had set himself up intently to watch this and was already revelling in the view, with Marie seemingly oblivious to his fixed attention.

What he admired was a young girl of twenty years, naked before of him. Her beautiful pale flesh was smooth and firm. The sweep of her thighs round her hips and into her waist was full and feminine. At her stomach there was the slightest suggestion of roundness, but it was firm and perfectly smooth. Below was a dark full mound of hair that tucked neatly and delicately into the soft fresh space between her thighs. Her breasts were the delight of her body, round and pert but with the most perfect suggestion of weightiness to them. Her slender shoulders and neck led to a round and soft featured face with brown eyes and a look of youthful innocence in every expression. At her back she was able to appear even more feminine, her curves amplified by the lovely round ripeness of her buttocks.

As Marie lifted her leg to dry her thigh Martin centred his gaze on the delicate pink flesh between her legs and felt instantly the rush of arousal start his cock slowly swelling.

"Have you set your alarm?" she asked him as she opened up her pyjama bottoms.

"Yes," he replied absently, for his attention was soaking up every glimpse of intimate flesh that was given. His thoughts were beginning to grow more animated now and he found himself thinking how much he would like to push her against the wall, heave both her legs up high and wide, and force his hardness in her vigorously before exploding onto her breasts like they did in pornographic films.

Having pulled on her pyjamas she ran a brush through her hair and once again surveyed her bags. Content enough she came to the bed and climbed over Martin, whose eyes watched her hungrily, and put herself beneath the sheets.

Martin's hands moved from behind his head and started stroking over the fine young body of his girlfriend, touching her bottom, the backs of her thighs and cupping a breast as she curled up next to him. For

Marie this was the usual conduct at night as she prepared for bed. Martin would touch her first affectionately and then more overtly sexually hoping that he could stir her towards consenting to have sex with him. He was rarely ever successful, however, as the touches over her bum, her breasts and sometimes forcing themselves between her legs did nothing to arouse her. They were an annoyance because when she went to bed she wanted to go to sleep.

It wasn't that she didn't love Martin. She loved him very much. She also found him attractive, sexually attractive, as he had a well conditioned, strong body. It was a sexual attraction that didn't often convert into the urge to have sex, however. They had had plenty when first together, both virgins, and she maybe even enjoyed it then. She had even initiated it at times. That passion had naturally eased. It had to, as Marie saw it, so that you could concentrate on doing well in your studies and interviews and in your career. Plus, penetrative sex had nearly always hurt her. Martin claimed it was because she got too uptight and nervous. He was right, though she never allowed him the satisfaction of knowing he was. When it came to sex she became very conscious of her own actions, very inhibited by the act of being sexually intimate. She would physically tighten so that, not only was penetrative sex painful for her, it was often impossible to achieve.

As Martin's hands continued over her, despite her cold response, she realised she must make some concession to his needs. In the morning she would be leaving for a new town and her first proper job working in a museum. It would mean her and Martin spending more time apart than they had ever done in their four years together. The prospect of prolonged physical separation meant Martin would need something of a 'goodbye kiss'. It had been a while since he had been allowed any type of 'kiss' so she felt an obligation.

Full sex she was not going to permit as she had showered ready for an early start tomorrow. She turned over in the bed until she was facing him and slipped her hand down under his boxer shorts and lightly took his penis into her fingers.

His response was instant. A sigh of pleasure at the contact came from deep within. The flaccid flesh she had taken into her hand was responding quickly, with no effort from her, growing in length and width until she had hold of his full erection, hard and hot and throbbing slowly in her hand as though willing her to action.

To allow better access Martin wriggled out of his boxer shorts and then turned onto his side slightly to face Marie. He kissed her eagerly, his tongue on her pursed lips, but felt a tepid enthusiasm reciprocated. He slid a hand beneath her pyjama top and gently fondled her breasts, rubbing his thumb over her nipples.

Marie built up the pace of her hand's movement from a gentle up and down of Martin's generously proportioned shaft to a quick handed pumping of his cock that had him gasping uncontrollably. A small amount of pre-come began to ease from the hard tip of his dick and Marie used her thumb to smear it over his cock's swollen head. It lubricated the quick motion of her hand and excited him massively until he was soon ready to explode.

Marie knew it was approaching the end because Martin was attempting to pull her pyjama top up over her breasts in the misguided hope that she would allow him to shoot his come over them. She had allowed this in the past but found it distasteful now and manoeuvred herself so that Martin was laid on his back. With her breasts covered again, and free of his groping, she turned her pumping of his cock up in speed until his accelerated panting and stiffening of his limbs intimated that he was seconds from coming. She quickened her pace further still, a furious pumping up and down his rock solid shaft until she heard him emit a low deep groan and felt the pulsing of come firing up through his length. It shot out far over his chest and stomach. She could see it firing out, thick and creamy in colour. It kept coming, still more as she pumped at his dick as hard and as fast as her hand would go until the last tame spurts emerged from his throbbing tip to coat her fingers in his sticky fluid, the evidence of his satisfaction.

She released him and wiped the come that was on her hand and between her fingers onto his boxer shorts. She then handed them to Martin so that he could wipe himself clean and rolled over to fall asleep. After a quick wipe Martin did the same, putting out the light and wrapping his arm around her.

Marie found herself thinking actively while she tried to sleep. She dwelt on the act she had just performed. Inside her there were terribly mixed emotions. Part of her wanted to make Martin happy in all things while another part of her found something unseemly in sex, or giving blow jobs, or even what she had just done.

A big part of her problem with sex was the aftermath, she realised. She always felt shame at being involved in the sort of behaviour that slutty girls revelled in. The shame was always there because, as she had felt a few minutes ago, in that instant when Martin exploded and she had felt his come running over her fingers, she had enjoyed it. At that precise moment she had wanted to be the dirty slut that enjoyed unseemly behaviour. Whenever she allowed sex or intimacy between them it was this feeling that invariably emerged and that made her feel very ashamed about how her mind worked. Whenever that feeling emerged, the desire towards the disgusting, depraved acts of common whores, she suppressed it mercilessly.

She felt it under her skin at all times, and attributed her constant highly strung nature to this fact. She felt it heightened when tossing Martin off, or the rare occasion when she let him inside her. It was a sluttishness that rose up and would betray her if she was not careful to deny it. It wanted her to lick the come from her fingers then kiss Martin wetly on the lips. It wanted to scoop up the come from his chest and smear it between her legs, pushing it past her lips while Martin wanked himself hard again. It wanted her to stand him up and for her to be on her knees sucking at his balls, licking his long shaft and to put his thick cock in her mouth until she felt his gushing semen, that huge amount of beautiful salty spunk, burst deep in the back of her throat. It wanted her to hold his ejaculation in her mouth and show it to Martin on her tongue. It wanted her to have pulled her pyjama top off when she was working his cock up and down and to take that blast of warm cock fluid all over her tits and to have lifted those tits to her mouth and licked every last drop of come off slowly while Martin watched with a look of ecstasy on his face. It wanted her to do all this but she never allowed herself to do any of it – or get anywhere near doing it. She ignored that urge because she knew that, if you did that kind of thing, you were a nasty slut. All a girl had was her reputation and doing that sort of thing gave you a bad one.

Marie was trying very hard to ignore it as she lay in the bed next to Martin, shamed by the thoughts that had already started to enter her head, embarrassed by the images some dark part of her thought acceptable. She tried to think of anything she could to displace those lewd thoughts but they were persistent and robust and her mind kept returning to the hand job and what she had really wanted to do. The images and the acts that appeared to her were incessant and urgent. They were starting to take hold of her physically as they sometimes were capable of doing. Her breasts felt more sensitive and full, her nipples hard and protruding embarrassingly, and the soft flesh between her legs was warming and moistening.

Unhappily she admitted defeat and climbed out of bed. Martin stirred slightly but did not enquire why she was getting up. She walked through to the bathroom, locked the door, and then removed her pyjama bottoms.

Standing by the sink Marie lifted her top up to expose her breasts. She lifted one leg up so that her foot was on the sink rim and turned so that she could see herself in the mirror. She was hugely aroused and she could see it clearly in the glistening pink flesh between her legs. Gripping her nipple with one hand she plunged the other into the broad gap made by her exposed position. It felt wonderful all through her. A huge wave of relief rolled over her just by that touch of her own flesh.

Her thoughts ran through the slutty behaviour she held within. She pictured herself handling Martin's stiff cock again. She was pumping it hard while she moved herself between his legs and sucked on his balls. She imagined him turning her over forcefully and how she would instantly get onto all fours and push her bum into the air, pushing herself back to invite him onto her. He would slap his hand over her bottom with a loud thwack and then again while, all the time, she tried to push out her cunt lips so that he would penetrate them. Then, with her bottom red from the force of his strike he would nudge his thick cock, searing hot, against the swollen and slippery lips of her throbbing hole.

Marie had her eyes shut. She vividly saw Martin holding his position against the entrance of her pussy, teasing her. He grabbed a fistful of her hair and, yanking her head back, he slammed his full length deep into her tight little hole. She imagined herself screaming out with the pain and the pleasure of such a forceful penetration.

The sensation of it was vivid in her as she worked her fingers up into her pussy, deep inside, her thumb rubbing hard over her clit that was so aroused it felt like it could burst. Her eyes closed even tighter, her fingers clamping down on her nipple as she pictured him at the back of her pumping in and out of her, hard and fast, with no regard for her pain, with only thoughts for the pleasure he derived from it. She wished it was real.

She heard herself in her head shouting out to him, so loud that his housemates would hear, or the neighbours and people in the street. She yelled at him to fuck her harder, telling him she wanted his come over her so bad, that she wanted to taste it and feel it blast warmly over her. She imagined his hand reaching round to squeeze her nipples so hard she would scream with pain and she saw her own hand reaching under her so that she could feel his balls as they pounded against her.

Stood in the bathroom Marie was reaching a fantastic state of arousal. She clamped a nipple between thumb and forefinger and twisted hard until the pain contorted her face and she had to fight to keep from screaming out. She held it there, the pain maintained through her. With the other hand she now worked the fourth finger inside her and started to thrust up inside her vigorously, her thumb still rubbing hard over her clit. The feeling through her was sublime. She was so close to climaxing that her whole body was starting to go into spasm. Her thoughts raged way beyond control.

She could feel Martin in her, forcing her down onto the bed with powerful, angry thrusts. She begged him to tell her when he was about to come. He gripped her nipples hard, pulling her breasts away while yanking her hair with his other hand, using his grip at these points to pull himself hard into her tight, sodden hole. She heard him call out. He was going to come. She quickly pulled herself forward off his glistening erection, turned to face him and started wanking his dick furiously as she put her lips and tongue to the tip. Her free hand cupped his balls. Soon she felt them contract and heard him shout out; "Take it all you little fucking slut!" and then the hot creamy come exploded out of his tip into her mouth, lashings of his beautiful spunk, and still more shooting into the back of her mouth, lingering on her lips and trickling slowly down her chin.

When she had every last drop of his climax in her mouth she imagined herself spitting it out into her hand. Some ran through her fingers, dripping onto the bed. As Martin watched, wanking his still hard cock slowly up and down, Marie spread her legs wide and rubbed the handful of come into her already wet cunt. She pushed it inside her hole with her fingers, rubbing its perfect wet stickiness over her lips and clit. Then, having fixed his attention, she pleasured herself hard and fast until the huge swell of ecstasy that was in her gathered between her legs. It formed as a pressure that hurt her deeply and then erupted beautifully through her, a massive relief, a convulsive, shaking pleasure that weakened her, giving her no power physically or mentally to do anything other than bask in her total satisfaction.

With the relief and the satisfaction there soon came a sense of shame. Her thrusting fingers, as she had pictured that act of depravity, had brought forth a powerful, deeply wrought orgasm, one that had emerged from so deep within her that she had actually squirted her juices onto the bathroom floor. Every emotion in her gave way to the heat of embarrassment. She cleaned up the mess with toilet paper before washing her fingers thoroughly to get rid of her smell and then slipping her pyjama bottoms back on.

Conscious that she had been engaged in this act for too long she returned to the bedroom as quietly as she could. Climbing onto the bed she felt Martin stir. He asked sleepily if everything was ok.

"Fine, just girl stuff," she replied, knowing that it was excuse enough to cover her absence.

She was in bed, willing herself to sleep. Her thoughts were slow to subside, however. She had to admit the intense physical pleasure of what she has just done. It had felt wonderful. That moment of climax was so powerful, a pleasure that was unique in life. But the pain she had now, of shame at her thoughts and embarrassment mixed with anger at the lack of control she had over herself, far outweighed that brief moment of pleasure. She concluded, as she had done many times before, that the lasting shame wasn't worth the fleeting pleasure. And, regardless, that sort of behaviour was plain wrong anyway.

CHAPTER 2

In the morning Marie roused and dressed quietly before Martin drove her to the train station. After a brief farewell she boarded her train waving Martin goodbye as he waited on the platform. She felt sadness that she would be away from him. He was kind hearted and loved her deeply. Sometimes she hated herself for taking advantage of those virtues.

She was headed for an unknown town. There she was to start work in a museum. It would be her first full time job. What most people called her first proper job, and hopefully the start of a career for her.

She had had several job applications turned down before she conceded that she would have to look beyond her home town. It was then she had found the Museum De Sade, and was offered the position without formal interview. She had no knowledge of their collection, the art or the artefacts, but expected the usual provincial museum items. Although hardly the dream start to a career that some might have hoped for, it appealed to her as it was likely to be a slow, steady, slightly dull position that would give her experience and would not apply too much pressure on her. She knew herself well enough to acknowledge that confidence was not something she had in any worthwhile quantity.

She had made arrangements to take lodgings at a house a few minutes outside the town centre. A couple were letting out their room on a casual basis. They had seemed very pleasant to Marie when she was finalising her plans. All she had to do was call them when she arrived.

After a long journey on a crowded train, she called and spoke to a man. Following a lengthy wait outside the station a large new Range Rover pulled into the car park. Driving it was a man in his early forties with a youthful feel about him. He had dark hair with a faint hint of greying, dark eyes and tanned skin with a slightly dishevelled appearance where he had let stubble grow through. The man singled Marie out, smiled and then pulled alongside her.

"Marie?" he asked.

"Yes," she replied, her voice sounding timid and girly. She found she was taken aback by this man's handsome features.

He climbed from the vehicle and lifted Marie's bags into the rear. He then ushered Marie to the passenger seat. As he did so she felt his hand touch faintly but intentionally on her hips. The contact struck her as inappropriate.

They started the journey back to the house. She was able to see him in profile and to admire his physique, which was quite muscular. He was nicely dressed also; a smart but casual appearance that made him look younger than he probably was but also gave him a look of someone who was confident and experienced.

"I'm John, in case you hadn't guessed already."

"Marie," she replied after a brief stutter trying to get her name out. She realised it was a stupid response. She had killed any conversation instantly.

Silence fell between them. John had penetrating eyes and Marie was very aware of him looking at her. They were not eyes that sought her own. He was quite clearly surveying her body in a rather lecherous way. It was making her very self-conscious, and she could feel his attention, whenever it diverted from the road, like a physical touch on her neck and chest, then her thighs and hips. Marie tried as hard as she could to look directly forward.

When they did make eye contact Marie found it unbearable. She diverted her look downwards instantly.

She wished that she had not worn such a tight fitting t-shirt that clung to her chest so revealingly. It made her breast look large. No wonder he was looking at her so intently. He must think I'm a cheap tart to turn up with my tits on show like this, she thought, mortified with embarrassment again.

"So you'll be at the Museum De Sade," he said, and Marie let out a sigh of relief to have the tense silence broken. "Interesting place. I've taken Issy there a couple of times. Powerful stuff they have there. You're into all that then?"

His question was a bit tentative, Marie thought. It was as though he thought it a bit strange that she should be 'into' history and art.

"Yes, very much into it," was her response.

"That's good to know," John said.

"I'm looking forward to starting," Marie said. "Lots to learn but it normally comes quick for me."

"I don't doubt it," he replied, with an expression that made Marie wonder if he was being ironic.

Overall something about John made her feel uncomfortable. He was a handsome, physically impressive, mature man. His eyes and his presence were quite impressive. He seemed a bit domineering given that they had only just met. Yet, despite the journey having an overbearing, desperately awkward air to it, it was also a nervously exciting experience that she was a little reluctant, in an odd way, to draw to an end.

They arrived at a large house and drove up the drive. Once inside, John placed her bags down and offered to take her on a tour of the rooms.

"Issy is out for the afternoon. She won't be back until quite late I'm afraid," he said to Marie as they walked up the stairs. Marie could still feel him watching her as he followed her up. She found herself, entirely against her will, accentuating some of her movements to feed his hungry eyes.

At the top of the stairs she halted. As he came up beside her he ran his hand over her bum, feeling its firm curve. It was fleeting, and unacknowledged by either of them. Marie felt a thrill of energy enter her through that touch. It quickened her heart with a fear that knew that his touches were inappropriate, and knew also that her letting them go without reproach was sending him the wrong signals. Yet the energy it gave her to know that this tall, toned, handsome man was lusting after her body was a new feeling for her. The awareness of his desire enlivened her.

"It's self explanatory really," he said indicating her room, "make yourself at home, unpack, familiarise yourself. I'm going to grab a shower." He walked across the landing and through the door opposite, entering his bedroom.

Marie, feeling even more curious about John's behaviour, started to bring her bags up to her room and unpack a few items. She was feeling a definite sense of excitement. She put it down to the new adventure she was on, embarking on a new career in a new town. There was also a more distant part of her that was excited, though. She tried to deny it before it could take shape.

Unable to control her curiosity she peered out of her door towards John's room.

She heard him stepping into the shower and the screen sliding shut behind him. An image of his nakedness was becoming fully formed in her mind. He was naked and there was nothing between them, no closed doors, no locks, nothing. It was an exhilarating feeling but she tried to ignore it, chastising herself for being this way. Close the door, she told herself, and mind your own business. The door stayed open.

Then John called out to her.

"Marie!"

He'd just shouted her from within the shower. It stunned her into a motionless terror. She tried to think of a suitable response but her mind was lost to disorder and panic.

"Marie!" he shouted again.

Shit, shit, shit. All she could think was oh, shit. Respond. Think of something to say for fuck sake. Think of something.

"Yes?" she called back, her voice loud enough to be heard but with a pronounced tremor in it.

"In your room, bottom drawer of the chest, there's some soap. Bring me one through." His voice held authority, staggering his delivery of the instructions for her easy comprehension.

Bring him some soap? The man she had known for less than half an hour wanted soap bringing to him in the shower. How the hell did you reply to a request like that?

"Bottom drawer!" he shouted again, more loudly than before.

Tell him no, she said to herself. But that would be a pretty bad way to start with a new landlord who had just picked you up from the station. But walk into his bedroom and pass him a bar of soap through the shower screen? When he was naked behind that screen? So pretend you can't find the soap, she thought to herself. No, that only delays the problem. Shit. The more she weighed up her panic-filled options the more time she was wasting.

She broke herself from her paralysis and looked in the drawer. There were several bars of soap. She picked one up and froze again.

"Have you found it?" John called out to her.

He must see that it is a totally unreasonable request for a married man to make to a young female lodger? Yet she knew that confronting him was not an option. She was too much of a coward.

Compliantly and fearfully she walked across the landing to the open door of John's marital bedroom. Looking in cautiously she saw the en suite bathroom with its door wide open and clouds of steam circling out. Through the steam she could see John's figure opaquely through the distorted glass of the shower screen. The adrenalin pounded with her blood and set her physical and mental state into a condition where she was not master over either. She was terrified.

She walked slowly to the shower. There was an excitement she could feel strongly in her. It was a nervous, sexually enlivening excitement, like the first initial encounters with a new lover.

The screen slid open. Marie's heart pounded so quickly and so suddenly that she jumped. John leant out his upper body from behind the screen and put out his arm to Marie, beckoning her to come forward so he could take the soap.

She stepped forward. Stood dripping wet in front of her, shrouded with clouds of steam, was a man of beautiful muscular definition, lithe and smooth and firm. He was like nothing she had seen before. More than this, the way he stood, facing her and pressed up close to the shower screen, meant she could not fail to see the blurred lines of his lower half. There was the dark patch of hair that descended over his stomach and broadened between the tops of his thighs. From there, unmistakable, was his manhood, hanging flaccid, full and long. Though she refused to look at it the fact it was there in her peripheral vision dominated her thoughts.

"Pass it here," he said with a hint of impatience in his tone.

Marie handed it to him mutely. He did not thank her.

The shower screen slid shut. Though seemingly absolved of her duties Marie lingered a moment to watch the blurred outline of this man showering. It was not a conscious decision, she just found herself pausing to soak up the impressive spectacle. He seemed to her the paradigm of masculinity. It was like wandering in to find a truly beautiful work of art on display.

She had dwelt on the view a moment too long.

"Make yourself useful while you're here," came his voice, deep, resonant and well spoken.

John slid the shower screen across again. This time he was stood straight, his full body on view, but with his back to her. She could see his nakedness, or half of it, clear in front of her. The nervous excitement accelerated in her as though a match had been taken to flammable material.

"I want my back washing," he said firmly.

He passed the bar of soap back to her and waited. She held it, deeply unsure of what was happening. Was this an elaborate prank? No, it had moved beyond that she realised. A misunderstanding? No, it was clear what was going on here, though she was reluctant to accept it was the case. John desired her. His touching of her was testament to it. He had it in his head, probably because she had let those touches go, or because of her tight fitting t-shirt, that she was the kind of girl to engage in spontaneous sex with a stranger. She was going to have to speak out. This had gone too far.

"I'm sorry Mr. Harmston, but I don't think…" she was interrupted.

"Just do as I said." His voice was firm. It sounded as though her speaking out had made him angry. Fearing further reproach she stepped forward and began hesitantly to rub the wet soap over his back.

She actually enjoyed how it felt. He had broad, muscular shoulders that were round and hard. All down his back she could feel the ridges of muscle definition beneath his skin, which was bronzed by the sun. The feeling of flesh on flesh was like a heat radiating down her arms and into her body and warming areas she normally denied warmth.

As her hands moved over him she dared herself to touch his buttocks. Taking a moment to pluck up the courage, she allowed her hands to slide symmetrically down his back and to his firm bottom.

The contact felt dirty and dishonest. He was a married man. She had a long term boyfriend, one she saw herself being with forever. Even that thought, summoned by a part of her that wanted her to feel guilt and to pull away from this man, only made the warmth sink deeper into her. It stirred through her in an elemental way, loosening primal regions that she had never known, even during her most dark and private moments.

"Wait while I rinse off. I want you to wash my front," he said, turning to allow the full jet of water to wash over his back.

He faced her. Without any sense of embarrassment he stood totally exposed before her shocked gaze.

Part of her desperately wanted to run from this. It was too sudden, too entirely unexpected. This was not how she thought people behaved. People were reserved and self-conscious about their bodies. People were deeply secretive about matters of sex. Yet here she was, confronted by the bare flesh – the perfect, muscular, smooth, bare flesh – of a domineering stranger. She was unwilling and unable to resist his demands of her.

She took the bar of soap and rubbed it slowly over his chest. His torso was like a slab of smooth rock. Both hands worked over him as he watched her eyes intently, looking into them and forcing her to lower her eyes submissively.

Inevitably her hands worked down over the flat muscular stomach, working the soap into the line of hair that ran down the centre. Spurred on by the electrifying sense of deviance that was already making itself felt as a dampening between her thighs, she allowed both hands to descend over the impressive length of penis that hung temptingly in front of her.

It felt wonderful in her hands. An object that she associated with unwanted pain, shame and a tarnished reputation was now a thing of deeply felt pleasure. Even to her, who had known only one penis, this was an object of impressive proportions and beautifully formed. Unsure how to handle it she let instinct take over and started to slide a hand up and down its length while she lightly gripped its base, her fingers gently caressing over his big balls.

"Good girl," he said quietly, a whisper to reassure her.

Continuing, she felt the soft flesh in her hands start to firm. It lengthened and widened from its already ample size to something even more impressive. It was intimidating for her to handle.

"Take your clothes off," he told her.

The fear that was in her and that was turning her stomach, and making her hands quiver, halted her. She was being coerced into a territory where she could not miss the serious consequences of her actions. Though half mesmerized by the body her hands touched, and the firming cock she held in her hands, she had alarms ringing violently within her.

Despite everything she believed in, all she had been raised to think proper, all she had hoped to become, she chose to ignore the alarm bells. She withdrew her hands from his erection and pulled her t-shirt up and over her head.

Without flinching or hesitating she reached behind her back and unclasped her bra, pulling it forward to release her deliciously round breasts. Then, stepping from her shoes, she unbuttoned her jeans and began to wriggle her hips from their close fit.

Tentative, she allowed her eyes to look up at his. His gaze held hers completely. Never had she felt so controlled by another person. She found that the demands on her were liberating. She had all decisions removed from her, and while the spell he had over her lasted she was absolved of all responsibility for anything that happened.

Stepping out of her jeans she stood opposite his nudity in only her simple navy blue knickers. John's eyes surveyed her.

The beauty of her body was natural. Her breasts were full and feminine, her hips round and smooth, her waist distinct and enhanced by the slight hint of roundness at the base of her belly. Her arms were slender, as were her legs, though she had a full, round bottom, as firm as a peach to the touch. It was her face that betrayed her naivety, not her body. In her face her features were young and honest, with her glasses and her hair giving an impression of suspicion, detachment and reservation. This was in direct contrast to her body which, in every aspect, was warm and inviting, feminine and open.

John was quickly aware of everything that her body, and the way she held it, said about her. As she began to slide off her panties he halted her.

"Take off your glasses first."

She did as instructed. Instantly she felt the sense of exposure and nakedness over her, more profoundly than she had when removing any garment. It was unsettling for her, who had such security behind her glasses. It was also exhilarating.

"Get in," he said sharply. He stepped to the side only slightly, allowing her very little room to enter.

Once she was in John closed the screen. He gripped her shoulders with his large strong hands and positioned her where he wanted her, facing him, her head directly beneath the powerful jet of water.

John then cradled her head and neck with his hand in a way that felt almost tender to Marie, though unmistakable was latent strength in his grip. She felt the flesh moisten between her legs.

His hand dropped to her pert, swelling breasts. He took hold of them firmly, each in turn, kneading them with his broad hands.

"You're a dirty little slut," he told her. "You're a filthy, cock craving, whoring slut."

The way he told her this startled Marie. The abusive words were nothing near how she was, yet they appealed to her greatly. She wanted him to abuse her more.

The hand on her breast dropped down over her belly and through her dark, untended pubic hair. It then slid beneath, immediately parting her warm, wet lips, sliding effortlessly between them. The thick fingers slipped over her swelling clit and then pushed up inside her narrow hole with a force that caused her to recoil from the sharp pain. She quickly settled back down on the fingers, embracing the swirl of pleasure that was running through her.

"That's a tight pussy you have there. I bet the boys love to fuck away at it, don't they? And I bet you let them fuck you raw, don't you, you slut."

She wanted more. She wanted to be made to feel guilty for things she'd never done, but longed to do.

"And you love it when their stiff little dicks are in you, don't you?" Still he worked two fingers up inside her. "You love it when their little pricks come up your hole, when they fill that dirty cunt with spunk. Don't you?"

The hand that had been holding her shoulder moved up behind her head. He gripped her hair. Between her legs he was now forcing three thick fingers up inside her. It was too much. It hurt too much.

"Don't you?" he shouted in her face, pulling her hair back so that her face was in the full stream of water.

"Yes," she spluttered, spitting water out of her mouth.

"Tell me what you love, you fucking slut." Still he held her head in the jet of water. She writhed against his grip trying desperately to find a moment of relief.

"I love," she spat and coughed, "their spunk inside me." Though tormented by the water she could hear the words coming from her mouth and they felt real. She was a dirty, cock hungry whore and he was making her pay for it.

"But you never let them near that cute, plump little bottom of yours. They never got near that did they? Those little bastards could do anything they wanted with you. They could fuck you in the pussy and squirt their pathetic dribble up inside you. They could go one after another, fucking that cunt and covering you in come; on your tits, on your clothes, in your hair. Anything they wanted but not in the ass. You never let them have you in the ass, did you?"

He had eased her face from the direct assault of the shower now and was staring at her with a look of burning contempt. She lowered her eyes and saw his hand buried deep between her legs and his huge erection standing thick and upright between them. It was glistening wet and smooth.

She savoured the filth he had used to describe her and the delightful feeling of his fingers penetrating her then responded to his tirade. "No, I wouldn't let them fuck me in the ass." It felt beautiful to speak it, to hear it in her voice. Every word of self-abuse she uttered served to heighten her arousal.

But John withdrew his fingers from her throbbing hole and released his hold of her head. Stepping closer, so that his erection pressed against the soft flesh of her belly, he reached up above her to the shower head. There was a jangle of metal and then John grabbed her by the wrist and raised her arm up to his. A clasp of metal swung around her wrist and clinked shut. Handcuffs. Her other arm was raised high above her head also. The handcuffs clinked shut again.

Marie was stood directly beneath the fixed shower head so that its powerful flow fell upon her head and shoulders. Her arms were raised above her head and the handcuffs fixed her to the metal pipe. She could not escape from this position, and could only make the smallest movements round or to the side.

"Sluts need punishing. They need to be taught a lesson."

He put his hands up to her breasts and squeezed her nipples tightly. She let out a yelp of pain.

He returned a hand to grip her hair at the back of her head then yanked her head back holding it against the rush of hot water.

"You loved the taste of it in your mouth, didn't you?" he barked at her, holding his hand firm against her instinctive recoiling from the water. "You loved the taste of their sperm on your tongue. You couldn't get enough.

You swallowed it down, and then licked their cocks clean. Then you asked for more. Didn't you?"

"Yes," she replied.

"You didn't care who it was, did you? You just got on your knees and jerked them off into your mouth, you fucking slut."

She pictured herself on her knees wanking a stranger's hard cock into her open mouth. "Yes," she spluttered.

"And what does that make you?" he asked sharply.

"A slut." She gasped for breath against the suffocating spray of water.

He pulled her head back and away so that the stream of water hit her swollen breast and engorged nipples. With his free hand he reached to the taps on the wall and turned one slowly. Her downcast eyes saw his hand then move from the taps to wrap around his imposing erection. He slid it up and down its length steadily. She wanted her own hands to be free so that she could be stroking that long, lithe shaft.

The water on her breasts was getting warmer, a lot warmer. It was uncomfortably hot, turning her breasts a radiant red. She twisted to try and escape, gasping with the emerging pain. Her bound wrists and John's uncompromising grip meant she could do nothing but suffer.

The heat continued to escalate, hotter still, too hot for her to endure and she began to scream out at the scalding pain on the tender skin of her breasts and nipples.

"Please! Please!" she shouted. "It hurts." Her face grimaced under the pain, contorted almost beyond recognition, her body flooded with agony.

John removed his hand from his cock and turned the tap quickly before placing his hand back round his thick shaft, pumping it up and down quicker now.

The temperature of the water on her skin eased instantly to a tolerable level, though the raw pain continued through her in waves. Strangely she wanted him to put his fingers back inside her to bring some kind of relief to the pain. Her body wanted that sensation as an accompaniment.

What she had just endured was beyond anything she had ever known in her life. Yet the pain had blown through her with a force that made her feel refreshed. Somehow she felt she could feel more acutely. She longed to have his fingers back inside her. She was aching for his thick, hard cock to plunge in her so that she could test her new awareness to sensation.

She was so consumed by this need she heard herself speak out. "Please," she said with a soft trembling voice, "push up inside me".

He let out a little laugh. "You little slut," he said and then placed his hand back onto the tap.

The water jetted out icy cold onto her breasts. Her breath was shocked from her so that she could only breathe in tiny gulps of air. Her eyes were wide with the startling cold powering over her.

He held her firm against the writhing of her body. It was pain again through her now, terrible, sharp pain that her every inch was instinctively desperate to escape. It was as agonising and as total as the scalding hot water a moment earlier. So precarious was her balance that she could not kick out, though her instincts called for it. She simply had to beg for his mercy again.

"Please. Stop it. Please," she whimpered. The unrelenting force of the cold was torture.

Again his hand released his erect penis and spun the taps. She felt the temperature of the water warm to cool and was able to steady her breathing. The shock faded slowly, along with the pain. The rapid changes from extremes of heat and cold on her naked breasts had left them with an intense tingling, like a thousand pin pricks.

John turned her round so that her back faced him. She felt his solid erection against her bottom and then felt his hand force her head forward. Her wrists were strained against the handcuffs that now dug into her soft skin sharply. Her arms were also twisted unnaturally and painfully, right down to her shoulders which felt the strain as a low burning sensation in her muscles.

"Sluts deserve punishment," he said solemnly. "They need to be corrected. But you, you disgusting little whore, need to be totally broken before you'll ever be anything but a cheap and easy fuck."

He reached round and grabbed her breasts and squeezed her nipples unmercifully hard. Again she screamed out, a low grunt of a scream. She could feel the warmth of his cock pressed against her wet buttocks and could think of nothing but how much she wanted it in her. She could not hold herself from pleading with him, though the desperation made her words confused.

"In me. I want it pushing," she said, panting, the pain raw on her wrists.

"Beg me for it slut," he said powerfully.

"Please. I want you up inside me. Please," she said, the neediness in her voice pathetic. She was trying to push her swollen sex back onto him.

He stepped back, releasing his grip of her tits. She could sense and hear that his hand was back pumping his cock vigorously.

"Beg harder slut."

"Please!" she yelled back at him instantly. It was a frustrated, imploring shout that was childish in its neediness and impatience.

He raised his hand and struck her powerfully on the soft flesh of her bottom, sending her lurching forward and struggling to keep her balance in the streaming water.

The force stunned her and the pain throbbed through her. She wanted him to do it again.

"Please," she begged.

His hand struck her again with an equal force. She felt minutely the impact and the shock shoot through her, then the pain building and hurting so fiercely at its peak, before easing slowly, until it calmed enough for her to feel the clarity of her senses.

She felt it most noticeably between her legs where she was swollen and wet with desire. If she could only free her hands, she would be able to plunge her fingers deep inside that sopping wet and pulsating hole. Oh, god, she needed him in her so badly.

"Don't whine," he said assertively. "Beg."

"I want you in me. I want you to push into me and to fuck my cunt hard. I want to feel every part of your cock through me and have you come all over me – in my mouth, on my face, my tits, my ass, and then I want to lick you clean, lick the come from your cock. Please, I'm a dirty, filthy slut. I know I am. I need fucking so bad."

"Why would I want to be inside that hole of yours, where every little dick you've met has had a spurt? Why the fuck do you think I'd want to put my dick there?"

"Please, just fuck me," she said, the frustration clear in her voice. In her anger at his refusal she wanted to hit out at him.

He grabbed her hair and yanked her head back brutally.

"Don't get shitty with me you slut," he yelled at her. "First lesson is you get what you're given and you're happy about it."

He released her hair and put his hand on her bottom, pushing the cheeks up and apart revealing her tightly sealed anus. His cock still in his other hand he guided it so that the very top rested against her puckered, delicate ass hole.

She held her breath anxiously aware of what he was about to try. She was worried that it was not possible. His cock was so broad that she doubted her wet aching pussy could take it without considerable pain. But he could never fit in her ass. It was too small and he was too large. She bit her lip and braced herself.

Slowly he pushed into her. Though scared of continuing Marie found herself doing all she could to help him inside her by pushing back against his slow entry to her anus. He succeeded in opening her, the bulbous tip pushing into her only a tiny distance, and yet already she was grimacing with the pain of his penetration. It felt like he must be deep already as the pain was so biting. But she knew he wasn't deep. She knew this was just the breaking of her virgin anus.

Patiently he worked his length into her until the tip was completely inside her, almost rending her in two. She was again experiencing the sharpest pain and it was arousing her every inch of flesh. She loved the fact that she was naked and chained by this muscular man and that he was forcing his huge length into her virgin bum. It was the real world mirroring her darkest, most repressed dreams and it was making her feel the exhilarating passions of being a filthy, debauched slut.

"Oh, you're one tight little bitch," John said to her, clearly enjoying himself. "But you're taking me all even if it kills you." With that ultimatum he gave a sharp thrust and managed to force his cock inside her another couple of inches, both of them letting out a groan of pain as he did so.

"Come on, slut, open up for me." He reached for a bottle of shower gel that was on near and squirted a good amount where his cock was stretching her hole.

John then bent himself over slightly so that he could reach one hand to grip hold of a nipple and one hand could circle under her to rub his fingers over her clit and the wet, swollen lips of her vacant cunt.

Marie closed her eyes and sunk down into the position, revelling in the sensations of pain and pleasure in her breast and on her clit and deep and wide and dirty in her ass. The shower gel was working, and with some gentle in and out movements of John's pulsing, veined cock she was soon experiencing at least half his length through her at a quickening pace.

The satisfaction was sublime. His domineering demands of her, the way he stared at her, intimidating her, the way he talked to her like she was some disgusting street slut who would spread her legs for anyone, made her feel so incredibly sexually alive. Certainly she had never known herself so animal in her urgency to be penetrated. Never had she been so consumed with hunger and single mindedness about handling an erection and wanting it to fill her with come. God, she wanted him to fill her with come so much. She wished he could fill every hole she had until it spilled out.

Oh, fuck. He was pushing deeper now. The pain was like nothing before, beyond hot water, beyond cold, beyond being struck. This was deep and internal. Each thrust was like a punch inside her, to areas that were afforded no protection. Tears were welling in her eyes. The deeper he went, the more pain she felt and the more she felt like exploding into an orgasm that would rip her apart.

He was in her now, all of him, pumping away furiously, his big, full balls hitting against the pouting lips of her pussy. His grip on her nipples was like a vice, crushing the tender tips and shooting pain through her breasts. His hand under her was rubbing hard with his thick fingers over her throbbing clit, working it firmly and quickly. It was painful and it was wonderful.

There was a rush of urgent, insistent energy rising in her. She started to moan uncontrollably, deeply and loudly. Then she felt it begin to work to the surface. Her face reddened, her chest flushed scarlet, she screamed without inhibition and then…

John let out a series of quick, loud grunts. His pounding cock in her anus accelerated, with both his hands now on her hips to keep her in place against the force he used against her.

He started to shout out at her. "You fucking slut! Dirty, fucking slut!"

He continued smashing his cock into her tight hole, as quick and as hard as he could. He shouted out again. "I'm coming. Fucking yes, I'm coming, you fucking slag."

She felt his twitching cock in her, made possible by her heightened senses. She could feel the contractions of his balls that were pushed up against her sex; then felt the shooting pressure of his semen as it erupted deep inside her. She could feel each pulse of his come flooding her.

A ripple of climax ran through her gently. Only a ripple, the full rush that she had felt was circling her still, as though it had been caged and was desperate to get out. All she had was a tremor over her, a contraction of her hole and a pulsing current through her cunt and clit. Her body needed more. She needed to take the sensations inside her to their limit.

She bucked and moved with agitation and eagerness as John slid his cock out of her.

"Good girl," he said disinterestedly.

"Let me lick you clean," she pleaded. She knew he would have to let her free from the handcuffs if she was going to do so.

"Suit yourself," he answered. He had lost interest in her now that he had spent his full load in her virgin hole.

He reached up and freed her wrists. Immediately she reached to turn off the shower and then spun round, sinking to her knees. She grabbed at his still firm cock and put it straight into her mouth. Her other hand plunged down between her legs and began rubbing violently over her clit.

The tip of John's cock was still seeping come and she lapped it up enthusiastically. His entire length was glistening and she licked it frantically, fighting against its fading.

"Go easy," he said, surprised by her energy.

She felt the rush rising in her again. It was back at her surface, pushing at the bars of its cage. She could feel the come dripping out of her anus, pooling directly beneath her. She wanted to scoop it up and lick it from her fingers but there was no time. It was on her now, the climax, ready and hard through her, like John's cock had been hard in her ass. It was spinning in her like the pain of his punishments, ringing and rising like the insults he threw at her. Slut. Dirty fucking slut. Come loving, cock craving whore.

It exploded, the bars that caged it obliterated. It pounded through her wildly out of control, sending her head back, her mouth open and a scream coming from her. Then it smashed down to where her hand thrashed over her clit and then forced itself from her in an ecstatic bursting of her sexual juices spraying onto the shower floor. Then she dropped, with the last twitching of her pussy and the last drips of her juices before the gradual reorganisation of her scrambled head and the slow realisation of where she was.

She removed her hand from the half erect penis in front of her. Her skin prickled with embarrassment. She wanted to spit the taste from her mouth and pull a dressing gown over her to conceal her nudity. Oh, what have I done, she thought to herself.

Her sense of disgust and her self-recriminations were put on hold. There was the sound of a key in the door, then the door opening and closing firmly. A woman's voice shouted out.

"John, I'm home."

CHAPTER 3

The two naked bodies froze momentarily. The forceful, dominant sexual aggressor now had a distinct look of worry on his face as he realised his wife had returned home while he was in the final stages of fucking their new lodger. Marie mirrored his expression, though quickly it turned to one of terrified panic.

"Get out, get out," John said urgently and in a whisper.

Marie clambered out of the shower, picked up her clothes and started to fumble through them looking for the waist of her jeans.

"No time, for fucks sake. Just get out," he told her.

She took her clothes into her arms and bolted out of the bathroom door. She knew her only hope was to sprint naked to her room and hope that John's wife did not make it onto the stairs as she passed them. If she was caught Marie expected to be violently assaulted by this unknown woman. She would be cornered and have her eyes scratched out for being such a slut with this woman's husband.

As she bolted, naked and wet, with the feeling of John's cock lingering in her anus and the taste of his come still on her lips, she could hear the footsteps of the woman below.

With a slam of the door Marie was in her room. Her heart felt like it was about to break her ribs. She couldn't believe what she had done.

The woman shouted from the base of the stairs. "John, is everything alright?"

She knew something was wrong, Marie thought. Her voice had a suspicious timbre to it. Marie reproached herself for ever getting involved in such behaviour. This was not who she was, so why the hell was she about to be assaulted for whoring? She had succeeded in not being caught at the scene of the crime, true, but had as good as shouted her involvement out by escaping in the only way she had available to her.

Still wet from the shower, Marie hurried to put her clothes on. She knew there was no excuse she could present that would justify her dripping wetness. She decided hiding was her best option. She stepped into the wardrobe and curled herself at its base, pulling the doors shut from within.

The footsteps were climbing the stairs now. Marie was churning with fear. She listened.

"John," the woman's voice called out uncertainly.

After a moments delay John's voice replied. "Just getting out the shower."

Issy, Marie remembered. Her name was Isabelle. They had sent a couple of emails to sort out the room. She was at the top of the stairs now, very near Marie's door. Terror was strangling Marie, so that she could barely breathe. If Isabelle came through that door there would be nothing Marie could do – her guilt was all over her body.

"What took you so long to answer?" Isabelle asked, her voice moving away from Marie's door.

"I was in the shower," John replied. "I didn't hear you come in."

"What was that noise?" Isabelle asked. Her voice had the hint of accusation. Marie feared the worst.

"Didn't hear any noise. Probably the cat." John answered, using a dismissive tone in the hope of breaking Isabelle's suspicion.

Marie found it slightly strange that the man who had demanded she remove her clothes, and whose intense eyes had made her submit to acts she found disgusting, would resort to lame lies in this way to his wife. He was changed massively in her eyes from the demi-god figure whose masculine body had taken from her a virginity she had never wanted to give up.

"I heard a door slam," Isabelle was persisting. She knew something had happened, she just didn't know exactly what, nor did she have any proof. Marie's only hope was that Isabelle gave people the benefit of any doubt she had.

"Strange," was all John responded with.

"Did you collect Marie?" she asked.

"Yeah. I went straight down after you'd gone. I think she has gone for a lie down. Long journey."

Thank you, John, she said to herself. That simple deceit, assuming it was accepted, ought to keep her safe from Isabelle for at least a few hours. Enough time, Marie hoped, for any suspicion to dissipate.

"Shall I put some dinner on?" Isabelle asked.

"That would be nice. And open a bottle of wine – the Syrah."

John had navigated a very difficult situation with something close to ease. Marie sensed that Isabelle had given up on her doubts. At the very least she had missed her best moment to strike with her accusations.

The movements of John and Issy settling back to their daily routine were audible through the large, beautiful house. Marie remained in the wardrobe listening, comforted by the darkness and isolation. John's simple cover story required her to stay as silent as possible. While she was meant to be asleep she could not be accused of impoliteness for staying in her room rather than going to meet her new landlady.

She curled up tightly and rested her head on old sheets and towels that were stored in the bottom of the wardrobe. She closed her eyes and remembered herself chained to a shower being penetrated in a disgusting place and it made her feel guilt and huge regret. Had she really done that? Was she about to wake up and realise it was one of her dreams, the filthy ones she had so often and that made her so ashamed? No, what had happened was real.

She thought of her boyfriend, Martin. She thought of his kind nature and his willingness to put up with her refusal to have sex with him all because it made her feel physically sore and mentally uncomfortable. And yet, she had just revelled in a stranger's generous endowment deep inside her bottom before licking that object of every last drop of come. She hated herself for what she had done. Every part of her flesh was now repellent to her, as though it had betrayed her deepest secret to the world. She never wanted to leave this wardrobe, or ever face the world again. If she looked another person in the eye they would surely know what she had done. It would be in her eyes and on her skin that she was a filthy slut, who cheated on her boyfriend and was fucked in the ass by a man she didn't even know. People would see it in her. She would be ashamed of this act all her life.

Marie closed her eyes and felt physical exhaustion. After a while the tension in her muscles, fraught with fear of detection, began to ease and tiredness fell over her like a thick fog, sending her to sleep. She felt uneasy as she drifted, as though nightmares were descending on her. Ones that were all too familiar to her, and that today had been shown as being dangerously close to prophesy.

Reality became confused and hard to recognise. A dream formed and started to pull her into its odd shaped world. She resisted listlessly but soon found herself entirely powerless against the floating, unpredictable flights that her mind conjured.

There was a yard with low brick buildings, old and heavily weathered. The slate roofs were rolling and uneven along their length. Broad wooden gates filled the lower half of entrances to the low building at regular intervals. Small bales of hay, a wheelbarrow and ropes identified the building as a stable yard, the one she had been to as a young girl.

Marie was in the centre of the square yard, lost as to her purpose. She was wearing jeans and a baggy, unflattering jumper but beneath she was highly conscious of her underwear. A bra of thin and sensuous material wrapped over her breasts. Stockings held up by perfectly weighted suspenders. Running over her mound and between her legs was a pair of silky knickers with an open slit that ran neatly over her sensitive labia. The feeling of those delicate, sexy garments beneath her made her feel arousal accompanied by concern that someone might know what she was wearing.

There were voices behind her, around a wall. She knew the voices – male, strong, purposeful and quickly approaching. A beat of excitement coursed through her.

"I have plenty to do yet," said one of the voices, deep and mature. "But I will get there before too long I think. She has the makings of a decent mare."

She knew the voice, but couldn't place it. Nor could she move from her position in the centre of the yard, though the thought of hiding was prominent in her thoughts.

"Patience is important. I have always to keep reminding myself of that. Patience and persistence," said the other voice – Martin's voice she realised with shock. "Training never is much fun while you're doing it but you forget the pain when they're as you want them," he continued.

It was Martin but why the hell was he here in a stable yard? Then instantly she placed the other voice. It was John talking to Martin; her boyfriend with the man who she had recently debased herself with in the most wretched manner. A terrible fear ignited in her. Would they have talked about what she had done? She prayed that John would not speak out about it.

"That's it," said John in agreement as the two rounded the wall and entered the yard.

The two men circled around her, barely bothering to look at her, and proceeded to a stable door that Martin opened and entered. Both men were strangely attired in high leather riding boots, tight fitting jeans and bold coloured polo shirts. The clothes were remarkably flattering to their physiques, accentuating the tightness of their buttocks and the carved splendour of their chests and arms. It seemed to her that Martin had become more muscular.

"Are you lungeing her for a start?" John asked Martin.

"I thought I would. Tire her out a bit before I saddle up on her," Martin replied with a confident tone not entirely characteristic of him.

"I'll get a lead rope on her then," John replied and then gathered up a short length of rope with metal attachments that had been hanging by the stable door.

Marie was surprised by how ignorant they were of her. She tried to say something but couldn't think what to say, or even articulate it if she had been able to think of something. She was mute. As John approached her he made eye contact and it was that moment Marie realised it was she who was to be roped.

John's hands moved quickly to take a grip of her chin and jaw. She tried to resist briefly but soon acquiesced when she felt his strength. He threw the rope over her and began to make adjustments. A piece of metal was in her mouth and straps circled her head keeping it fixed in place.

Martin emerged from the stable with a long length of rope and proceeded to attach one end of it to the harness at a point at the back of her head. In his other hand he held what looked like a fishing rod to Marie, but clearly could not be. As Martin walked away from her, unfurling the rope, the purpose of that item revealed itself. It was a whip, a long leather horse whip.

"In the yard?" John asked.

"As good a place as any," Martin called back. He was now stood with the rope fully extended. Both men faced her. John took a few steps back to the edge of the stable yard. Marie was uneasy about what was intended for her now, though not fearful, for she was in the presence of Martin. While uneasy, she felt happy for these two men to use her as they saw fit.

A sharp crack in the air behind her made her jump and alerted her. She turned to face Martin, the wielder of the whip, who had a look of stern disapproval on his face.

"She's stubborn alright," called John with a smile on his face.

"She'll learn one way or another," Martin replied. Then, raising his arm swiftly and elegantly he brought it down so that the leather tip lashed sharply and painfully against her backside sending pain ringing from the point of contact. She knew what Martin wanted her to do but could not bring herself to start running round on that length of rope. It was a stupid, pointless and humiliating thing to expect her to do. She cast him a disapproving look which he appeared totally oblivious of.

"I wouldn't be so sure," John called back, much amused by Marie's refusal to trot round the yard. "Get those layers off her," he continued with more seriousness in his voice, "or you'll never get the mare to move. Is she in season?"

"Probably," answered Martin as he approached her, a slight look of frustration about him.

Effortlessly, in a single movement, Martin removed her baggy jumper to expose her pale flesh, a tiny part of which was covered by the delicate bra supporting her juicy, appealing breasts. With similar ease she found herself stepping out of her jeans – with stiletto heels on. Burning embarrassment came to her face as she found her stockinged legs and scarce concealed pussy on display.

Martin threw the two garments to the perimeter of the yard and walked back to his starting point, the rope fully extended. Marie felt both men's eyes on her exposed flesh like a coarse touch. It made the embarrassment more potent and seemed to send the red hot flush to her chest and circling down to the flesh that was lined by her crotchless knickers.

She knew she was without any protection from the bite of Martin's whip, dressed as she was in this fine and beautiful underwear. Sure enough the whip came down directly on her backside. She heard it before she was able to feel it, a sharp crack that split the air before the pain built and then broke over her skin. It hurt, a burning pain that made her jump about in the vain hope of making that pain vanish. Reluctantly she admitted that the horse whip was too much to invite another strike and set off in a shamed jog around the yard.

The sense of humiliation in her was heavy, subduing her sense of self worth. She felt that this was about all she was good for. All her hard work, all her study, all her effort at presenting herself well was for nothing. Perhaps all she was good for was servitude, slavery and obedience.

Within her dream she trotted around in her black lingerie as the two men observed her. When she slowed her speed Martin administered a crack of the whip on her rear that burst pain through her and sent her pace up suddenly. By increments of whipping Marie found that she was running at considerable pace on Martin's length of rope. Her heart was beating powerfully and she was starting to warm in her face as sweat began to drip from her. The sustained exercise tired her quickly. Perspiration on her skin gave her a peculiar feeling. She was aware of it on her breasts and between her legs. Each drip that ran over her skin felt like the gentle touch of a finger.

She was exhausted. The physical activity was wearing her down. She felt she could fall to her knees at any moment. Mentally she was defeated also. The eyes of the two men made her self-conscious and nervous. The way they were debasing her, the way they commanded her, was, paradoxically, liberating for her. There was no expectation of her here. Her own control over her behaviour and her ability to make decisions regarding her conduct had been fully removed from her by her boyfriend.

With Marie dripping wet with sweat and panting for air Martin finally brought the ordeal to an end, gathering the rope in as he walked towards her.

"She tired quickly," John said as he walked towards Martin.

"She's short on fitness. Not too sure whether I ought to ride her after that," replied Martin as he removed the rope from the back of Marie's head.

"A quick ride will do her good," John advised. "Don't ask too much of her. Perhaps just have her in the trap for bit."

Martin agreed that she was fine for a spell in the traps, whatever that was. He took hold of Marie's harness and pulled her towards what looked like a small chamber, something like the cages that a race horse is ushered into before setting out around the track. Marie was forced in, bent over at the waist and had her legs pulled up into the ledges at the side. He was being rough with her.

Her position was such that her bottom was the most elevated part of her body. Her hands clung to the sharp edges of the trap, her only way of preventing herself from falling onto her face.

Martin walked round to where Marie's head was and attached a set of leather reins. He threw them over her back and circled to her rear. Taking the reins he pulled back firmly so that Marie's head was jerked back.

She could hear behind her Martin was undoing his belt. His zip descended. Though she could see nothing she was conscious of his penis naked and hot close behind her. She could feel the pumping heat that was enlarging it.

The hard tip, guided by his hand, touched the split material of her crotchless knickers. They were sopping wet from the sweat that was still dripping from her. This wetness was heightened by the arousal she was experiencing, prompted by that exciting sensation of having a hard cock near her exposed pussy lips. She was very aware of his hard cock pressing against the soft hairs around her wet, parted flesh. It sent a thrill through her like an electrical current.

The gentle first touch of Martin's cock against her softest flesh was deceptive. He had merely been lining up his entry. Pulling on the reins sharply he pushed his length fully into her, smashing past the tightness of her entrance in a quick thrust that made her yelp like a hurt dog. He sighed with the satisfaction of that tight, nervous pussy around his shaft.

Pulling on the reins he began to work himself in and out of her hole. It was dripping wet now, his abrupt entry seeming to open up a reservoir of arousal in her. She could feel it running out of her hole and over her swollen clit, flooding in her knickers so that they sagged.

She gave no thought to resisting Martin. Though she was in considerable pain she endured it, knowing that he was feeling pleasure from being inside her. She derived a certain pleasure from it herself, a source she had never derived pleasure from in the past. She wanted him to come inside her so that she could know he had been satisfied.

Martin quickened his pace and his pulling on the reins became more forceful. Soon he was breathing deeply and cursing at her for being an easy, dirty slut. His abuse and his vigorous use of her continued to escalate until she heard him call out long and low, as though pushing with all his strength an unmoving object. Then she felt in her wave after wave of his spunk pulsing deep into her, creating a warm feeling inside her. It left her with a simple, beautiful elation at having given her man such satisfaction.

As he pulled out, a trickle of his come and Marie's own arousal fell out of her onto the yard floor. Martin watched it drip from her cunt with a vacant look on his face, one of a man pleasured to a point close to oblivion. He broke himself from it and pulled his jeans up, fastening his belt. He stepped down from the trap.

"She's got the makings," he said to John.

CHAPTER 4

The sound of shouting from inside the house woke Marie abruptly so that she was confused as to where she was. She was unsure what of the last day had been real. It was a sobering and unpleasant realisation that not all of her behaviour had been a dream. She had indeed acted in that revolting manner.

Her drowsy senses gradually tuned into the cacophony of shouts from downstairs. It was a blazing dispute between John and Isabelle with voices shouting at full strength. Marie had never heard such intensity in an argument and was at once concerned and enthralled. They were arguing and shouting so fiercely that they must have been audible some distance down the street, and would obviously be heard by their new lodger. Yet they seemed not to care in the slightest.

Intent that she should be able to discern every word of the argument Marie moved from the wardrobe and towards the bedroom door. She did so as quietly as she could.

She couldn't make out what the subject of the argument was, though Marie had a dreadful suspicion as to what it might be. Her curiosity was consuming and gently, silently, she opened the door. She listened with total concentration. Her heart beat quickly and powerfully.

"You're a cheating bastard. And again! Here! When you're away I accept it. But here! Our fucking home!" Isabelle was screaming with passion, the power of her anger affecting her voice.

"You don't know what the fuck you're talking about," was John's instant, firm and dismissive reply.

"Don't I? You really think I'm that stupid?"

"I know you are."

"You wish I was. You wish you could fuck anyone and everyone and never have me know. You probably do. But I fucking well know this time you callous bastard."

Marie was frozen with fear. She knew now what she had feared was happening. The argument was about what she had done earlier in the shower. She felt an idiot to have entertained the thought that she might have got away with it. She now worried for her own safety in this house. She thought through how she would defend herself when this woman came to kill her. Still she listened.

"I can't say anything when you're paranoid like this, can I?" John said loudly, though with much more self control than his wife was currently capable of.

"You can say you fucked her," Isabelle bellowed back at him, her voice so pained and angry that it was turning hoarse.

"Fine then, you stupid bitch, I fucked her. I fucked her in the shower this afternoon and it was a bloody good fuck as well. Does that make you happy? Is that what you want to hear?"

Marie began to shake with the adrenalin through her. Though she had only awkward control of her body she edged out through the door and to the top stair so that she could see what was happening below.

She saw Isabelle absorbing what had just been admitted. In her face she looked broken, as though she had wanted desperately to be wrong. As she assimilated the infidelity she seemed to change in her expression quite markedly. Rage came back to her, and any sense that she was interested in discussing the matter, vanished. She looked set on violence.

"That's what you wanted to hear, wasn't it?" John said to her, eager to break the unnerving silence that had followed his confession.

Isabelle reacted by picking up the object nearest her, a wine glass on the table, and propelled it, including contents, at her husband. She let out a scream as she threw it, a release of pure rage.

Instinctively John moved his head away, raising his arm to deflect the object from his face. It smashed against his arm and then again as it hit the floor.

"What the fuck are you…" John tried to protest but no sooner had he raised his head than another object flew directly at it. He ducked and it smashed against the wall.

Isabelle continued, grabbing anything that she could and hurling it in the direction of John's head. Each smashed object was accompanied by a terrifying scream. When nothing else was available to throw she charged at John and threw her clenched fists at him, connecting firmly with the side of his head.

Marie watched excitedly. Never in her life had she seen something so exciting. She had no conception of a woman capable of being so uninhibited, so overtaken by her anger. It was exhilarating to be so close to it, and so sexually exciting to be the cause of it. Marie could feel the heat between her thighs.

What followed startled her beyond amazement. John rose upright against the flailing strikes of his wife and grabbed both her wrists tightly. She twisted and hissed against the restraint. When she tried to kick him he released a wrist and struck her powerfully against the side of the face. The blow was of such force it shocked Isabelle, and she was left without any sense or strength. John seemed to be dangling her from the grip he had of her wrist.

Despite the blow Isabelle still summoned the bravery and strength to come for him again. Her free hand swung lamely at the side of John's head, making barely enough contact to warrant John flinching. Immediately John swung his large open hand at her, making contact with her cheek with a force entirely disproportionate to the offence. It rattled all sense from his wife. She was left with a shocked and confused look on her face.

Isabelle's legs gave way beneath her. She sank to her knees, spared the ignominy of total collapse by John's grip of her wrist.

"What do you say?" John asked her calmly.

There was no response. Isabelle looked as though she was still lost in the confusion of those punishing blows she had sustained. That or the realisation of her husband's adultery had left her feeling vacant of sense and dull to emotion.

Unmercifully John shook her to elicit a response. "What do you say?" he asked of her again.

She looked up at him. "I'm sorry," she said.

"What else?" John's voice was calm and controlled.

"I would like to be punished," she said in a whisper.

"No."

She tried again. "I deserve to be punished."

"Correct." John used his free hand to undo his belt and loosen his fly.

Marie watched with astonishment what was happening between the couple. Below her, Isabelle, whose glazed expression was being replaced by one of concentration and eagerness, pulled John's penis from his loosened trousers. As Marie had done earlier, much to her deepest shame now, Isabelle used her hand to caress its considerable length and placed its soft tip to her lips and tongue.

The act was being performed willingly it seemed to Marie. Even enthusiastically, for Marie recognised the look of enjoyment in Isabelle's eyes. But how could this beautiful woman, who had come home to that betrayal, and who had been struck down with such violence, be so apparently happy and enthusiastic about performing fellatio on the man responsible for her suffering? It made no sense to Marie. And then Marie's own acts with the same man came vividly back to her and she realised that this was the power of the man.

Below, Isabelle's enthusiastic and expert hand and mouth had made John's penis long, thick and hard. As Marie watched she could not avoid having a further flicker of excitement between her legs just to see the perfection of that manhood. John had released his grip of Isabelle's wrist now and allowed her unconstrained access.

He pulled Isabelle's top up over her head to reveal her thin, smooth and beautifully formed body with its porcelain skin. Her breasts were modest but well shaped. She wore a delicately patterned black lace bra that complemented her dark hair and eyes. She looked wonderfully attractive engaging in the act of oral sex, and Marie watched her with envy for everything she was and everything she had at that moment.

Suddenly Isabelle jumped up so that she was facing John and spat full in his face before swinging a hand at great speed into the side of his head. She connected with a sharp sounding slap that made Marie jump. Nearly as quick John grabbed Isabelle by the hair and wrenched her back and down so that she could not reach him to continue her assault.

He wiped the spit from his face with his free hand before leaning over and putting his face directly in front of hers. He had a look of impatience on his face that was terrifying to Marie as she watched on the stairs. She felt compassion for Isabelle and admiration for her courage.

John addressed his wife in a tone that he might use to address a misbehaving dog. "I'm going to make you regret that."

Still gripping her hair John dragged Isabelle along the floor to the coffee table and, with a broad swipe of his arm, sent everything that was on it to the floor. He then pulled Isabelle up so that she was laid face down on the wooden surface.

While she lay on the table, suddenly unresisting, John reached into an open drawer and removed from it a length of thick, coarse rope. Reaching beneath the table he pulled her arms together and tied a quick knot that tightly bound her wrists. The force that he pulled the knot tight with brought a whimper of pain from Isabelle. Having her wrists tied beneath the table, while she was laid face down on top of it, pinned her in a very uncomfortable position.

John forcefully pulled off Isabelle's smart, black trousers, wrenching with them her black thong. Marie heard the sound of material ripping from the force of his abuse. With the excitement of her voyeurism Marie felt the flesh between her legs grow hotter and more moist.

Isabelle tried half heartedly to prevent John tying her ankles. She could see nothing, however, and John soon had them pulled awkwardly together beneath the table so that her body was pulled taut against its surface. Her buttocks and the tender flesh between her legs were parted. Marie looked at the view before her with wide eyes. There was something incredibly beautiful about Isabelle and her helpless exposure. The elegance of that delicate pink flesh between her legs, with the faintest suggestion of hair coming up from her mound, was beautiful. The wondrous roundness of her bottom, and of her breasts that were squashed beneath her, made Marie feel a very pronounced sense of envy. Marie wanted at that moment to be Isabelle, especially so that she could feel what she was about to feel.

Standing a pace back, John surveyed the position he had engineered for his wife. He wanted her to feel the rope's coarse weave sharp and abrasive on her soft skin. He wanted the pressure on her breasts to start to hurt her and the strange pull on her limbs to be transmitted uncomfortably through her.

"I'm going to make sure you really suffer."

"Please," Isabelle said meekly. "I'm sorry." She sounded close to tears, her gentle voice faltering.

"Quiet," John replied to her sharply.

From where he stood John moved to an area out of view of Marie's crouched position at the top of the stairs. When he came back into view he had in his right hand a wooden paddle. It had a handle wrapped in worn, soft leather. As John held it the paddle looked an intimidating weapon, especially so near to the pristine skin and beautiful, tender arousal of the insolent Isabelle.

Marie continued to watch excitedly. Sensations of heat were rolling through her insides. She was fearful for Isabelle, to whom she had already developed a close attraction based on empathy and admiration. She almost wanted to intervene and spare the porcelain skin that was bare on the table below. To Marie it had the look of some virgin sacrifice in a barbaric sex ritual. More of her, however, wanted to watch everything that was about to unfold.

She crouched, fully aware of the consequences if she were caught. She was acutely conscious of how shameful her behaviour had been already that day and now she was compounding the shame she would suffer. She was disgusted at herself but was unwilling to retreat until she had satiated the throbbing urge of her curiosity.

John stood side on to Isabelle, raised his right hand and the paddle it held above his shoulder, and then brought it down at great speed to make a brutal, reverberating contact with her bottom. A short scream of pain came from Isabelle. Marie winced in sympathy for her. Her own bottom felt the absence of pain like hollowness. She envied Isabelle everything she was now feeling. Her mind ran through the feeling she had had when John's hand had struck her in the shower, desperately trying to resurrect that pain.

"This is for your disobedience." Another resounding thwack exploded on Isabelle's bottom, the descending paddle wielded with vigour and precision by John's thick muscled arms.

The scream that the strike forced from Isabelle was distressing, the startling pain she was experiencing obvious. Where contact had been made her bottom was scarlet. In her reaction to evade the pain she writhed and bucked on the table, but the rope that bound her did not permit her to escape or even ease the throbbing, burning agony.

Marie's hand descended down her stomach, unbuttoned the trousers she had hastily put on earlier, and worked over her pubic hair to touch the warming flesh below. She did not want to. As her hand lowered, as the button had been undone, as her mound had been glided over she had said to herself internally; "Stop". She willed herself to halt the progress but she was not strong enough to break the insistency of the flesh to be touched. And when her fingers slid through the warm, wet flesh she felt the most wonderful pleasures easing up inside her, her eyes focused intently on the raw skin of Isabelle's bottom, bright like a burn.

"This is for your insolence," and John's arm descended with terrifying force to strike his wife.

"I will fuck who I want to fuck." Thwack! The paddle struck her brutally, the sound shaking through the house.

"You will never question me." Thwack! Isabelle's bottom was raw, the blood vivid beneath her skin. She could do nothing but scream out, her body writhing and bucking desperately on the table to dissipate the agony.

Marie's finger began to move more vigorously between her legs. She was incredibly wet, dripping into her trousers. She was thrilled by how wrong her voyeurism was. Though she wanted to be a part of what was happening below, she would not break from the wonderful arousal she was now feeling. It was laced with adrenalin, like the thrill of theft, and it made her feel alive in a way that was unknown to her until today.

"You are a dirty," Thwack! "You are a cheating," Thwack! "You are a deceitful," Thwack! "Disobedient," Thwack! "Whore!" Thwack! John rained down strike after strike on the tied flesh.

The last strike was the most vicious by far. It had within it all John's impressive strength, coupled with an anger that was shockingly intense. Marie could feel the intensity as though it was physically present in the air. It made the fine hair on her body stand up and her skin tingle. This was no contrivance. This was no game playing to ignite an extinguished sex life. There was passion between these two. Attraction, yes, instinctive and powerful, but also conflict and even hatred and distrust. The sincerity of it all made her pussy ache for release.

"What do you say to me?" John asked of her in an aggressive, half crazed way.

"I'm sorry," she said weakly, her breathing broken and heavy with the pain that clearly dominated her senses and her thoughts.

John made no response other than to unbuckle the belt on his jeans and slide them down to his ankles. He wore no briefs. His large cock swung out into the open space before it, the flesh already firming. His hand grasped it and began a rhythmic stroking bringing it to its fully erect impressive size. Marie could see the animal lust in his eyes as he worked up and down his cock. He was looking at Isabelle's bottom and her pussy and pumping harder on his shaft, his arm revealing the power of its muscles.

His erection was huge now. Marie marvelled at its size and splendour. Two fingers worked hard over her clit, rubbing quickly, the pressure as much as she could bear upon its tenderness. When she felt a twitch inside her, as if the climax she was building towards had got too much to contain, she slid the two fingers further under and pushed them up inside her wet hole, slowly easing them in and out as the urge to come eased off enough for her to return to working over her clit. She was desperate to release the orgasm inside her but also intent on getting every last voyeuristic pleasure out of this spectacle of sadism.

John pumped over his cock furiously now. He was stood over Isabelle. Her buttocks were still bright red. Marie watched his dick being pumped with unblinking eyes. A contortion came over his face. His breathing deepened and his legs seemed to give way beneath him slightly.

Abruptly he stopped, removed his hand form his erection and took hold of the paddle. Instantly he brought it down onto her bottom with a powerful strike then repeated it again and again. There was no break in the assault. One blow succeeded immediately by another. Thwack! Thwack! Thwack!

Isabelle's screamed violently. It was a long cry of agony that made it clear she was being pushed to the limits of her endurance. It was the cry of the tortured. Marie, from her elevated and distant position, could see the lines the paddle had made on Isabelle's bottom. Her skin looked like it had been subjected to repeat branding.

Marie was forced to give up her efforts to prolong her pleasures. She had to come. Three fingers rubbed hard and fast over her wet clit, building up the intensity of arousal inside her. Hard and fast she rubbed herself as she watched John discard the paddle and put his grip back around his pulsing erection. He pumped it hard again, his arm going as quick as was possible. Marie focused on the erection and found she was matching his furious rhythm with her fingers. She could feel the climax pushing powerfully inside her, swollen and beautiful and painful. All she wanted now was for it to burst through her, a wave of ecstasy to gush from her hole. She knew it was near. It was so fucking near.

John groaned out loudly. Marie knew the sound already. It was something she would always remember. His face contorted again, spoiling his handsome features. His arm pumped vigorously. His legs quivered, then his mouth opened wide like a yawn as a scarcely audible grunt came from him, followed by a powerful spurt of come looping out of the purple tip of his cock and falling onto the burning red buttocks below. Spurt after spurt gushed out and over her buttocks. It seemed to keep coming, shooting out under the pressure of his balls.

Marie rubbed hard. As she watched John's spunk shooting out over Isabelle she pressed down on her flesh, making her clit hurt. It was the trigger for the huge build up of slutty arousal to explode and she had to fight the urge to shout out as it rushed through her insides. It flowed in changing speeds, then suddenly pushing through her to soak her hand and her trousers, leaving her head bewildered by the power and the length of pleasure that the climax had brought.

John had slowed the movement of his hand and now squeezed gently the length of his erection, a few last drops of semen falling onto his wife. Already her bottom was covered in unmoving puddles of his thick come. He appeared to be bringing himself round slowly to a reality that his passion and his climax had temporarily removed him from.

Marie watched in a warm glow. She removed her hand from between her legs and, without thinking, put her fingers beneath her nose an inhaled the strong scent of her climax. She pulled them away quickly when she realised what she was doing. Now she was starting to feel the self-hatred washing over her. Then suddenly John turned as though startled and looked up into the dark corner where Marie squatted.

He had seen her. Or had he? She could not discern from his face. In the panic of the seconds he held his gaze Marie was unable to make any sense of what she should do. Convinced she had been spotted she stood and rushed to the bedroom, the door shutting firmly behind her. Like a little girl who was scared of the monsters she thought lurked in the shadows, she dived into her bed and hid herself beneath the sheets.

Her breathing was deep and fast, almost hysterical, and her heart was rampant as she listened. John was coming up the stairs.

CHAPTER 5

Marie was wide eyed with fear that John was about to enter the bedroom. He had seen her watching. How could she be so stupid?

The steps reached the top of the landing. She listened, not even breathing. He had paused at the top of the stairs, within reach of Marie's door handle. She could feel him, his presence, his physical power, naked and angry. What was he waiting for? Please, she begged silently, please, do not come in this room. Yet part of her, the treacherous, irrational part of her, wanted to see what would happen if he did enter.

Mercifully she heard steps moving away from the door into the room opposite. John then closed his bedroom door firmly behind him.

Marie allowed herself to breathe again. She tried to calm her heart and her shaking hands. The relief she felt was total, as though the thing she had wanted most dearly had been given to her. She wanted to cry she felt such relief. Then came the realisation of her situation. What the hell was happening to her?

Tears came to her eyes. Initially her eyes welled up blurring her vision. Then the first tear broke, streaked down her cheek and she fell into hysterical, uncontrollable sobbing.

She couldn't make sense of anything. This new place, these new people, these new, unimagined areas of sexuality were all too much for her. She longed for the chance to erase this from her life. She wanted to be back with Martin, wrapped up with him in a warm bed.

For so long she had maintained her reputation and standards so that no person could look at her with an accusing eye. She took pride in knowing that she had never lowered herself in the way that every other girl she had known had ended up doing.

It had not been easy for her. Not because the things those girls were doing appealed to her. She found it hard because she seemed to have a dark, powerful urge inside her that wanted to go far, far beyond what the other girls, even the dirtiest and sluttiest, could even conceive of. That part of her she had suppressed with a puritanical zeal. It had tried to steer her towards acts of the flesh that she was disgusted by, yet simultaneously aroused by.

She had never let this dark part of her take hold. When she felt it swarm in her head, manipulating her thoughts into lurid forms, she punished herself and beat it down inside her. She would stop physically, remove herself from contact with Martin or take herself from the view of the man, or woman, who had aroused that part of her. Eventually those forms in her head would fade. Only occasionally did she have to give into it through masturbation. If she could have cut that part of her body off that gave rise to these thoughts she would have done. But she could not, and had instead learned to control it. Or so she thought.

She had come on the train to this new town and it was as though her control over these urges had been left on board. Was it because she was so many miles from home? Or that she knew nobody here? There had been times when the urge had told her to run away to a distant city, overseas even, and be free to commit whatever acts of depravity she could think of. It was all such a mess in her head. Had she even consented to John? She tried to remember back to how it had unfolded earlier in the shower.

She was shocked to recall it. She had had his penis in her mouth. She had enjoyed it. It had made her feel the most perfect feeling throughout her. She had had his erection in her anus, pushing through her firmly and it had given her the most amazing, unprecedented rush of pleasure. Most of all he had hurt her. He had hurt her bottom with spanking and penetration. He had hurt her breasts with the water and his cruel grip, and she had loved it. She knew the images of her acting this way would be with her like a life sentence. She would never be absolved of the shame.

Gradually she calmed herself. Her eyes dried and her shaking gave way to steady breathing and a resolve that she would never let herself fall as she had done today. She would stay with John and Isabelle, unless they asked her to leave, and she would work hard at her new job. She would act as though this day had never happened.

Marie realised with concern that no sound had been made by Isabelle. She must still be tied to the table, Marie thought. She may have passed out from the brutal assault she had been subjected to. Marie knew that, as much as she wanted this day to end, she had to go and see if Isabelle needed help.

Summoning courage that she had not known was in her Marie slowly and quietly climbed from the bed. With only the faintest of creaks she opened her door and exited; her every effort was directed towards stealth. John would only be able to hear her if he was listening and from the sounds of deep slow breathing from the room he was probably asleep. Marie began descending the stairs terrified at what she might find.

A few steps down and Isabelle's naked flesh again revealed itself to her. She was awake and conscious and she turned her head to face Marie. There was a look of understanding and gratitude in her face that was apologetic – her eyes seemed to be saying sorry to Marie. There was no embarrassment between them, even though they had never met. There seemed instead an instant mutual understanding as though they had been friends for many years.

When Marie was level with Isabelle she was able to see up close the startling marks that John had left on her. Isabelle's buttocks still burned red with the distinct lines of the paddle. The evidence of John's satisfaction was puddled on the surface of her skin, pools and strips of his ejaculate covering the red flesh like a salve. Some had run over the curve of her bottom into the parting of her buttocks, over her pinprick hole and down to the still engorged lips of her beautiful sex.

Marie looked Isabelle in the eye. "Can I untie you?" she asked in a whisper.

Isabelle paused as though taken aback by the kindness in Marie's voice. "Yes," she replied, barely loud enough to be heard.

Marie knelt down near to Isabelle's head. It felt pleasant to her to be in this position with a naked, bound woman of such beauty and femininity. It felt good to be able to help her.

Reaching below the table, her head still above it and looking at Isabelle's divine body, Marie felt her way along Isabelle's forearm towards her tied wrists. She could feel the fine hair on Isabelle's arms and then the coarse rope that was digging into her skin. Feeling over the rope delicately, being careful not to cause any more pain to Isabelle, Marie managed to push a finger into the tightness of the knot. Working it gently she began to pull at it, squeezing the rope backwards and forwards to break its grip. Gradually her manipulation eased the rope's pressure from Isabelle's wrist.

The sense of relief on Isabelle's face was apparent and Marie felt a strong attraction towards Isabelle at that moment.

Soon she was in control of the knot. With both hands she hit the point where she knew she had solved it. She smiled involuntarily and pulled at it, slowly unravelling its length, letting it fall to the floor. With gentleness she ran her fingers lightly over Isabelle's wrists, feeling the marks of compression gouged on her skin.

Taking her hands from beneath the table Marie raised herself from her knees, tenderly brushing Isabelle's hair from her eyes as she did so. No words passed between them. Words were not needed. Like so much of what Marie had felt that day it was a primal contact they had, not sullied by the pretensions of words.

Marie moved so that she was directly behind Isabelle and facing her. She could see the prefect curve of Isabelle's form, more impressive to look at now that she was able to raise her upper body from the wooden table, supporting herself on her elbows as she rubbed the pain from her wrists.

Reaching under the table Marie again felt for the knot, letting her hands dwell on the skin as much as she could, calmed by the way it felt to brush her fingers over it. She went down the rope, felt blindly over it for a gap to slide her finger into, and having done so pushed into the tight knot with satisfaction.

As she worked the knot loose below the table Marie was leant forward so that her head was only a few inches away from Isabelle's exposed pussy, as well as the red skin of her bottom with the spunk covering it. She was so close that she could smell Isabelle's scent, different from the way her own moistness smelt. Marie could see that Isabelle's arousal from her punishment had not faded yet. She was drawn to the scent as she was once drawn, embarrassingly, to sniff her own knickers after a day of being constantly aroused.

Around Isabelle's little hole and on the softest of flesh around her sex there was no hair at all, nor any mark or blemish. It was perfectly, beautifully smooth. The lips of her pussy were pulled apart by the awkward position she was tied in.

The knot was pulled apart. It fell to the floor as Marie held her hands gently over Isabelle's ankles, caressing them. She did not want this to end. It felt too special to just return to her room. She felt like she had been stripped of her facade by Isabelle's eyes looking into her own; and that the disparity of what she wanted to be seen as and what she was had been resolved into harmony. She did not want to step away, as she knew that this balance would be disrupted the moment she did.

Isabelle turned her head and looked Marie directly in the eye. The look seemed designed to impart reassurance and strength. Marie knew that it meant she was to do what she wanted so much to do.

She released Isabelle's ankles and raised her hands to gently rest on her beautiful thighs. Marie then kissed the back of Isabelle's thigh. It felt wonderful to have her lips on Isabelle's flesh, to be this way with a naked woman. It was a dark, disgusting fantasy of hers that she repressed but that was now alive. It felt as magnificent as the brazen parts of her had promised it would.

She worked her kisses slowly up Isabelle's thigh. Isabelle was instantly receptive to the sensation, her breathing becoming deeper. There was a feeling in the air around them that what they were doing was illicit and dangerous.

Marie ceased her gentle kisses when she reached Isabelle's bottom. She looked closely at its redness and felt compassion for the pain that came with those marks. Every part of her wanted to kiss it better. She had no intention of denying herself anything at this moment.

With her tongue and lips, as though kissing tenderly at Isabelle's mouth, Marie softly kissed over the sore flesh of Isabelle's chastised bottom, licking up John's come as she progressed along the lines left by the paddle. The sensation for Marie was exquisite, with the taste of John's thick climax strong on her lips with the heat from Isabelle's bottom on her tongue.

She swallowed down John's fluid happily. Having it in her mouth and sticky around her lips made her feel connected to the act that had brought it gushing out initially. The strikes of the paddle, the powerful wanking of that brilliant cock, the endless spurts of thick, creamy come were all in Marie's head. They were warming her pussy, still sore from the intensity of pain and pleasure it had already known that day.

Soon Marie had lapped up all the come from Isabelle's red buttocks. Without hesitating Marie put her hands up to pull the buttocks apart and let her tongue enter that valley. She licked at the spunk that had gathered on Isabelle's tight anus, loving the debauchery of the act. She dwelt on the small hole, circling over it and swallowing every bit of come her tongue found. Then, with an expertise that she had no right to be capable of, she stiffened her tongue and pushed it past the tight clenched entrance of that gorgeous bum hole. She began flicking her tongue in and out.

Isabelle began to squirm with the sensations running through her. A deeply felt sigh of satisfaction came from her. Marie was emboldened by it and increased her tongue's pace as well as how deep she pushed it inside. She moved her hand quickly to undo her trousers and pulled them over her buttocks urgently.

Still flicking her tongue into Isabelle's beautiful ass, and holding the raw buttocks apart, she began to use her free hand to strike her exposed bottom, hitting it as hard as she could. The pain was not enough but there was a sense of impropriety that had her arousal climbing. She struck hard and fast, the sharp slaps mixing with Isabelle's sighs of pleasure.

Isabelle was near to coming. Marie could tell from her movement, pushing back onto the invasive tongue, willing it to plunge deeper. Marie wanted desperately to make her climax. She wanted to know that she had made this beautiful women feel the sweet liquor of an orgasm spill through her. The prospect pushed Marie's own arousal spiralling, as close as she could get, unable to control it. Harder still she struck her bottom.

It came beautifully and powerfully and endured for a long time. As Marie plunged her tongue as deep as she could force it, the pants of delight from Isabelle changed to a high pitched, stuttering whimper. Marie knew this was it and could not escape, nor wanted to escape, the onset of her own intense finish. Desisting from spanking she pushed a finger into her own anus and banged it in and out as fast as she could manage. It built up in her quickly, layer on layer, with Isabelle's whimpers and her tongue licking over that beautiful anus, both their wet cunts dripping and the taste of spunk still on her lips, and then with a low groan Isabelle broke out with her orgasm, her body twitching and twisting, her tight hole throbbing and her pussy pulsing and then a little squirt of liquid fired out onto the table beneath.

Marie's own finger continued thrusting into her ass. She moved her mouth from Isabelle's anus to her still twitching pussy and licked eagerly at the juices that coated her delicate, pink flesh. The taste of John's semen was still there. The smell was beautiful, strong and hot and dirty. It was the smell that went deep into Marie, and then she could feel a rush of energy firing into her sore cunt. Oh fuck. It worked through her like something collapsing, all of it centring on her ass. She closed her eyes and breathed out completely. Breathless, she let her finger slowly beat out the last waves of pleasure from her bum.

Marie slumped down exhausted. The intensity of what she had just felt through her had made her weak, incapable of any act or thought.

Isabelle raised herself up from the table and knelt beside Marie, her arm placed around her comfortingly.

"Come on," she said gently. "Let's get you to bed."

CHAPTER 6

Marie woke to her alarm and pulled herself from beneath the covers rubbing sleep from her eyes. She felt recharged after an excellent night's sleep. It took a few moments before the events of the previous night came back to her.

The memory descended like a heavy weight dropped on her shoulders. She recovered the events trying to establish what had really happened, wishing it had been one of her vivid dreams. No, only one modest part of what she recollected had been a dream. She wanted to cry.

There was little time to think over her actions. It was her first day at work and she had fought to get this job and she was not about to throw the chance away. She showered and dressed quickly then descended the stairs with a deep breath to face John and Isabelle.

Marie's worries proved unnecessary. John and Isabelle were busy preparing for work with a hasty breakfast and swiftly drunk coffee. It was as though the astonishing sexual acts of the previous day had been as inconsequential as a gentle stroll in the park. Marie found it difficult to comprehend the casual way the three were conducting the morning – there was not even an undercurrent of tension detectable – but she was also hugely relieved that what had happened was not going to be disruptive.

Marie walked to her new work having taken directions from John. Standing outside the place he had directed her to she was struck by the beauty and curiosity of the building. It was like a stately country home tucked in a city centre with spacious grounds and ornate columns. It had a powerful presence to it and Marie felt inspired as she walked up its steps to the grand arched entrance.

A beautiful dark haired woman of about forty sat behind a desk in a large foyer. She had a mass of long, dark hair. Marie was taken aback to realise the woman wore a corset. It looked vintage as well, incredibly tight and restrictive around the woman's waist, while pushing up her pale breasts so that they made beautiful pressed spheres. Marie struggled to take her eyes away from the woman's chest.

"Yes?" the woman asked curtly.

"I'm Marie. It's my first day." The woman merely stared at Marie. "I spoke with a man," she continued. Her mind went blank. She could not recall the name of the man she had spoken to.

"A man?" the woman said sternly. "Well, no one has said anything to me so I'm afraid you will have to leave."

Marie was flustered. "But, please, I spoke to a man. He said come here..." Marie's pleading was interrupted by the entrance of a tall young man into the room.

"Marie?" he asked in a confident voice.

"Yes. Yes." Marie replied, ecstatic that this handsome man had been ready for her.

"Come with me," he said.

Marie was led down a long corridor. The man who she looked on now as her saviour was well built with broad shoulders and a thin tight midriff. His face was classically handsome, Marie noticed. He had an upright stature, brisk manner and confidence that were directly linked to his beautiful features. Marie instantly disliked his cocksure attitude, even as she struggled to deny that he was a stunningly attractive man.

He stopped outside a door and looked directly at her.

"That was Daniella," he said. His voice was very well spoken. "She is our Cerberus. Her blood runs cold which keeps undesirable people out. It doesn't make for good conversation." He opened the door and led Marie through.

They entered a huge room. Every wall was adorned with huge paintings while the floor was interspersed with glass cabinets and large statues. It was an impressive sight. She felt a rush of satisfaction. A little smile crept to her lips.

"My name is Aiden," he said to her. "I am your contact for all matters. A brief tour as induction now."

The paintings he showed her were stunning. They were neo-classical and all of them featuring nude or partially clothed figures in various types of conflict. Some contained quite explicit sexual acts. She was familiar with the style but had never seen it presented quite so openly.

Aiden paused in front of another huge canvas. It depicted a plump but beautiful woman being forced back. The man gripped her arm powerfully. The woman's face was full of terror.

"A seventeenth century Dutch copy of Titian's Rape of Lucretia. A very expensive work of art." He led her onwards.

They stopped in front of a large glass display. Inside was a cracked piece of stone work or plaster, it seemed to Marie. It showed a faded picture of a woman naked and on all fours with a muscular, naked man entering her with his long, stiff penis. Marie felt embarrassed.

"In Pompeii the brothels were decorated with these frescos, no doubt to set the customer's blood alive. This came from the largest brothel in Pompeii. I rather like the work, though the act is rather trite and tame." Marie tried to offer up her opinion but Aiden had already moved on.

He led Marie out of the room and they descended a flight of stone steps. At the bottom was a small wooden door. Above the door was a weathered key stone that had a stiff phallus and balls carved deeply into it. Around it was the inscription "HIC HABITAT FELICITAS". Before she could open her mouth to ask it was translated for her.

"Happiness resides here." Aiden pushed open the door and walked in. Marie followed.

Aiden set a few dim lights flickering on. The room was stone floored and walled. A set of drawers were pushed against the far wall. There were cast iron rings set into the wall on all sides. From one of these there was a length of heavy rope tied to a pulley in the ceiling and falling down to suspend ominously in the centre of the room. On the end of the rope was a heavy looking metal hook.

Aiden walked to the drawers and took out a heavy looking bundle of leather straps. He then hung it from the hook, a confusion of leather and metal buckles.

"This is one of the finest artefacts in the museum, idiotically hidden down here. It is a sixteenth century harness, crafted in Italy, principality unknown, for the amusement of the very wealthy aristocracy."

Marie wanted to speak when she heard him pause in his speech but her voice froze.

"It is exceptional, probably one of a handful at most scattered around the world. Not one link, not one line, has been replaced such was the skill of its creator."

They both stood looking at it hanging limply from the hook. Marie still had no idea what it was made for.

"Come here. I want you to feel the genius of the man who crafted it."

Marie was reluctant, yet Aiden's eyes did not seem to permit her to make a decision. His manner was such that she didn't have opportunity to formulate an excuse. Instead, under the pressure of his manner, she meekly acquiesced.

She stood next to the harness and looked at it with suspicion. Aiden took hold of her arm and pulled her half a step towards the harness. He then started to wrap a piece of the leather around her waist.

Realising he intended to put her in the harness Marie resisted.

"I'm alright thanks." Her voice quivered with nervousness.

He paused and held his look into her eyes. His expression went beyond annoyance. It was angry. What right had he to be angry at her, Marie thought.

"Listen," he said. "You will try this harness on because it is one of the finest artefacts of its kind in the entire fucking world. I am granting you the opportunity to experience what only an incredibly small number of people have had the pleasure of experiencing in nearly five hundred fucking years. It is your chance to be physically entwined with a genuine Renaissance masterpiece, an incomparable work of craftsmanship, and your reply is; 'I'm alright thanks'." He paused, the anger bright in his eyes. "I'm going to put this harness on you and you are not going to say another fucking word."

She did as she had been instructed. Aiden worked around her tying knots, wrapping lengths of leather around her and fastening buckles with varying tightness. His hands worked around her waist, then her thighs and then near her breasts all of which unsettled her greatly but she was too full of fear to protest.

He stepped back to look over his work, reaching to make minor adjustments. His interest in the harness rather than in her eased some of her worry. She was underwhelmed by this supposed masterpiece. The fit was not right for a start, with some bits tight and other bits so loose that they were not worth having. Aiden was a self obsessed jerk, she thought. He was very good looking though, that she couldn't deny.

He walked to the wall where the length of rope was tied to a metal ring. Marie wondered what he was doing when, with a huge effort, Aiden pulled down on the rope, passing it through is hands and fixing it back to the ring in the wall. Marie shrieked loudly as she was jerked from her feet. The ropes that had hung limp around her now snapped tight. She was lifted off her feet and thrown back so that she was almost horizontal. She continued to shriek, partly from the pain of the ropes, partly from the exposed position the harness had put her in. Her legs were spread wide apart, her knees raised up.

Aiden walked over to her with a satisfied look on his face, as though he had just pulled off an elaborate magic trick. As he circled her, testing the ties he had made, her shrieking ceased. Her panic was still audible in her erratic breathing. She was completely bound; no part of her had freedom of movement. Suspended from a metal hook her wrists and ankles, her shoulders and chest were tightly trussed.

The sensation the harness created was entirely unique. She could feel it at once. It instantly set her sexuality alive in a strange way. The exposure of her crotch, though still covered by her light linen skirt, the pressure of the slightly painful constraints and the way those constraints pulled her open set her instantly warming with lust. She concentrated on suppressing it.

Aiden was trying to unsettle her, she thought. He wanted her to panic so that he could boost his own ego at her expense. She would be damned before giving him that satisfaction, the jerk. She used what determination and stubbornness she had inside her to at least look undisturbed by her vulnerable position.

Aiden looked over her body. "Many attribute the birth of the Renaissance to the discovery of Alexandria's ancient texts – to the entombed works of Aristotle, Euclid et al. But it wasn't these. What ignited it was the discovery of sex as an indulgence. Sex as exquisite pleasure. Pieces of parchment were dusted off that revealed the richness that could be added to life through the cock and the cunt."

She tried to answer him but was unable to. She was at once fearful, aroused and determined to show neither.

"Of course people fucked," he continued, staring at the centre of her spread legs. "I'm sure they fucked plenty and some did it for fun. But it was not done with any art. They did it as dogs. Suddenly they had revealed to them the sex that Cleopatra knew. A world of cunnilingus, cock sucking, orgies and anal done with great skill.

"There are wonderful stories of French aristocratic females who were addicted to pendulums like these. One account tells of a Lady who bound herself in it for days on end welcoming all comers – servants, swineherds, neighbours, guests, chambermaids – anyone."

His talk was distracting her mind. Marie felt heat concentrating between her spread legs. She was getting warm and wet. She could see her nipples were engorged and were giving her away to Aiden. He had looked at them more than once.

"You should feel quite privileged. The harness you are in has held the most prized and beautiful women of age after age. Naked in these constraints, warm chested, their cunt lips heated and parted, they would be entered repeatedly. They would have been used by man after man who spent his seed deep in her hole. But the genius of the artisan who made it was to ensure the real pleasure was the woman's. For her there was pleasure that was inconceivable to the uninitiated."

She was really wet now. She worried that it was possible he could see her wetness forming, or that he could smell the sweet pungency of her arousal.

With the faintest of touches Aiden touched the skin on the inside of her knee, pulled her towards him, and then released her swinging gently.

His touch riled her. It was taking a liberty, yet she had been half wanting him to touch her flesh. The fleeting touch sent flashes of heat through her. It set aflame carnal sensations that were shameful to her.

Aiden walked over to the drawers and removed a black cloth then walked to the rear of Marie. She could not turn to see what he was doing. This unnerved her considerably and she gave into her panic. "Aiden, please," she bleated, but had scarcely spoken the words when Aiden swiftly pulled the black hood over her head, shrouding her in darkness.

Again she exclaimed loudly. "Take it off, Aiden. Take it off for fuck's sake. I don't like this sort of thing." The anxiety was terribly evident from the breaking of her normally soft voice. She could see nothing through the hood.

"Come now, Marie, play along. It's hardly worth going through all that to just untie you, is it?"

"Please, I really don't like..."

"Be quiet now," he barked, his tone of voice suddenly changed. He softened it again. "It isn't that you don't like it, it's that you don't know."

She complied meekly. His tone and his manner were calm and assertive, making this whole horrible and improbable experience seem perfectly acceptable. Such was his power that Marie felt genuinely that she was being unreasonable to protest so much.

A period of silence followed. She felt his hand stroke over her calf, up to her knee and then over and down the soft flesh on the inside of her thigh, easing beneath the light material of her bunched up skirt.

She summoned some courage. "No, Aiden. I want you to let me down now. Please."

"You don't really want that."

The hand, a stranger's hand, continued slowly down her thigh towards her already wet panties. It was working her to a state of desperate urgency that was unfamiliar to her. Her breathing was deep and quick. The sound of her breathing was strong in her ears because of the hood. On each breath her stomach muscles involuntarily contracted lifting her hips up as though pulling the hand into her. In her head she was desperate for this to end and she hated the pleasure her body was feeling.

"Just stop. Now, Aiden. I mean it." Her voice was raised but weak. She was starting to cry as it dawned on her how vulnerable she was. She fought to suppress them but they persisted.

"No more talking," Aiden said sternly. "Understand?" She sensed that he was angry at her. There was a very real threat in his voice and she was not prepared to challenge him any further. Oh, stupid girl, she thought, what have you done?

His hand was resting on the very soft flesh where her thigh met her warm and open pussy, albeit concealed by her wet panties. A finger pushed up the edge of the undergarment and his hand progressed inwards. It brushed lightly through her untrimmed hair, his fingers playing in it gently. His large hand inside her panties pulled them up and across so that there was pressure against her soft, wet flesh. The gusset of her panties narrowed and dug in between her swelling lips releasing some of her wetness.

His fingers dropped to the centre of her hot flesh, sliding firmly down the centre, pressing over her clitoris, making her hips twist, and then down to circle round the entrance of her hole. His finger slid effortlessly and gently feeling the pulsing of her arousal. The feeling through her was lovely, even through the tears. She was being sexually assaulted and her cursed body was glorying in it.

Aiden firmed his thick middle finger and slid it directly inside her wet opening, easing past the resistance it met as she tried in vain to deny him access. Slowly he started to slide in and out of her, curling his finger up as he withdrew and pushing his thumb against her wet clit as he slid back in.

His other hand was placed on the flat of Marie's stomach, just above the line of pubic hair. It had been pressing down to keep her in place and to heighten her arousal by bringing her g-spot into play. This hand now slid up to undo buttons on her shirt, exposing her pale skinned breasts. He slid his hand under the cups of her bra and pulled the full breasts out, caressing the swollen nipples with his thumb.

Through shame and tears and disgust Marie was unable to avoid the exquisite pleasure Aiden's skilful hands were creating in her. It was all part of the cruelty, all fuel for his ego, she thought. He was empowered by his ability to arouse her despite her desperate efforts to avoid it. In her head she was already formulating plans to never speak to anyone about this.

His hands had strength in them and they pushed waves of sensual pleasure through her constantly. She had never felt so hot and wet between her legs, nor so flushed and full in her breasts. Her pants were sodden and the wetness was spreading down over her thighs and buttocks. She could feel it wet over her anus.

He moved. Both hands were still in place, though changed, and he was up nearer her head. With the hand between her legs he now used his fingers and her wetness to rub broad circles over her clit, smearing wetness over her skin and pink flesh. His other hand took hold of her breasts with more force. She then felt his mouth kissing over them, his tongue circling her nipples. The leather straps dug into the underside of the soft flesh of her breasts and began to spread pain through her. It was sharp and persistent, but seemed, strangely, to be appropriate to the pleasure she was receiving from his mouth and hand.

He removed his hand from between her legs and smeared the wetness roughly over her tits. He then locked his mouth onto the beautiful orbs and sucked and licked her juices off. Using his teeth he began to pull at the nipples sending an excruciating pain flashing over her chest like a sting.

He released her and she knew he was moving again. The hood was adjusted slightly to reveal her mouth and nose only. She sensed him directly over her now. She heard him unbuckle his belt and his zip descend.

Her heart quivered with a shot of adrenalin. She steeled herself to resist what she was certain was about to be demanded of her. She was powerless but she could still make it hard work for him, the bastard.

Her heightened senses heard his trousers slide down and his manhood drop naturally into the open. She knew it was near her face. She could sense it near to her mouth. She waited for him.

He stroked his hand up and down his cock's length. She could sense it was large. She then felt him put the tip of it to her lips. She clamped shut against him turning her head blindly to avoid it.

"Be a good girl, Marie. There is only one road open to you here; you know that, don't you? So stop fucking about and take it in your mouth."

She heard some impatience in his voice. She screwed her face up and continued to turn to prevent him from guiding it into her mouth.

Thwack! The open palm of his hand smashed against the side of her head. For a moment she was stunned, lost as to her whereabouts or situation. It hurt her entire head and sent a ringing through her brain.

"Must I hit you again, Marie?" he bellowed at her.

Still shaken and unsure she reacted instinctively and raised her head slightly with an open mouth to receive his cock. It was a half conscious act of self preservation. Without thinking she began to rock her head back and forth, circling her tongue over his fat tip and sucking him firm.

His groans were audible. He was enjoying the sensation of being inside her mouth, fucking away at it gently. His dick quickly reached full firmness so that it was like stone inside her mouth. She couldn't tell how large his dick was but she felt it must be big as she could fit little more than the thick tip into her mouth.

As her thoughts became clearer after the shock of his strike she found herself hugely turned on to have a stranger's cock in her mouth. She could feel her arousal in contractions between her legs, and in the heat and the wetness that was building up there.

She sucked at him vigorously without realising. Her tongue circled hungrily round the tip of his manhood each time she tasted any pre-ejaculate seep out. The creamy salty taste seemed to spur her on to more enthusiastic sucking, trying to draw more of his fluids out. When she realised what she was doing she checked herself. Still the tears were in her eyes but she was enjoying the act, her shame pressed down by the eagerness of that sexually driven side of her to indulge in this man's cock.

He pulled his cock from her mouth and she gasped for air in quick breaths. She was nearly hysterical with the conflict inside her. She was being abused and yet her body, the source of so much shame throughout her life, was alight along every nerve fibre with arousal like she had never known.

Aiden stood between her spread legs and lifted her skirt. He gripped the soaked crotch of her knickers, his knuckles brushing against her swollen vulva and making her ache for satisfaction. Using his other hand to grip her thigh he wrenched hard at the knickers, then again, pulling at them forcefully until the wet material bit into her skin and tore apart completely exposing her beautiful flesh.

Marie felt the tip of his cock rubbing slowly around the wet entrance to her cunt. She could sense his size better now. She could tell his cock was big and long and was going to stretch her wide when he pushed into her. And she was at such a state of arousal that she was desperate for him to be inside her. And yet a sudden fear struck her. She was small inside. Her boyfriend, Martin, was too big, and he wasn't nearly as big as what was waiting at the entrance to her hole.

"No, please, you'll rip me," she implored.

Her plea received a disdainful response. With a violent thrust he powered the full length of his formidable erection into her, right up to his balls so that his muscular torso and pubic hair put pressure on her swollen clit. He let out an animal grunt as he entered, her extreme tightness making his entry at once painful and hugely satisfying, as though he was fucking at a virgin pussy.

The power of his penetration forced a sharp scream from Marie. It hurt desperately. She clenched her teeth and groaned against the pain of having his large cock suddenly inside her tight hole. She felt certain he had damaged her inside. It stretched her so that she felt he was close to tearing her flesh open. Underneath this pain, flashing in the same way as the pain, was an amazing sexual arousal.

Aiden began to work his length out of that beautifully tight pussy. As he withdrew Marie felt ecstatic relief wash over her. He left his broad tip just inside her lips and held it there a moment, using his hand to rub it around the entrance to her hole, feeling it slowly contract from the shock. He then took a tight grip of her waist, his fingers digging in sharply, and thrust himself powerfully inside her again. He let out a groan of delight and then a distinct peel of laughter as Marie screamed out.

Again he slowly withdrew and again he thrust his full length into her. He continued in this way, sliding out, letting her hole narrow, letting her feel relief, and then smashing back inside her. Marie's screams lessened with each entry. The painful invasion still hurt her but increasingly the pleasure of it was becoming more prevalent.

All her life she had avoided pain with a neurotic, irrationally obsessive fear. And now, exposed to it like never before, she was enjoying it in a horrible, perverted way. Shame brought tears to her eyes and set her sobbing again. Each thrust was making her feel more aware of her body than she had ever been, aware of herself as a physical being, alive to pain and pleasure.

Aiden's pace built. He was thrusting in and out of her aching hole without stopping. He was frenzied now that Marie could accommodate the full girth without causing him any pain. She could sense the shape of his cock, the contours of it; the blunt round tip. Sensual pleasure was overtaking her. Heat was building inside her and was being forced deep by Aiden's long, hard cock. She could feel everything. His balls were slapping against her where her cunt was dripping juices over her buttocks; his hands were digging their nails into the skin at her waist. The feeling of pressure and the need to urgently release it was moving rapidly through her, pushing down to where that huge cock fucked her so hard, and then burst through her like a volcanic eruption, spewing forth and running through her, smooth and thick. It was the most delicious, indulgent, perfect feeling of pleasure she had ever known. She didn't know if she was crying from shame or pure delight, so confused were her feelings in the aftermath of her orgasm.

Aiden moved his hands so that they gripped Marie's nipples tightly. He used his anchorage to pull her soaked and sore pussy onto his thick cock, pounding into her manically. Marie felt the pain of his grip and it reignited her lingering orgasmic pleasure. Her mind focused suddenly on what she could not see – the young, muscular man, trousers around his ankles, fucking her glistening cunt with his thickset, throbbing cock. She heard his breathing become loud and she felt that he was going to come soon. Marie wanted it. She was desperate for his groans to be his climax and for her cunt to flow with his sperm.

It came for her at that moment. With a sustained moan of satisfaction he pushed into her as deep as he could and held it there. She then felt the stream of spunk open up, shooting into her quickly, then more come was pumping out of his twitching cock, every sensation felt deep inside her cunt. He slowly worked his cock in and out of her, the last little firing of ejaculate flowing out of him, mixing with her own flooding juices.

The heightened sensations and the awareness of being pumped full of thick spunk from a stranger's cock, and of it running out of her made her feel such a slut that she was again incredibly aroused and in a state that was desperate for more. She felt him withdraw his fading erection and, without knowing it, she implored him not to leave her unsatisfied.

"I need to come again. Push it back in."

She heard him pulling his trousers up. She desperately wanted just a few moments more from him to release the swelling arousal inside her. Anything, just a finger pushed up inside her, would be enough to bring it on.

He did nothing except untie a single knot that bound her hands. He then turned and walked from the room.

Marie quickly shook her hands free and then pulled the hood from her just in time to see the door closing. She immediately pushed a hand down between her legs to the swollen flesh while she used her other hand to squeeze hard at her tits. It was sublime satisfaction, uncomplicated by any thoughts other than how great it felt to have her fingers rubbing hard over her pulsing clitoris and to have that hot pain through her tits again. It took a few seconds of this desperately needed masturbation for the pressure that was in her to force itself out in gushes of juices from her throbbing hole.

The rushes through her body slowly lessened. The beauty of that last powerful orgasm was easing from her and self awareness was replacing it. She was appalled that Aiden had treated her like this, but more ashamed at the way she had enjoyed the act.

With effort she removed herself from the harness. He legs were weak and her balance uncertain. She smoothed her clothes, covering her exposed breasts and put on her torn knickers as best she could. And as best she could she wiped away Aiden's come from between her legs, spreading it on the inside of her skirt's hem in a way that truly appalled her when she reflected on it. With a deep breath she contemplated her options. She would keep silent about this episode and pray that Aiden would do exactly the same.

Marie's first day at worked passed without any more distress. Aiden was absent the entire day, much to Marie's relief. Though she was in a fragile emotional state, close to tears all day, she was full of determination to see her first day through professionally. With considerable pride at her resolve she made it to five o'clock and set off for her new digs.

The torment of her behaviour was torture for Marie. Each moment of her cruel use at Aiden's hands was continually playing back in her mind. She had not been forceful enough in telling him "No". Oh, god, she had begged him to fuck her, she had no excuse. Her pain, embarrassment and self loathing were at levels she had never known – and her whole sexually mature life had been coloured by these feelings.

When at her new home she spoke briefly with Isabelle then made her excuses and retired to her bedroom. Should she be going home now, she thought, away from this place where so many of her hidden desires had already been revealed? She was lost as to her way forward. Something told her that she must not quit so early and this was how she resolved to act. Stick it out and put the past behind her.

Martin called on the phone, full of enthusiasm and affection. For Marie the phone call was expected but unwanted. She tried to reciprocate but the ordeal of her first day would not permit any joy, however feigned. Her patience with Martin finally broke when he suggested he should come and see her the following weekend. She just couldn't bear to see him with what she had done so fresh in her memory – it was hard enough speaking to him on the phone – and her reply was abrupt to the point of callousness. No, he could not come as she had only just arrived and needed to be left alone. Martin was taken aback but concurred.

Tired, sore and still quite shaken, Marie fell asleep.

CHAPTER 7

The next day at work Marie was instantly deflated by the reception she was given. Her new work colleagues, few of whom she had been introduced to, were looking at her and laughing and talking in whispers about her as she passed. Marie was instantly worried they knew what had happened with Aiden. He would never have told people that he had fucked her, surely? She was being paranoid. This whole damned place was making her head a mess.

Marie had the issue cleared up for her when she bumped into Aiden.

Feeling urged to speak through her pronounced and evident chagrin she said, "I'm prepared not to speak to anyone about yesterday if you are prepared to do the same."

His reply was cold and curt. "Too late for that. I told them all how much you enjoyed yourself and how you begged for more."

Marie's heart missed a beat. Shock and anger mixed together and set her body shaking in the rush of emotion.

"You bastard," she managed to say, her voice quivering. Aiden had already started to walk away as she uttered the words.

Distressed, Marie ran to the toilets. She could feel tears starting to well in her eyes. She stood solemnly looking at herself in the mirror and contemplated what she had done and what she had become. She had given in. She had always known not to give into the urges because they were wrong and now here she was suffering the consequences of submitting to them.

Daniella, the dark haired receptionist, walked into the toilet and immediately put a comforting arm around Marie's shoulder.

"Don't give him the satisfaction," the beautiful, older lady said, her dark eyes full of compassion. "He thinks he owns you and so he'll treat you like shit. But you can't let him."

Marie wiped a tear from her face and looked up. "He thinks he owns me?"

"Oh, honey," Daniella said softly. "That is exactly what he's been telling everyone. He's like this with all girls. You have to stand up to him. Show him it's about you, not him."

Daniella gently wiped a tear from Marie's face. She looked into the young girl's eyes earnestly and sympathetically. Marie suddenly felt a huge sense of gratitude that someone should be caring for her now.

"I've been so stupid," she said meekly.

Daniella, her arm wrapped tenderly over Marie's shoulders, drew closer and kissed Marie in a motherly way on the forehead. That gentle contact was like a spark that instantly invigorated the two that shared it. Looking deeply into one another's eyes Daniella kissed Marie passionately on the lips.

Marie was caught in the moment with its rush of emotions. Instinctively she was reciprocating. It felt good on her lips and was already moving quickly to tingle her whole body. Then the nagging thought entered her head telling her it was disgusting to enjoy kissing a female. She panicked and withdrew.

"I'm sorry Daniella. I really don't want this," she said, feeling satisfied that, at last, she had done the right thing.

"You're safe with me, sweetheart," the dark eyed lady whispered.

Daniella saw uncertainty in Marie's eyes and seized on the opportunity with another embrace. Her tongue pushed between the young girl's lips and circled the tongue which slowly began to reciprocate. She then began to kiss and delicately bite along Marie's jaw line and neck, pulling her hair back so that her flesh was fully exposed to her passionate efforts.

It felt so good to Marie. The gently licking and soft lipped kisses mixed with the sharp bites and firm grasp of her hair all melted into one delightful sensation that circled her body and made her forget the emotional anguish of moments before. Something inside her admitted defeat at this point – she could not resist this wondrous feeling washing through her. She would indulge every sensation and endure the shame afterwards.

Daniella sensed this in Marie. She released her grip on her and stood erect, reaching around her own back to undo the tight fitting corset she was wearing. Her gaze did not move from Marie's eyes as she worked at the elaborate binding. It began to loosen and fall, exposing more of her large breasts bit by bit. Marie watched full of eagerness and arousal as the corset descended, revealing the dark circles and firm points of her nipples. They were beautiful breasts: large, high and splendid. They were the type of breast Marie had dreamed of having and now, to her surprise, longed to kiss.

With a final sharp pull Daniella sent the corset dropping to the floor exposing her bare upper body. In her hand she held the length of binding. Taking Marie's hand she pulled her over to the toilet cubicle and began to tie the young girl's hands to the top of the frame.

As Daniella did this her breasts were pushed close to Marie who could not resist dropping her head to kiss the luscious, pale skinned flesh. With total self indulgence she kissed them as she had kissed Daniella's lips, with her tongue circling the nipples eagerly whenever the older lady's upward reach brought them towards Marie's mouth. Marie could feel the familiar tingle of arousal between her legs, the sensation working through her and moistening her knickers.

Marie was now firmly bound to the cubicle frame and facing inwards towards the toilet. Daniella brushed past her and yanked the girl's top high above her breasts. With similar abruptness she pulled down Marie's trousers exposing her plain underwear. The older lady ran her hands over Marie's exposed flesh, stroking over the fullness of her breasts and down to the delightful pertness of her bottom. The lingering touch electrified Marie. She closed her eyes and let the feeling please her. She was hungry for more. There was a release of wetness in her knickers.

Daniella undid the belt of her trousers and stepped out of them so that she was stood only in her black lace panties, stockings and suspenders. Marie tried to turn her head to see the beautiful woman undress but struggled with the sureness of her binding. She wanted to be touched. She needed to feel contact to ease the building sexual arousal.

The contact came with a crack and a sting of pain as Daniella's belt lashed against Marie's young bottom. It was a raw pain that burned through her and had her writhing to dissipate its effects. A second lash quickly followed, this time reddening the backs of Marie's thighs. Oh, that hurt so much more. She could not avoid shrieking at the instant pain. It hurt desperately, but she gritted her teeth and pushed her bottom out to invite another lash.

"Oh, you like this do you?" Daniella said, impressed by the young girl's moment of bravery.

The belt struck with much more venom this time, just as Marie had wanted, lashing her buttocks so forcefully that her plain white knickers tore slightly and Marie worried the blow must surely have drawn blood as she could feel a dripping moistness about her gusset.

Another blow from the belt licked her bottom. Then it licked her thighs and then once more against her back and side so that the leather rasped against her tender breast. Oh, it hurt so fucking much but, god, it was such a beautiful feeling to be beaten like this.

Daniella was clearly something of a master of knowing when she was letting a lover indulge too much. Just as Marie steadied herself for another lash Daniella withdrew and dropped the belt to the floor.

The older lady walked past Marie and faced her. Their eyes met and it was clear from the subtle smile on Daniella's face that she was relishing the total control she had over this innocent young beauty.

Daniella kissed the girl forcefully again. As she did so she pressed her naked breasts on purpose against Marie's. The effect this had on the younger girl was powerful and she began to raise one of her legs up to press between Daniella's thighs. Marie couldn't help herself. The cruel binding of her hands limited the means with which she could satisfy her urges. She wanted desperately to feel Daniella's soft pussy lips moisten, and her leg was all she had available.

To Marie's huge pleasure, Daniella's arousal was obvious. She could sense the heat and wetness on her leg as it pushed up against the experienced cunt. The older lady began to kiss and bite at Marie's tits, pulling her bra down to expose her nipples and sucking hard on them. Her fingers dropped down into Marie's panties and forced their way over her already dripping lips and into her tight hole. The feeling was perfect for Marie. Her cunt ached for it and as those feminine fingers pushed slowly up into her she sank down on top of them and quivered inside with happiness.

Daniella continued to play with Marie's cunt artfully. Still biting at her nipples she allowed her other hand to reach behind Marie and toy with her delicate rear hole. A finger at first traced around it, adding to the wonderful feelings already working through her, then pushed inside her just a little, penetrating her, opening her, and thrusting in and out very quickly so that the feeling in her ass was so wonderful that it was all she could focus on. She felt that fast finger fucking her ass and knew only a little more and she would come like the eruption of a volcano.

Sensing the orgasm was close, Daniella stopped. She gave Marie one last lingering kiss and then licked provocatively over her fingers that had penetrated the girl. Marie's arousal was complete. She was so desperate for satisfaction that she felt close to tears with frustration.

Daniella moved back and stepped up onto the toilet so that her feet were on the toilet seat and she was squatted over the bowl. Eying Marie with a purposeful stare and a playful smile she pulled her knickers to one side and let a stream of golden water run through her engorged cunt lips.

Marie watched in aroused anguish. It was so depraved, so perverse, so wrong in so many ways to her prudish sensibilities that it was somehow the most sublimely erotic spectacle she had ever seen. If she had not been bound she would have pressed her fingers against those pussy lips and felt the stream through them. That would have been enough to secure her climax.

Sitting down on the toilet seat Daniella pushed a foot up between Marie's legs and into the soft flesh of her pussy. She had soon worked a toe past the girl's panties so that it found the entrance to her hole where it began fucking in and out. Her other foot reached to pull the discarded belt towards her. Taking it into her hand she began to lash it against Marie's exposed breasts, striking against the engorged and sensitive nipples, shooting pain all through the girl's body.

The lashes from the belt were constant, one after the other, not hard but with enough force to shoot a lovely pain through her tits. The working of Daniella's toe was crude but it was just what Marie's pussy craved. She felt sensations building up, each lash adding to the last, each shock of pain sending her further into her own pleasure. Her body was responding to the thrusting foot hard in her hole and over her clit, hard and hurting, so that her whole body was feeling it acutely. Oh, fuck, she knew it was going to come soon. It was there in her womb like a ball of fire causing her pain. Each strike of leather on her tits was intensifying the heat. One more hit, across her nipples; one more crude thrust of the woman's foot, was all that she needed and she would come like a great fucking earthquake.

Oh, fuck, there it was. A lash, harder, more direct, stung her raw breasts and she could do nothing but give into its urgency to push out of her. A flood of youthful pussy juices came pumping out of her hole and onto Daniella's foot. Then more still came gushing out. Marie's legs gave way. They were too weak to hold her up. She was breathless, unaware of anything of her situation, and lost in the splendid aftermath of an intense orgasm.

The moment the final rush had subsided Daniella stood and untied Marie's hands. The weakness of her body was such that she fell to her knees. The older lady slid her soaked knickers down to her ankles and kicked them away. Sitting back on the toilet seat with her legs spread she pulled Marie's face firmly to meet with her dripping, throbbing cunt.

"Lick it hard you little bitch," Daniella said, vitriol in her voice.

Marie tried to bring herself round from her post-climax stupor but was struggling. She began to lick over the wet, sweet scented labia, circling her tongue around the firm clit, but she was still drowsy and weak. It was a listless performance and Daniella was in no mood to tolerate it.

She wrenched Marie's head back by her hair and bellowed into her face. "Try harder you little slut!" and then she slapped the girl firmly on the cheek.

It worked. Marie was awake again and aroused by the dirty act she was engaged in. She saw that luscious pink pussy glistening in front of her face and wanted it. She needed it.

Pushing her mouth into the scented flesh she worked her tongue and lips, sucking and kissing, licking and biting, with a frenzied eagerness. Daniella began to writhe on the seat and pushed her legs up and out against the cubicle walls to completely expose her hole. "That's good, Marie. That's really fucking good," she said through half clenched teeth.

Urged on by this response Marie eased a finger into the tight little ass of the older lady. Her buttocks were spread wide and the hole was wet with cunt juices making entry easy. First one finger, then two, stretching the hole wide while she continued her eager licking of cunt lips and clit.

"That feels so fucking good, Marie. Keep going."

Marie eased a third finger into the lady's ass and began pumping it in and out. She was stretched wide but Marie dared herself to try stretching her more. The groans of exquisite pleasure from Daniella, and the pleasure she had already given Marie, demanded it of her.

She shaped her hand so that she could fit a fourth finger up inside the woman's ass and pushed. Needing a little more lubrication she spat onto her knuckles and began pushing her whole hand, little by little, into Daniella's taut hole. It was difficult at first getting it to that widest point but when that was reached she could ease her entire hand, up to her wrist, inside the beautiful woman's hole.

The effortlessness of the last few inches was hugely satisfying for both involved. Daniella released a high pitched squeal of pleasure, revelling in the raw but sensuous pain. Her face was contorted, her eyes closed.

"Fuck me hard. I want to come so hard into your face."

Marie needed no further invitation. Licking hard and quick over Daniella's clit she simultaneously began fisting in short and quick motions at the woman's anus.

"Oh, yes. That's it you little bitch. That's it. Keep going. Keep fucking going you slut. Oh, fuck…"

Daniella's body contorted, her limbs stiffening involuntarily, her ass contracting around Marie's hand. She wrenched the young girl's head back as she screamed into her face.

"Oh, fuck my ass bitch! Fist my ass! Harder!"

A loud, shrill scream came from Daniella's gaping mouth. She held Marie head so that her face was close to her throbbing hole. Marie could see the wet cunt lips pulsing. A little squirt of thick, clear liquid fired out into the young girl's face. Then again and again in regular bursts. Then suddenly, as Daniella curled her body up a vast spray of come fired out of her cunt into Marie's surprised face. It dripped down her chin and ran onto her breasts.

With a huge sigh of relief Daniella released Marie and slumped back on the toilet seat, totally spent.

"You're a good girl," she said softly.

The door to the toilet swung open and a beautiful young woman entered, startling both Daniella and Marie.

The girl did not seem in the least perturbed by the scene in front of her.

"The Master would like to see Marie at once," she said dispassionately and then walked back out.

CHAPTER 8

Marie waited patiently outside The Master's room. Mrs Ryder, The Master's demure, middle-aged secretary, had instructed her to wait until she was called in. Mrs Ryder also assured Marie that she shouldn't worry. Despite this Marie was exceptionally nervous. This was her first meeting with The Master who she had been informed was the most important person bar none at the museum. She had a terrible feeling that she was being summoned because of the appalling way she had conducted herself since starting work.

After a long wait Mrs Ryder came and informed her that The Master was ready for her. As she walked through the dark wooden door into his office her hands began to shake.

The office was large and grandly decorated with dark wood and leather furniture. It had a Victorian austerity to it that Marie had never seen before. Antique volumes filled imposing bookcases. Beautiful paintings of female nudes hung on the walls.

Behind a huge desk sat The Master. He was a man of around fifty years old, strongly built and handsome. Slightly greying hair was medium length with a subtle wave through it. His eyes were bright and powerful. His suit was smartly tailored. An air of classic style was obvious about him as well as a sense of strength and authority. Marie was no more at ease having seen him at last but she was captured by the power of his presence nonetheless.

The Master remained seated and silent. There was no chair for Marie. She stood meekly in front of the desk, her eyes downcast as was her natural reaction in the presence of a dominant man she found attractive.

"You have made quite an impression since you started," he said.

"I'm sorry," she replied nervously.

"Remain silent until I ask you to speak," the Master replied sharply. When he was certain she understood him he continued. "Everything that happens in this museum comes back to me. I know you have been enjoying your new freedom from home. I know who you have fucked, how you have fucked and where you have fucked."

Marie coloured with most powerful feeling of embarrassment and shame she had ever felt.

"I've been reasonably happy with what I have heard. The chance I took on you might just be vindicated."

The comment startled Marie. Had she heard him correctly?

"As far as I'm concerned, however, you have had your fun. Any liaison you have must benefit your education. It must improve you. To merely float from tryst to tryst is folly. You learn nothing and ultimately you become numb and empty. You become worthless to anyone."

Marie was increasingly confused. The Master continued.

"I have taken you on to improve you. I believe you may one day have some value. The free rein I gave you was a test and you behaved tolerably. But now you must come within my control and learn my lessons."

His voice was deep with experience. It was incredibly sexy, Marie thought, as was the intensity of his manner and the thoughtful way he spoke.

The Master stood erect from his seat. "Allow me to demonstrate."

He ushered into his office the same beautiful blonde young woman who had summoned Marie from the toilet earlier. The sophistication and allure this young woman carried made Marie feel instantly inferior.

"Bare your rear and bend over the desk," he said to the blonde girl as he walked to the corner of his office and retrieved a thin length of cane.

The blonde girl obeyed his order without any word or hesitation. She lifted her skirt up above her waist and then eased her thin black panties down to reveal her deliciously round and firm backside. As she bent slowly over the desk to rest on her elbows Marie became transfixed by the spreading buttocks revealing her little pink crinkle of ass and, below it, the delicate light hairs and soft skinned slit of her pussy.

Marie could not control her thoughts. She became excited and aroused and wanted access to those two wondrous holes.

The Master stood behind the young blonde and ran his hand over her bottom, circling every part then sliding his hand to feel the soft flesh between her thighs. A faint smile came to his mouth at what his fingers met there.

Grasping the cane in his right he thrashed it from above his shoulder onto the girl's porcelain-pale rear. It sent her lurching forward. An involuntary, but quickly suppressed, whimper came from her. Marie watched with envious eyes. She was filling with sexual urgency again.

More strong armed blows came down. After three or four brutal strikes The Master would run his hand over the scored flesh and feel through his fingers the marks he had made. The poor blonde was scored with long red marks across her bottom that must have been excruciatingly painful. Marie was astonished by how graciously the young woman took her punishment, she knew she would have been screaming through her tears had she been in the same position.

Another series of vicious blows rained down onto the poor girl's bottom. She was struggling desperately to bite her lip and avoid giving voice to her pain. It was not all suffering for the young blonde, however. Marie, whose eyes remained fixed on the bare flesh, could see clearly that the girl's exposed pussy was opening and glistening with sexual dew.

Placing the cane down, the Master looked into the beaten girl's face. "On your knees and pleasure me," he said and stood tall, awaiting her response.

Turning to face him the perfectly formed blonde girl settled onto her knees directly in front of his crotch. Marie looked at her delicately featured face and was full of admiration for her classic beauty. She could also see how the pain had brought tears welling in the girl's eyes making them brilliantly bright.

The young woman did not hesitate in her actions. She was clearly well drilled. Undoing the Master's belt and trousers she gently lowered them to release his well-formed penis and full, tightly set balls. His package hung beautifully in front of her face. Marie was feeling a sharp pang of envy. She could not believe what she was seeing.

Taking the flaccid length in one hand she began to gently and sensuously caress it. Her other hand massaged expertly at his balls.

"Very good," he said in a whisper.

The blonde's gentle working of his genitals was obviously highly skilled. With only very subtle use of her hands she had worked her master to firmness and now brought her lips to kiss over the engorged tip. Her tongue circled his head and then ran up and down his full length of well-proportioned cock. Her hands continued with their slow caresses.

Marie was sopping wet in her knickers. She was so sensitive to her arousal that she could feel how her pussy lips had opened and moistened and were now pulsing. She wanted to push her hand between her thighs and finger her pussy while she watched, but didn't dare. She knew that the Master would not approve. She stood and watched, the heat between her thighs making her fidgety.

The blonde girl had begun to build up the pace of her sucking. She was now taking a considerable length of the Master's erection into her mouth. Marie had heard talk of this way of fellating a man. Seeing it done directly in front of her was a torture of temptation. She was desperate to push that cock down her own throat.

Marie could not hold herself. "Please, sir," she stuttered. "Please let me do that to you."

The Master looked up in surprise. The beautiful girl sucking his cock continued without any disruption.

"You may assist this whore in pleasing me, yes. But I will punish you for your impertinence, be assured of that."

Marie knelt beside the blonde girl and felt a wonderful, exhilarating sense of excitement pump hard inside her. As the blonde girl circled the tip of his erection with her tongue Marie began licking and sucking his tight balls. She tried to emulate the slow, skilful technique of the girl beside her that was clearly so effective.

Generously the blonde passed control of the Master's cock to Marie. Marie put it straight into her mouth and began sucking and flicking her tongue over its tip. She could taste the steady seeping pre-come of his arousal and sucked harder to draw out more. That taste thrilled her and she longed for him to shoot the contents of his balls into her mouth.

"Deep throat me," he said to her.

She was unsure how. Opening her mouth wide she pushed her head forward so that his cock was filling her mouth and pushing the back of her throat. But still only a small amount of that length had passed her lips. The blonde had taken it all, right to the base. What was she doing wrong?

The beautiful girl beside her manoeuvred from licking the Master's balls and, disguising it as a flick of her hair, whispered quickly into Marie's ear.

"Swallow."

Marie swallowed and pushed her mouth forward on the Master's cock. It worked. With a sudden sucking pressure the length of his erection was pulled into her throat in what was the most peculiar sensation she had known in her mouth. The groan of delight that The Master let out when she had taken his full length told her she had pleased him.

The two girls began to exchange his pulsing erection between them, each deep throating for a few seconds and then sliding it out so the other could take it in. The rhythm they built up was driving the Master to deep breathing and uncontrolled groans of ecstasy.

"Filthy, whoring bitches," he muttered.

Marie was lost in the act. She loved the feeling of swallowing his cock to the back of her throat and having her tongue at the base of his shaft. She loved the taste of him and the way she was bringing drops of come from his balls. She wanted his come so much. She was greedy for it.

When it was next her turn, Marie seized him and swallowed him down, determined she would make him blast his sperm in her mouth. She pushed down as hard as she could and swallowed again and then again while it was in her throat so that his cock was gripped. The pace of her bobbing was frenetic. She knew it was working. He was building up to his climax. She wanted his spunk so badly.

The Master groaned loudly. It was coming. Marie felt the twitch of his balls as her hands worked over them. She was grinding her mouth down hard to the base of his cock, swallowing and sucking to bring that come gushing. He shouted out that it was coming. It was nearly there.

With a rough shove the Master pushed Marie aside and took grasp of his cock in one hand and the blonde girl's hair with the other. Pumping at his shaft powerfully he breathed out and then sprayed a huge thick thread of sperm into her face. Pumping hard, more shot out, firing into her face and open mouth, running down her cheeks and chin.

As the final shot of sperm looped onto her lips the spunk-covered blonde took the Master's cock back in her mouth and slowly licked it over, sucking the very last drops out of his shaft.

Marie looked at the blonde jealously. She had wanted him to come in her face more than anything at that moment. She had wanted to taste it and feel it fill her mouth, hot and salty and running out over her lips. Instead she watched as the girl beside her wiped the come from her face with her fingers and licked those fingers clean. She had a happy smile on her face, content at having been rewarded with his ejaculate. Her final task was to lick the Master's soft cock clean and put it back into his trousers as though the garment had never been disturbed.

Walking back round to his desk he said sternly, "Leave. I'll speak to you later, Marie, about your punishment." He sat down and began work with some papers.

Hugely aroused and deeply disappointed Marie exited with the beautiful girl. There was emptiness inside her and Marie already knew that the only thing that would cure it was a good fuck. She sensed that she was losing control of her desires. She was becoming addicted.

In the corridor the blonde girl snatched Marie's hand. "Come with me," she said and pulled her to a door with furtive looks up and down the corridor to make sure nobody was watching.

CHAPTER 9

Marie was pulled by the blonde girl into a tiny room, scarcely big enough for two people to be in. There was nothing in there except a dim, flickering bulb and a shoebox.

The girl whispered to Marie, "We'll get in trouble if Master finds out but when he is being cruel and won't let us come we sneak in here."

Marie was more than a little confused by the explanation.

"I'm Tilly. Now, do you want to go first or second?"

"First or second?" Marie replied hesitantly.

"For coming," Tilly replied with a smile, amused at Marie's naivety. "Some girls like to come first and some girls like to come second. I like them both. Which one are you?"

The peculiar question suddenly made sense and revealed the situation she was in. She was uncertain. So much had happened today alone, so much that she was starting to feel uneasy about. Yet she was also aware that she was becoming less and less uneasy about it, desensitised to the shame. More prominent in her mind were the words of advice the Master had given her, stating that she should be working to improve herself. She was not sure in what way but she doubted that another wanton act in this broom cupboard would be what the Master thought edifying.

Yet she was still simmering with arousal from deep throating the Master's cock. And Tilly was exceptionally beautiful. Quite tall and slender but endowed with gentle curves and gorgeous breasts that made Marie, whose own breasts had many virtues, feel considerable envy. She was older than Marie by a few years which were revealed more in her confidence and her mature sophistication, despite a slightly ditzy tendency in the way she expressed herself. Most impressive was the classical beauty in her face. Well defined features and bright blue eyes that sparked with light. Marie wanted to know her intimately.

"First," Marie said, startled by her response and willingness.

Tilly reached into the shoebox and pulled out a glass dildo, contoured and tapered to a point. Rummaging in the box she also pulled out what looked to Marie like bulldog stationary clips. Marie's heart flushed with a shot of excitement, the sort that made your hand tremble. She was fearful but excited at what was going to follow.

"We have to be quick," Tilly said as she knelt down and pulled Marie's trousers and knickers down to reveal her delicately haired mons.

"That's a pretty pussy," Tilly said sincerely. She then widened Marie's stance giving access to her moist cunt. For a brief moment Marie wanted to clamp up and prevent this going any further but more of her, a lot more, needed to come.

The blonde slid a finger over the already parted pussy lips exposed before her. It glided over the flesh with perfect smoothness that indicated she was well lubricated. Tilly then pinched at one of the labial lips and pulled down at it slightly giving a little shock to the younger girl. What was to follow made this feel as nothing, however. Still holding the thin lip of labia Tilly clamped a bulldog clip onto it.

The excruciating pain which shot through Marie was brutal. There was no respite, just constant, searing agony over her whole pussy. She fought hard to keep from screaming out but her whimpers were becoming quite noticeable.

Tilly reacted swiftly stuffing the discarded knickers into Marie's mouth and using a length of ribbon from the box to tie them in place. It worked to muffle the hollering that was coming from Marie.

The pain was about to get worse. Another bulldog clip was clamped on the other pussy lip before Tilly placed another clamp on each of Marie's tender and erect nipples.

The pain was as horrific as any Marie had ever known. Worse, the pain was constant. Though her hands were free it did not occur to Marie to simply remove the source of the pain. In her writhing, contorted agony she was not prepared to prematurely end it.

Tilly comforted her with a kiss on the cheek. "Good girl," she said delicately.

Marie was then turned around so that she faced away from Tilly. She was bent at the waist with her legs spread. Licking over the glass dildo to lubricate it, Tilly proceeded to feed it slowly into Marie's tightly furled ass.

It was something more than pain through her, though masked slightly by the pulsing shocks of agony through her labia and nipples. The glass dildo was pushed in against Marie's natural resistance, but Tilly did not seem to be struggling, spitting a couple of times into the valley between Marie's buttocks to ensure progress. Once deep penetration was secure Tilly began pushing and pulling the object in short movements through the stretched hole.

Marie was warming to the sensation, painful though it was. The feeling in her ass was superb and Tilly was supremely skilled in her movements. The pain of the clips crushing her nipples and the agony of the clips on her labia were swirling through her insides and bringing tears to her eyes.

A groan of deep satisfaction was released through the gag. It was a mix of pleasure and pain that she had not known before. It was simultaneously horrible and wonderful. And already she felt the pressure of an orgasm building up inside her.

Tilly sensed the heightening arousal and increased the depth at which she worked the dildo. With her free hand she worked between Marie's legs and passed a finger over her wet and throbbing clitoris., Tilly played over the already engorged nub expertly so that it was full and erect. Marie's knees began to weaken. She felt the now familiar orgasmic tension inside her. She would come soon and she would come hard.

To Marie's horror Tilly reached to pick up another bulldog clip and clamped it directly onto her swollen clit. The profound pain hammered up through her clit and made her scream hard into her gag. She kept screaming because the pain wouldn't go. It was crushing her most sensitive area of flesh. The agony was scalding, erupting inside her and burning her body deeply. Oh, God, please let this end, she said within herself. Please, I can't take any more pain.

Tilly waited. She was trying to time it perfectly. Yes, now was the time. As quickly as she could she wrenched the full length of the glass dildo from Marie's ass. The shock of its removal made Marie's screaming cease to a whimper, her legs wobble, her body begin to contort and then her cunt burst with a massive gushing spray of come all over Tilly who knelt behind her. It came at once in a powerful eruption of orgasm.

Marie's legs gave way. She slipped down onto her knees, her head lolling in her outstretched arms. Tilly removed the clips and released the improvised gag.

With a deep release of breath Marie whispered an exhausted, "Thank you."

Tilly was in no mood to wallow in the afterglow. "Your turn to do me now," she said and turned Marie to face her. Tilly then stood over Marie's reclined head and guided her beautiful, red-hot pussy over the girl's mouth. She then spread her legs wider so that her cunt lowered and contact was made.

"Lick my pussy really hard," she said, her voice already giving signs of how pleasurable that mouth on her pussy felt. "Lick it really hard. We haven't got long."

Marie was suddenly full of vigour now that she had such a delicious and beautiful pussy in her face. It was smooth and tasted of sex and female come ready to rush out. Marie wanted to be responsible for it gushing out of her. She licked and sucked as hard and as fast as she could, her tongue circling up into the hole and then back to find the swollen clit for her lips to close round it and for her to suck at it hard, her tongue flicking it as she did.

Tilly was close to breaking. She had put a clip onto each of her nipples and was reaching back to finger her little ass hole. Her breathing was long and deep with each exhalation bringing a groan of the purest sexual delight. Then she began to quiver. Her whole body started to shake violently and her finger in her ass moved quicker.

"Oh, that is so fucking good. I love that fucking mouth. I'm gonna come. Suck it out of my cunt Marie. Put your tongue in my hole and take it all in your mouth."

Marie did as she was asked. Shoving her rigid tongue deep into Tilly's hole she felt the shaking of the blonde girl's body and the twitching of her ass. Then it came with a shrill squeal and a rush of sweet juices flowing from that delicious pussy, down Marie's tongue and into her mouth. It felt and tasted exquisite and decadent, like honey was being drizzled onto her lips.

Tilly shook the last spasm of orgasm out, still holding Marie's head in place between her legs. With a sigh of satisfaction she released her grip of Marie's hair and leaned against the wall to regain her composure.

Both girls dressed quickly realising that they had been absent from work longer than they should have been. They did not want to face the punishment of being caught.

"Ready?" Tilly asked with her hand on the door.

"Yes."

They listened for noise of anyone in the corridor and then Tilly gave a quick nod and both girls exited the tiny cupboard.

Marie's heart sank instantly. Stood watching them with arms crossed and a stern look was the Master. Both girls froze. His anger was obvious.

Addressing Tilly he shouted, "Get to your room you nasty slut." She scampered off down the corridor, her eyes downcast.

Marie was shaking with fear. After a moment of contemplation the Master spoke to her with a firm voice.

"You clearly paid no attention to anything I said to you. Well, listen now or you will be gone from here forever."

Marie was terrified of him. The threat had her heart pounding. She did not want to be fired from the museum. Realising how much she enjoyed being there, and dreaded no longer being allowed to experience these previously unknown sensations, surprised her.

"In two days' time you will report to Mrs Ryder at this exact time. Between now and that time I advise you to exercise some discipline upon yourself. Now get out of my sight and get on with some work."

He returned to his office shutting his door firmly behind him. Marie was disgusted at herself. She had not wanted to disappoint the Master nor ignore his advice but she had done just that and, worse, got caught. She was acting like such a wanton slut and he was trying to steer her away from such behaviour. Yet, she was uncertain about what his motives were exactly. Everything is becoming such a mess in my life, she thought.

A storm of emotions was inside her as she walked back to her work. She resolved to follow the Master's instructions no matter what temptation was presented to her.

CHAPTER 10

The next few days passed quietly for Marie. She was occupied at work with learning new tasks while outside of work she had several affairs to arrange in her new home town. But her time at the Museum didn't pass entirely without incident.

On one occasion she walked through a door to find Daniella, the beautiful older woman of the museum, being sodomised by a huge, muscular and unknown man. Marie's natural reaction was to flee but the image stuck with her throughout the day and made her wonder what it would have been like to join them.

She became increasingly aware of a change within her. She felt more attractive, more confident and more capable of dealing with a world of unexpected challenges. When she undressed for bed she was lingering to look at her naked body in the mirror – something she had never done in her life. She was very attractive, she acknowledged, blessed with a natural beauty that many girls must surely envy. In the shower each morning this new appreciation was taken further. She found herself sliding her hands over her breasts, buttock, thighs – anywhere that made her feel pleasure. She had never had a sense of happiness from her own body before.

There were still very mixed feelings about the carnal behaviour she had engaged in. Her thoughts kept returning to Aiden's cruel treatment of her that first day, she had not reacted as she thought she ought to have. Instead of being tormented by the memory, part of her was aroused by it. Instead of recoiling with the sense of violation she found she wanted to experience it again.

The same could be said of all the sexual experiences she had known since arriving, if she was honest with herself. She had done what she had once considered only ex maniacs would. The acts were evil, immoral and the reserve of the unbalanced and dangerous. While she had told herself this her body had been drawing her towards these lascivious acts. The more her body wanted them the more she trained herself to despise them. For years this turmoil had been a constant source of discomfort in her. She had never known happiness. She distrusted her body too much. Although she had a boyfriend she knew that neither was fulfilled. It had been an awkward way to live and yet she felt she had no alternative. In the space of a week the Museum had taken from the prison she had built herself and shown her the world. At first it terrified her. Now she saw it spread wide before her, limitless, full of opportunities for elation and excitement.

There were thoughts that tempered this happiness, however. Her relationship with Martin must be over. It could not survive the infidelities she had committed. She could not live without confessing them. She would let the dust settle from this mad week and then break it off. The prospect of admitting to the acts she had done terrified her. She did not want people to know about this, despite her new confidence.

This fear was exploited by Aiden one afternoon. Earlier in the day he had cornered her and thrust his hand into her knickers and groped coarsely at her pussy. She managed to squirm free. His hand had done enough to moisten her but she was unprepared to let him feel superior to her, even though her pussy would have appreciated it.

Later that day he approached with a smug look. In his hand he had a mobile phone. To Marie's horror it was hers.

"This is an interesting situation. I found this phone and, looking through it, there are some lovely, sweet natured messages to someone called Martin. I bet Martin would be all ears to hear about your first week on the job. Shall I call him?"

"Don't you dare," Marie said with a sense of panic engulfing her.

"How about I call Mum and Dad?" Aiden said as he fingered the buttons.

"Please don't do that."

"Well, let's strike a deal. You take my cock in your mouth and I return the phone. The alternative is you don't take my cock in your mouth and I have a conversation with Martin and the folks about you."

The blood drained from Marie's face. She could not call his bluff – he was totally without compassion.

Sat in her chair she drew it closer to Aiden and undid his belt. She chose not to look him in the eye. This was necessity, not pleasure.

Unzipping his trousers she slid her fingers through the opening in his underpants and pulled his flaccid length out. It was large and thick. She had recalled it often over the last few days, disbelieving it had really been that big. Now she knew it was.

Gently working her hand over it she felt it grow firmer. It lengthened and thickened and became hot in her hand. She could feel the blood pumping through it. She began to grow warm herself.

Marie wrapped her mouth around the tip of Aiden's cock and closed her eyes, instantly sinking into a state of sexual bliss. The rapidly building erection that she was responsible for made her feel a peculiar pride. The heat of it in her mouth and the taste of it on her tongue was a filthy but wonderful pleasure.

Aiden had reached his fullest. Marie could feel the straining power of his cock and instinctively took this as her moment to escalate her activity. Running her hand in long, twisting motions over his shaft she sucked eagerly at its head and flicking her tongue over its surface.

"Blackmail was hardly necessary, was it, you little slut?" Marie bobbed her head quickly on his large dick.

He took hold of her hair and pulled her head back, her mouth coming from the end of his erection with a trail of spit running down her chin. Taking hold of his hard length in his other hand he slapped it against her face, a big grin on his face. Marie, hungry for cock now that she had tasted it, was moving her head around trying to get it back in her mouth.

Releasing his cock but still pulling her head Aiden struck her face with the back of his hand. He repeated this firm strike a number of times in quick succession. Marie was in shock. There was a vacant look over her face as she struggled to cope with the sudden pain. Aiden laughed out loud then pushed his cock back into her mouth.

Marie came round quickly. She moved to pumping her hand faster over his shaft and taking him deeper into her mouth.

"Oh, yes. Here it comes you dirty bitch."

Aiden gripped both hands on the back of Marie's head and pulled her mouth onto him. He let out a low groan and then fired a powerful jet of semen into the back of her throat. She loved the sensation. She loved having induced this amazing eruption. She wriggled to try and release Aiden's grip so that she could satisfy her urge to have him shoot more come onto the tip of her tongue and lips but he was too strong. More sperm shot into her mouth. Each twitch of his hips brought another spurt of thick fluid. This feeling in Marie's mouth brought on a delicate quiver of orgasm in her dripping panties.

Aiden let out a satisfied moan and pulled out of Marie's mouth. She licked over the tip of his cock and sucked the last few drops of spunk from him. Looking up she saw a smug smile on his face. Without even glancing at her he did his trousers up, threw the phone into her lap and departed.

Marie was left bitterly disappointed. The pleasure of blowing Aiden, even though he was a bastard, had ignited her ardour. Now she was left to dwell uncomfortably in it as it slowly faded.

Later that day, as she was finishing her work, opportunity presented itself. As was leaving she passed a door slightly ajar. Her ear picked up the distinct report of leather striking flesh. She stopped in her tracks. She listened for more. Again the report of leather on flesh this time followed by the muffled whimper of a woman. It was unmistakable. A nervous, voyeuristic panic and rush of uncontrollable heat pumped through her.

She thought of walking past, of leaving them to their business and controlling her dirty desires. But she knew she could not resist. These feelings through her had become an addiction.

Silently Marie moved so she could see through the crack in the door. Her heart raced. At the far end of a long room stood the Master looking tall and powerful. His shirt was half unbuttoned exposing his broad, muscular chest. Sweat glistened on his brow and he held a long bullwhip. In front of him was the beautiful, dark haired Daniella. She was nearly naked wearing only knee high leather boots and a corset that had been twisted down her body revealing her gloriously large breasts. She was stood at the centre of a large wooden frame, with her wrists and ankles bound into each corner. On her thighs and across her hips were red lines where the Master's whip had struck her. The lines ran over her bar pubic mound. Here the lines blazed bright and made Marie wince and moisten between her legs simultaneously.

Across the beautifully formed breasts burnt more lines from the whip. Marie instinctively felt empathy for the pain that lash must have produced.

The Master paced slowly within the room with the coiled whip in his hands. He looked deep in thought, as though what he did was as much vigorous stimulation for the intellect as it was for the body. He daubed the sweat from his forehead with a handkerchief then stopped pacing and let the whip unfurl beside him.

Marie sensed what was impending and seized the opportunity to squat down, lift her skirt and plunge her hand into her already wet knickers. She was so turned on from the day's sexual frustrations that this spectacle of domination was like a flame to kindling. Her hand on her cunt felt beautiful, at once a relieving her and demanding relief. She rubbed her fingers over the swelling, rising clit and along her pouting labia then sunk them up inside her pulling out more silken pussy fluids and spreading them around her young cunt.

The Master pulled his hand back and ripped it forward, straining his muscular body to bring the bullwhip over his shoulder with a force that made Marie recoil. The strike was a crack that reverberated through the room, as loud as a rifle shot. It was followed by an agonising wail of pain, slowly subsiding to a whimper from the beautiful woman.

The strike had been directly across Daniella's pale skinned breasts. The impact had drawn a small trickle of blood that ran over the contour of her bosom to drip from beneath her pert nipple onto the floor.

The effect upon the Master was profound. He cast the whip aside and moved quickly to the rear of Daniella. Her head hung weakly on her chest and her face trembled with the lingering pain. She looked physically exhausted by what she had endured.

The Master was unconcerned. He had designs on only one thing. He unfurled his belt, unbuttoned his trousers and let them drop to his knees. Clasping his hands upon Daniella's hips he pulled her back putting her bound limbs under further strain and causing her a sharp shock of further suffering. With one hand he grasped his already erect penis and manoeuvred it between the woman's thighs, working his wet tip into the wet, soft haired entrance of her pussy. When he was secure beneath her he thrust his cock up and pulled back firmly so that his massive length rammed inside her. The Master's roar of satisfaction was resounding, punctuated only by the defeated whimper of the dark haired woman he was fucking.

"Yes, you've been good slut. You've earned a good fuck. You took your lesson well. Oh, you take this well too," he said to her as he thrust his cock into her again and again.

"Thank you Master."

Marie had full view of Daniella's front and could see well the Master's cock working up between her legs. The bright red marks over her body were distinct and strangely beautiful, for they compeimented her curvaceous form. The spectacle was beyond anything she had ever conceived. Marie could feel the heightened sexuality all over her. She worked her fingers hard over her pussy and her pent up sexual frustration and newly heightened arousal were at full capacity. She longed to come but she wanted to continue enjoying the spectacle.

Unrelenting in the power of his thrusts, the Master continued fucking deep into Daniella's dripping hole. He grunted in an animal way that Marie had not expected of him, then wrenched even harder at the woman's hips. It was now a brutal energy that was about him, all his muscles straining and defined, as powerful as a man half his age could only wish to be.

The woman lifted her head. She grimaced from the pain of his cock hammering into her. Then opening her mouth she let out a wail that rang unmistakably with an exquisite and excruciating climax. She screamed out in Italian, words Marie did not understand, beautiful, angry sounding words. It was building up in her with each rough thrust. Everything now converged: the pain from the whip, the strain of her limbs, the deep ache of the Master's cock inside her, until she could do nothing but relinquish what little control she had remaining, and allow the rush of her own coming to blast her out of any consciousness. Her body fell limp.

Marie struggled not to come herself when she watched Daniella spend but she wanted desperately to see the Master finish and let the sight excite her beyond even her current intense state. She did not have long to wait.

With Daniella only half conscious there was no resistance in her body and this allowed the Master to rip into her deeper, faster and harder. Marie watched the thick length thrusting up and played hard on her clit, using her free hand to full her knickers to one side. He thrust into the woman completely so only his big balls were visible under her and then his knees began to give and his body visibly spasm as he fired up his come deep in her throbbing, sore cunt. He pumped in and out of her again, each push firing more come into her, his cock glistening with the mix of his creamy spunk and her watery juices.

Marie rubbed hard and felt it build and then it started to break through her in burst of sublime release. Her eyes were fixed on the sight in front of her and she lapped up the perversity of the spectacle. When the Master withdrew his dick from Daniella's cunt a gush of come ran out onto the floor, then dripped out slowly, like honey being poured from a jar. The sight sent Marie into a higher plane of orgasm and she burst with a delicious, muscle-straining, pussy-hurting rush of come that dropped her to the floor and left her weak against the waves of pleasure slowly rolling over her.

She soon came round. Though her legs were unsteady, she made good her escape.

CHAPTER 11

That evening Marie had some peace to reflect on what had been happening to her. She felt she was giving into the perverted side of her nature with every opportunity that presented itself. The realisation upset her. But, she thought, what was the real harm in her acting this way? If anything she felt happier for what she had done, and the pleasure was now outweighing the shame. What she had done surprised her, that was true, and she would hate for others to know what she had done. But she felt less and less that she was some sort of depraved pervert for enjoying herself during sex.

There were problems ahead, she realised. If she continued on this path Martin could not be a part of her life. This thought made her emotional and she pushed it aside as best she could to stay the tears that were welling. Similarly, that careful plan she had for her future would have to be relinquished. Many other difficult choices presented themselves to her mind that night and no answers were forthcoming.

As she lay in the bed awake the familiar urges descended on her. It was prompted by the sounds coming from the kitchen. Tonight, much like every night since she had arrived, Isabelle was getting a good, robust fucking from John. Marie could hear plates and glasses tumbling. Loud grunts came from both of them and deep moans of pleasure and physical exertion. There was also the regular sound of flesh being slapped.

Marie could picture perfectly what they were doing. She was tempted to spy on them but tonight she had a distinct desire to be spanked. Turning so that she was on her stomach she lifted her nightdress up and pulled down her knickers revealing her round, smooth bottom.

Pushing one hand underneath herself to access her pussy she took her hairbrush in her other hand and proceeded to strike her buttocks as hard as she could from her slightly awkward position.

The first strike created a beautiful warm feeling through her, touching the corners that other contact only glided past. It hurt but that was what was so good about it. The strike enlivened her cunt to the movement of her other hand, made her breasts tingle and brought her to that heightened psychological state only attained when she knew she was doing something naughty.

With the sound of passionate intercourse coming up from the kitchen she set about spanking her bottom and fingering her pussy. She hit herself hard and quick, a strike every few seconds, imagining that the Master had her bent over his knee. It was his fingers she imagined were pushing up inside her. She hit as hard as she could, now imaging the exquisite pain Daniella had known earlier. She wanted to draw blood and feel it run over her skin.

The fucking from the kitchen turned increasingly intense. The sounds were of John and Isabelle fighting each other towards their climax. The thought of John's big cock working through Isabelle's pretty cunt or stretching her bum wide thrilled Marie. It was happening now as she was fingering her wet hole and beating her bottom raw.

Her orgasm came suddenly and in a way she had never experienced. Feeling each strike of the brush in layers of pain on her skin she thrust the handle of the brush into her tight bum, pushing all of it in quickly and without lubrication. She screamed out in pain, it was too much to shove in so quick and dry, but it brought out of her almost instantly a powerful climax that pushed her body up so that her bum was high in the air and then fired from her twitching cunt fine jets of come that sprayed up the wall.

The jets of her juices subsided and she slumped down into a quivering heap, her fingers gently rubbing over her pussy. Below her, in the kitchen, John and Isabelle were still fucking vigorously. Marie had no strength to do anything but pull the bed sheets over her clothed body, remove the hairbrush from her bottom, and fall into a deep sleep, oblivious to the disruption that was about to impact upon her life.

CHAPTER 12

A few uneventful days passed for Marie. She busied herself at work and thought to control her urges, though not deny them, as the Master had instructed her. She felt that she was starting to understand his rather opaque philosophy and this pleased her. She was on the whole content, though several issues hovered about her.

She was forced to contemplate one of these issues when she returned home from work and found John, Isabelle and her boyfriend, Martin, sat drinking tea in the front room. Marie coloured with embarrassment instantly, the shock knocking her dumb. With transparent nervousness she wrapped her arms around Martin and kissed him.

John and Isabelle made polite excuses and left the room.

"I said I would tell you when a convenient time was," Marie said through a tense smile, her voice shaking. "Now isn't really a good time to surprise me."

"It's lovely to see you as well, Marie."

"You should have asked. John and Isabelle don't want people arriving unexpectedly." Marie was now pacing the room.

"I have asked. Plenty of times, and it's never convenient. And now, I'm finding, it isn't convenient to call you. Oversensitive I may be but I couldn't help but feel messed around." Martin's tone expressed the anger that had built up inside him.

"So you come all this way to have a go at me?"

"I've come to see what the problem is. I'm smart enough to know when I'm being fucked about." His voice was increasingly loud.

"You're not being fucked about. I'm busy. I have a new job and a new home and new friends and I'm sorry for making the best of it," she said sarcastically. Then, turning her back on him, she began to cry.

A long silence fell between them as they each considered the situation. Martin then asked the question that had been tormenting him for some time.

"Have you been unfaithful?"

Marie's crying instantly turned to sobbing.

"You have, haven't you, you whore," he shouted.

Still she was sobbing, her head low and her back to him. Thoughts of lying and thoughts of her future and whether she loved him all spun through her mind. But everything was telling her to be honest.

"Yes," she mumbled and then descended into hysterical crying.

"Who with?" he asked, the rage crackling in his voice.

"A few," she whispered after a long delay.

"You fucking whore!" he bellowed and seized her about the shoulders. With his face blazing with anger he slapped her viciously across the face. Grabbing her by the hair he wrenched her head back and struck her again before throwing her powerfully across the room. She fell in a heap holding her cheek and sobbing.

At that moment John and Isabelle rushed in, John stepping in front of Martin as he was about to set about Marie again. Isabelle crouched beside Marie and held her.

Martin was pulled from his rage and a look of disbelief took over him. "I'm sorry. I'm so sorry, Marie," he said gently as the reality of his violence became clearer.

John ordered Isabelle to take Marie from the room. He then sat Martin down and tried to calm his emotions further. Martin was shaking with adrenalin and had a disbelieving look on his face, pale and despairing. He continued to apologise, uttering it over and over in a feeble voice.

"Come on, snap out of it. Act like a man," John said firmly.

It seemed to work as Martin sat upright and looked John in the eye.

"I can't believe I've just done that," Martin said. "She said she had been cheating on me. I lost control."

"There are a few things you need to know about Marie and what has been happening. Since she has been working over here she has started to uncover a side of her that she had been keeping down since she was a girl. She's started to accept that this is a part of her. Yes, she has been unfaithful in your relationship. But that doesn't cover what is going on with her. It's not that simple. Marie is a natural submissive in all parts of her life, including sex. It's only through recognising this that she is ever going to be happy, and that's what she has started to do since she has been here. It isn't about you or your relationship. It's about her understanding that she needs to be who she really wants to be, to act how she wants to act, if she is to be happy in life."

Martin thought through what had been said. He was struggling with all that had happened to make sense of anything.

John continued. "What you have just done here, Martin, in hitting that girl, was understandable. These are natural reactions to heartfelt emotions. It is foolish not to respond to these physical urges. This was Marie's problem. She denied all her genuine feelings and it got her into a mess. It can't work like that. You can't live your life like that. You felt the honest desire to hit her and so you hit her."

"It felt good," Martin replied. "I wanted to hit her again."

"I wish I had let you, Martin. You're as naturally dominant as Marie is submissive." John smiled. "Neither of you have realised because you're both to busy confusing yourself about what you *should* do rather than what you *want* to do. You need to bring that dominant side out more."

"It's over now so it hardly matters."

"No. It's over when you say it's over. And, trust me, you don't want to end it with this girl." John paused a moment and thought through the options. "She needs to be punished. Yes?"

"Yes, severely," Martin answered.

"So if you fucked someone else and made her watch that would settle the score?"

"I suppose so."

"Then fuck my wife and make Marie watch."

"This is mad! I can't."

"You can if you want to. That's what I'm telling you."

After a long pause Martin agreed. "She needs to be punished," he said sincerely.

John called Isabelle and Marie into the room. He took a length of rope from a drawer and threw it to Martin.

"Tie her up."

Martin, a little hesitantly, tied Marie to the corner staircase. He was surprised at how compliant she was. He started to feel aroused.

John took a cane from the corner and passed it to the younger man. "Do whatever you want with Isabelle," he said. "And do it hard."

Taking hold of Isabelle gently Martin moved her over to a chair and had her bend over its back so her bottom stuck out. He let his hand run over her slender curves, reaching up to cup her breasts and down to stroke her thighs, letting his hand linger between them, feeling her warmth through her trousers. Isabelle gave no resistance.

Martin looked over to Marie who was wide eyed but not showing any distress. John was stood placidly by, although his eyes gave away the excitement he was feeling.

Unbuttoning her trousers Martin slid them down to expose her luscious bottom which was covered by delicate black panties. He rubbed his hand over then stepped back and gave her a tame rap with the cane. He tried again with more vigour. Isabelle gave no response. They were passionless efforts at discipline.

John was about to intervene when he saw Martin eying Marie. There was a quick change in the young man's face with some of the earlier anger burning up again. He raised his arm and struck Isabelle forcefully, branding her with a bright red mark and making her cry out.

Martin was now breathing deeply, excited by the reaction and his own anger. He struck her again and again, only stopping to fondle her lovely tits or rub her moistening pussy through her knickers. His cock was hard and straining the confines of his clothes.

He could not contain himself and after a volley of vicous strikes with the cane he undid his trousers and pulled out his long stiff cock. Ripping her knickers down he gripped her at the hips and worked his thick cock under her, impatient to find her hot hole. With his swollen tip at her pussy lips he pushed up hard, the whole thick length sliding smoothly, though tightly, into her. Both he and Isabelle gasped out with delight and pain.

Once in, he began to fuck up into her hard and fast. He was a strong young man, tall and broad and the situation had made him rampant. Isabelle was being thrown around by the power of his pumping, the chair knocking against the table, the table knocking against the wall. The colour of Isabelle's cheeks and the smile coming over her face made it clear how much she was enjoying this rough fucking.

Martin was flushing as well. He called out and dug his nails into her hips.

"Yeah, fucking hell. Oh, I'm gonna come. Fuck. I'm gonna come so fucking hard inside your pussy you fucking bitch. Ahh, yeah."

And with a series of deep, wide mouthed groans his body convulsed and he came deep inside her in long, powerful spurts of thick fluid, flooding her cunt so that it was dripping out as he continued to thrust into her. Finally he withdrew and collapsed onto the sofa.

Isabelle pulled her knickers and trousers up and then knelt down between Martin's legs. Taking his shrinking erection into her mouth she gently sucked its glistening, come covered shaft. Sliding it into her mouth she let her tongue circle it softly and expertly. Soon Martin's breathless exhaustion gave way to excitement with his cock once again hard.

Isabelle undid her blouse and exposed her lovely pert breasts. She moved herself so that the hard tips of her nipples rubbed on Martin's balls while she sucked the swollen tip of his cock. His excitement was reaching its peak and he began to pump his hips upwards into her mouth. He was approaching climax. Isabelle placed a finger under his balls to work his perineum and prepared herself to take his come into her mouth.

Martin had other ideas. With his eyes fixed on his girlfriend he pushed Isabelle abruptly aside and stepped over to face Marie. Grabbing the cane he lashed it down on Marie making her scream out with pain. He struck her legs and arms, her breasts and her bum, back and belly, as she writhed within the confines of her bondage.

He then threw the cane down and took his stiff cock into his hand, pumping it hard.

Marie, still ringing with a new sharpness of pain, lifted her head up and opened her mouth desperate for him to shoot his sperm down her throat.

"Come hot in my mouth. Please, I want your spunk on my tongue, all over my lips and mouth," she said, the sexual excitement peaking in her.

With a shout Martin began to fire great jets of his come into her face, coming every few seconds, a jerk of his cock and a looping string of pearly white come firing into her mouth, hitting her chin and dripping down onto her beautiful breasts.

Stepping forward he let Marie lick his cock. Marie worked over it hungrily, loving the taste of his hot spunk on her tongue and relishing the feeling of it around her mouth and on her tits. A swelling of heat rose inside her leaving her with a delicious, contented feeling all over.

Martin sank to his knees and untied his girlfriend. As soon as his hands were free they embraced passionately with the smile of lovers reunited after too long apart.

CHAPTER 13

When the excitement of that passionate night had calmed, Martin spoke with John about where his relationship with Marie could go. John advised speaking to the Master of the Museum. Leaving Marie at home Martin went the following morning to speak with him.

Martin was welcomed into the Master's office. He spoke in a slightly shamed tone about the developments of the previous night and also of the problems he and Marie had experienced in the past.

"You are a fortunate young man," the Master said in his usual sage manner. "You have the love of a special girl in Marie. In the course of my personal and professional life I have had the pleasure to know and educate some very special girls indeed. Only a handful would I venture to call exceptional. Marie engenders the same feeling in me that those exceptional ones did when they started out in their learning. She has a huge amount to learn but what excites me is the potential.

"I would like to continue her education a while longer and in a more formal, structured way than she has had so far. I will be more explicit. I will educate her in the subtleties of submission, of pain, and of pleasuring her Master. I will, of course, waive tuition fees in this instance."

Martin was lost in thought trying to keep up with all these new developments, and trying to understand exactly what this man was offering. The proposition appeared rare and generous. And when he compared the years wasted on passionless sexual interaction with Marie against the frenzy and ecstasy of last night he felt that there was only one course of action. His curiosity sought more information though.

"In this education," he said hesitantly, "Marie will be having sex with people?" He felt he was asking a stupid question.

The Master replied. "Sometimes there will be sex in one or other of its forms. Other times there will only be punishment and discipline. I will be her Master while she is here. I will be the only one who takes her unless I decide otherwise."

"And what will she be like when she has finished her education?"

"She will be highly skilled in the sexual arts and will be utterly dedicated to pleasing you. She will be completely submissive but more confident than you have ever known her. She will also be happier than you have ever known her as this is what her innate nature desires."

"John said I might be a naturally dominant person. Is this something I need to develop?"

"You must acknowledge whatever desire is within you and you must have her fulfil it. Punish her, discipline her, but do not abuse her. Exercise her routinely and treat her generously occasionally. Share her, by all means, but you must be her master through the day and through the night. Enjoy her. All she wants is to make you happy."

It was agreed. Marie would stay at least three months longer to advance her education. Martin, at the Master's advice, would return home and make preparations for her eventual return to him.

Martin and Marie parted on good terms that night. Their relationship had undergone a profound shift and both were closer to their natural state. They felt the thrill of young love again but it was mixed with something more permanent, undeniably linked to the Master.

Returning to work the following day Marie had no expectations that her routine would be altered. Martin had not conveyed any of the discussion he and the Master had the day before. So when Aiden approached her from behind, lifted her skirt and pushed a finger into her barely moist pussy, she felt the day would be unexceptional.

"Get off me," she said, struggling against his grasp.

"I like a fighter," Aiden replied. "Nothing gets me quite as hard."

Marie continued to struggle from his invasive fingers and strong grip.

"But I don't like all this melodramatic acting up. It's too transparent." With this he clamped his hand firmly over her mouth.

Still holding her tightly, and with one finger roughly penetrating her, he pushed her face first against the wall. Taking hold of her knickers he gave them a few hard tugs, ripping them so they hung around her waist like ribbons. With unrestricted access he rubbed his fingers over her forcefully, spreading the emerging moisture over her swelling cunt lips and clitoris.

"You've got my blood up this morning, you little whore." He lifted his fingers to his nose and took her odour in with a deep breath. "What a powerful drug lies between a woman's thighs."

He hastily undid his trousers and pulled out his full erection. Wrapping his arms around her hips and pulling her up onto her toes he managed to work his twitching, massive member to her tight entrance. Securing his glans inside her hole, an act that caused Marie considerable discomfort, he then pulled her back and down while pushing up causing his broad cock to stretch her terribly in one slow, smooth, painful impaling. She could only scream into his hand as her pussy burned. Aiden made sure he had pushed his entire length into her, right up to his big balls.

He started to fuck at her hard. His deep penetration had lubricated his length with her silky juices and he could now pump into her without any discomfort to himself. He slotted it up inside her with powerful thrusts that lifted her off the ground and pushed her hard into the wall.

The act was beginning to thrill Marie. This was such a carnal act of fucking that her cunt was already dripping juices down his shaft. The pain his depth of penetration caused was pronounced and pleasurable. His strong arms gripping her added to her spiralling arousal. She was acutely aware of the sexual heat inside her rising. More of his brutality and she would be coming hard down his stiff dick. She focused her mind on the sensation of this huge member inside her, stretching her and hurting her, degrading her. Though she loathed this man who was fucking her up against the wall she was undeniably consumed by his vigour and the proportions of his cock up inside her. She wanted the ordeal to be over, but not yet.

Aiden started to lose control of himself. He slammed her harder and harder and cursed her more loudly. "You little cock lover. You love a good fuck. You love a man coming in your cunt you whoring slut!" And on that last shouted insult he thrust his cock right up to his balls and shot their full contents into the neck of her pussy, his cock twitching with each thick wad that burst out.

He withdrew and released his grip on her. She still hadn't come though the pressure in her had taken her very close. The abrupt end left her desperate for more. Vainly she pushed her bottom out hoping Aiden would at least finger her to climax but he showed no interest. He wiped his fading erection on her skirt and then tucked it into his trousers and walked off as though she did not exist.

Marie, not for the first time, was left at the height of her arousal with no means, bar her own dexterity, to bring herself off. Her hand had only just made contact with her dripping, sperm flooded pussy when she heard footsteps nearby. She quickly adjusted herself.

It was the Master. "Come with me," he said sharply.

Marie followed obediently. A trickle of semen was running down her thigh, past her own panties. She was walking behind so she discreetly used her skirt to wipe her tender, and needy, cunt clean. The act brought a flush of shame to her face.

She was led along corridors she was unaware of and then into a small changing room where the Master instructed her to undress and clean herself. She would then exit, he told her, naked, through another door on the far side of the room. He left.

She stripped naked and carefully cleaned herself. As she worked a warm and wet sponge between her thighs she was tingling with arousal but did not dare touch herself more purposefully in case she should be chastised by the Master who seemed to know everything. He must surely know that she had recently been filled with come or he would not have demanded she clean herself.

She dried herself and examined her naked body in the mirror. Satisfied with what she saw but feeling fearful she exited the door as instructed. What she walked in on shocked her.

The chamber she entered was stone walled and windowless. Along the far wall were three girls with their wrists tied above their heads to fixed metal rings. They all faced the wall. Two wore delicate corsets with stockings and suspenders; the other was completely naked like Marie. The Master stood in the room still in his suit. Most astonishingly, Mrs Ryder was present and wearing tall heels and a full body leather suit that had slits revealing her breasts and the fine haired flesh of her pussy. Marie was stunned and aroused instantly.

Mrs Ryder took firm hold of Marie and pushed her against the wall. Raising her hands high above her head she clamped her wrists. Then, quite tenderly, she brushed the hair from Marie's face.

Marie looked at the other girls. All were ashen faced with fear, their eyes not daring to look up.

The Master unleashed an ear-splitting crack of his whip. "You have all behaved in a manner demanding severe punishment." His voice was booming, deep and stern. "You will get nothing less."

Then, with considerable skill, he lashed the girls across the back with the whip, each in turn. The first three girls all shrieked and whimpered but Marie was determined to show her strength. She endured the searing strike in silence.

"Well done, Marie. I am impressed. You will all follow Marie's stoicism and not let even a heavy breath leave your mouth." He then unleashed four more lashes against the girls, this time on their legs.

The first three shrieked again. Marie remained silent. The pain in her was excruciating but she closed her eyes and focused on the way the pain tingled through her body as though it was switching on her senses.

"I will have silence, girls, I assure you." Again the whip flew through the air, striking each girl on the bottom this time.

Only two girls shrieked. Four more lashes across the girl's shoulders. Still one girl persisted, yet all the girls were punished. Their backs, bums and legs were burning red with whip marks.

The Master struck each one, low on the backs of their thighs. Miraculously all four were silent, though their bodies writhed in an effort to dissipate the pain.

Marie kept her eyes tightly shut. She felt like she might faint with the agony that was overwhelming her. It was worst of all on the backs of her legs. It had sent her body into a state of hyper-sensitivity. She could feel the blood pumping through her body, stiffening her nipples and swelling the flesh between her thighs.

"Mrs Ryder, would you do the honours please," the Master instructed politely.

"Yes, Master."

Mrs Ryder, looking sexually exquisite in her outfit, turned the girls around so that their backs were to the wall. She kicked each girl's legs out wide exposing their young, perfect flesh. She then took her horse riding whip and struck the first girl in the line directly between her thighs. The girl screamed and danced around in agony.

"Master?" Mrs Ryder asked, seeking his guidance regarding the girl's indiscipline.

"Twice across the breasts," he replied.

Mrs Ryder thanked him and struck the offender with two powerful lashes across her small, rosy tipped breasts. The girl just managed to hold her tongue, though the pain was evidently testing her limits.

The next two girls took similarly firm strikes upon their tender young labia with only whimpers that the Master felt should go unpunished.

Marie, knowing it was her turn, pushed her hips out slightly as though inviting the whip. She wanted Mrs Ryder to hit her hard on her pussy lips. She wanted to feel that beautiful sensation of pain burning through her cunt.

The blow connected hard and her flesh instantly began to throb with a fierce heat that instantly had her pussy getting wet. She let out a scream of pain. She hoped that this would be punished with more strikes up between her thighs.

Mrs Ryder turned to the Master for guidance.

"Marie," he said with a smile, "I thought you would have coped with that better. Two between her legs, Mrs Ryder, and two upon her nipples."

Mrs Ryder obliged with stinging strikes upon Marie's bright red cunt and two quick, accurate rasps upon her nipples.

The pain rushed through Marie in the same way an orgasm does. She was so wet between her legs she could feel her juices running down them.

The Master removed his jacket and rolled up his sleeves. He took the riding crop from Mrs Ryder and walked in front of the girls. As he did so he rubbed the leather end over their swollen pussy lips and inspected the whip for wetness. When he had inspected Marie he raised the whip to his face and breathed in her scent. His eyes closed and he seemed to be enjoying the smell of her arousal. The thought of him smelling her pussy juices made Marie want to fuck him all day and all night.

"Would you get me erect please Mrs Ryder," the Master said as casually as if her were ordering his morning coffee.

"Yes, Master." Mrs Ryder then settled to her knees in front of him.

Pulling his length from out of his trousers she set to stroking her hand over it and kissing and licking over its head. She did this slowly and sensuously but clearly with amazing skill for within less than a minute the Master's cock stood upright and as hard as stone.

Marie looked at it in awe. It was a huge erection but beautifully proportioned. In her head she was pleading for him to take her, to push that huge dick insider her. She wanted it so much she could feel the pulsing of her pussy.

Mrs Ryder stood up from her task. Receiving a signal from the Master she walked over to the first girl against the wall and roughly pulled her by the waist so that her bottom stuck out and her sore flesh was on display.

Without any preliminaries the Master walked up behind this young girl and pushed his big, thick erection up inside her tight hole. The girl screamed out, the sudden invasion of this monstrous cock causing her to erupt in agony. She thrashed around as much as her restraints, and the Master's tight grip, would allow. Even the Master was suffering slightly from the tight fit of his length in her cunt. The grimace on his face soon turned to a look of satisfaction.

"Yes, you felt that, didn't you? You little creaming whore." He gripped her hair and pulled her hair back as he pushed into her.

Marie watched jealously as the Master worked in and out of the girl's sore hole in a slow, rhythmic movement. The girl was clearly in great pain. Tears were running down her face and she was breathing only in hysterical whimpers and gasps. The Master was working her like a maestro, testing this girl like a musical instrument. He had the look of intense concentration on his face. He was testing the girl, judging how good she was at submitting to and pleasing a man.

"Strike her breasts Mrs Ryder. Firmly," he said as he continued to work his cock into the girl.

Mrs Ryder obliged and struck the girl with six good lashes across her young breasts. A terrible shriek came from the girl.

The Master thrust up into the girl harder and faster.

"Again," he shouted. Mrs Ryder applied six more brutal lashes of the riding whip across the girl's breasts. They were showing clear red lines criss-crossing their pale flesh.

The girl was wailing in pain now. Marie winced half in sympathy and half in envy for the girl's suffering. She could feel her own juices trickling down the inside of her thigh, her pussy wet and wanting punishment.

The Master was pumping into the girl with great vigour now, his thick cock plunging her depths. The girl had changed from screams of pain to a low, animal grunting like someone lost in the pleasures of carnal sex. Marie could sense it. The girl was building up to come.

"Clamp her," the Master ordered. "Quickly."

Mrs Ryder rushed to attach metal clamps to the girl's nipples and then to the girl's swollen clitoris. Such was her excitement that she let out only the faintest whimper before being lost again in the maelstrom of arousal around her.

"Yes, that's it. Give in to it," the Master uttered almost in a whisper. He then started to fuck her harder still so that he was pounding her like a machine.

She gave in. Tossing her head around wildly the girl let out a volley of expletives, her breathing erratic, her face as red as her burning tits.

"Oh fuck. Oh fuck, oh yes. Thank you. Fuck me. Fuck me. Oh, fuck, yes."

She went silent. Her breath was held and her face contorted. Her eyes were tight shut. Then, with an exclamation of raw, sensual exhilaration her body released all of its tension with a gush of pussy fluid running down her legs, coating the Master's length. After a few seconds of muscle twitching ecstasy she fell completely limp, held off the floor only by her bound wrists.

"Leave her bound, Mrs Ryder." The Master then withdrew his glistening cock from her quivering hole.

He stepped back and turned his attention to the second girl. Deep in thought he approached her and pushed a finger up between her thighs. He felt inside her as though checking her state of arousal and the size of her entrance.

Marie was becoming impatient. She wanted only one thing and that was to be fucked into oblivion like the first girl had been. There were no other thoughts or desires within her.

The Master withdrew his finger and moved to guide his erect penis towards the girl. He did not push it ininto her wet pussy but to her tightly shut ass.

The gushing of the first girl had lubricated his cock and the first inch was pushed in easily, although not without a great deal of pain for the girl who he was forced to grip very tightly. He could push no further, however. She was putting up too much resistance.

"No," he said, defeated and removing his tip from her anus. "Mrs Ryder, if you would."

"Of course, Sir."

Mrs Ryder came round to the girl's bum and, kneeling, she pulled the buttocks apart and thrust her tongue into the tight little hole. Pushing in and out quickly she used her fingers to circle over the girl's pussy lips. She then spat twice directly at the girl's bum hole and pushed a finger inside, fucking it in and out vigorously. She then stood up and stepped aside.

The Master stepped forward and guided his cock back to the entrance of the girl's ass. Pushing forward he gained access easily again. He then pushed hard against the natural resistance and his thick dick slipped in further. The girl was in terrible agony, her face screwed up and her teeth gritted. But the Master was merciless. He proceeded to push harder, and to move in and out of her, ramming on the push, going deeper in than he pulled out each time. She wailed and squirmed and tried to fight back somehow but his strength was too much and her restraints too tight.

"Strike her on her tits and on her cunt. But be careful to mind me."

Mrs Ryder picked up her riding whip and struck the girl a series of lashed upon her tits.

"I said strike her," the Master shouted out.

Mrs Ryder, looking the perfect dominatrix in her leather suit, stepped back and swung a series of brutal strikes against the young girl's fine breasts. A wail of suffering ripped through the room.

Marie's envy was consuming her. She felt another trickle of cunt juices break over her lips and down her leg.

Mrs Ryder alternated blows. Several quick strikes against the girl's chest and a couple of well placed hits on her labia and clitoris. The girl wailed out with each strike but there was undeniably something in the noises she made it clear that was enjoying the pain.

The Master increased the rate at which he was fucking into her ass.

"Harder now, Mrs Ryder. On the labia."

"Yes, Sir."

The older woman lashed up between the girls legs with ferocious power expertly placed. Again and again she struck the swollen pussy lips, making them crimson.

The low scream coming from the girl was unending as the Master thrust into her bum and Mrs Ryder lashed her labia and clit.

The young girl broke suddenly. Her low scream ceased and she let out a series of grunts then suddenly let flow from her cunt all her fluid and her tight asshole squeezed hard the cock that had so powerfully fucked it.

Limp, dazed and lost, the girl lent her head against the stone wall and sought to get her breath back.

Marie was so expectant. Surely it was her turn. She had watched the two girls enjoy the most exquisite pleasure and suffering. It had pushed her into a frenzy of voyeuristic arousal. Had her hands not been bound above her head she would have fingered her hole so hard that she wouldn't have come round for hours. But, powerless, she had had to endure. She wanted fucking desperately. She wanted physical contact. She wanted everything she had watched and more. The Master hadn't come yet so he must move on to her.

He turned to look at Marie. The intensity in his eyes excited her.

"Put the appendage on, Mrs Ryder," he said as he worked his hand casually over the length of his erection.

Mrs Ryder stepped from Marie's view. When she came back she had attached to her waist and protruding out fearsomely a huge, thick strap-on phallus. Marie's heart accelerated.

The Master and Mrs Ryder then set upon Marie. The Master was behind fingering her tight little bum hole and Mrs Ryder was in front rubbing her fingers over Marie's sopping wet pussy lips, smearing the juices over her flesh.

It felt so wonderful to Marie that she shut her eyes and sank into the delightful sensations. She felt she could come very soon with this fingering alone.

The finger in her ass was replaced by the Master's still-hard cock. It was a so tight. She was being stretched so much. It hurt like she was being torn in half but she wanted it all inside her so much and she put all her thoughts into taking more into her. The pain fired through her like electricity, shooting everywhere and then ricocheting back to her bum.

At the front Mrs Ryder adjusted her own stance and started to feed the monstrously large rubber phallus up into Marie's welcoming cunt. The strap-on was thick and studded, shaped like a cock but with its contours grotesquely amplified. As it entered her cunt the lips strained to admit its irregular shape. She was wet and hot like she had never known, dripping constantly down her legs, but the entry was still difficult, painful and delightful.

The Master had pushed his erection in a good deal deeper now. Mrs Ryder's entry had clearly eased the resistance in her anus. The two started to work up a rhythm, each pushing into her at the same time, each building up layer upon layer of pain in her.

She was burning through her entire body. He ass was stretched so far she could faint. At the same time, in her cunt, a monstrously long strap-on was causing shooting pain to pierce the deepest part of her vagina. These two combined set her head spinning, the pain bewildering her. She felt as if she was going to black out.

The Master must have sensed her ailing. "Keep her concentrating," he barked at Mrs Ryder. With that the lady struck Marie on the cheek and then dug her nails into Marie's breasts eliciting a yelp from her. The girl was back wide eyed and in raptures of suffering and delight.

"Good," the Master said. "Keep them there."

She locked her nails into Marie's breasts, using her grip as leverage in her continued thrusting.

"She's close," the Master said and then dug his own nails into Marie's hips.

She was so close. Marie had felt close to coming the whole time she had been bound. All the while she had watched the other girls being fucked she had felt she could explode. Now, with lovely stinging pain all over and inside her body, on her tits and hips, in her pussy and her ass, she was boiling inside with arousal. She focused on what these two were doing to her, how slutty it was to be fucked like this, how debauched and wild. The pressure began to rattle inside her. It felt like it could break her body open it was that intense. But she wanted the Master to come inside her at the same time. She didn't want to be like the other girls. She was greedy for his come.

Amazing herself she managed to contain the climax at the very second it was ready to burst out of her. The strain upon her body was making her shake, her breath held tightly, her eyes watering and a low groan were evidence of her struggle.

"Yes, that's it Marie. You know how to please your master. Keep going," Mrs Ryder whispered encouragement into Marie's ear, sympathetic to what she was enduring.

The Master continued to pound hard into Marie. His face was contorted with pleasure and there was a glow of sweat on his face. His head rocked back, his mouth opened and a huge shout of released tension came from him as his cock spurted deep inside Marie's ass, the first blast of come shooting powerfully, followed by more firing deep into her hurting hole.

Marie felt it shooting up inside her. With that first thick jet of spunk she knew she had achieved what she wanted and could let go all that she was damming. The fierce rush of orgasm broke inside her with the force of a tidal wave. She screamed out with each quick breath, her nerve endings popping like fireworks under her skin, beautiful and burning. Then it moved through her, physically rushing down her body, making her buck involuntarily until it hit the point where the huge dildo stretched her pussy. The rubber cock was like a plug in her pussy and the pressure of her juices literally built up around it before bursting past and squirting out the sides in a fine spray of come that kept on for several seconds, wetting the legs of all three involved.

The last drips eased from the Master's cock as he pulled it from Marie's ass. A trickle of semen ran from the shrinking hole down her cheeks.

"Have the girls cleaned and returned to their duties, Mrs Ryder. Light duties for the rest of the day, in fact." And with that the Master tidied himself up and left the room.

CHAPTER 14

Marie received a note in her pigeon hole. It was an order from Mrs Ryder. It read:

"Report to my office at 2pm today. Important duties. Do not be tardy.

Mrs R."

Marie had never received a message in this way before. It was the first thing she had ever had in her pigeon hole. It made her feel rather that she was part of the Museum now and she was quite pleased with herself for some time. Why Mrs Ryder should need to use this system didn't quite make sense to Marie, but the duties she referred to must be very important. That thought started to make Marie a little nervous. But the good thing of it all was that contact from Mrs Ryder normally meant you were to meet with the Master, probably for a thrashing, but that could always be endured and enjoyed.

She occupied herself with her tasks about this remarkable museum. She had been set on with cleaning duties about each room, wiping down the statues and feather touching the paintings. It was one of the more enjoyable of the routine jobs as it brought her close to the beautiful art that the museum held. The statues, so exquisitely carved, by wondrously skilled artists who knew the physiology of the human body minutely, that Marie felt almost the same feelings through her hands as if she had been wiping over a living man of muscular physique, or a living, breathing woman of subtle, elegant curves. The close visual contact with the paintings also brought new depths of stimulation to her. Stood so close she could see the exquisite detail employed by the artist, detail that would only be perceived by the very few people who ever got so close to their work. So, there before her were sexual acts in the frankest and most precise detail, beautifully depicted and full of excitement and energy. For these reasons cleaning the art work was no chore. It was a delight to the senses, and a source of heat under her volatile libido.

It was whilst so engaged, lost indeed in the pleasure of the task, that she heard the slow chiming of a clock sounding for two pm. It snapped her away from her pleasant reverie and plunged her into a pool of panic. She shot from the room and upstairs as quickly as she could, well aware that even thirty seconds late was too much for Mrs Ryder to endure without meting out punishment. Stupid girl, she thought to herself. Every chance to impress and you make the most blunderingly stupid mistakes and set everything back to scratch.

Mr Ryder was displeased. Sat behind her desk, looking smart, professional, elegant and very attractive, with her chest just tastefully on display and her skirt cut just at the right height to emphasise her long, slender legs quite evidently covered in finest quality stockings, she looked at Marie sternly.

"It was a quite simple instruction, Marie. Simple to even a simpleton. Yet here you are, late and out of breath."

"I am sorry Mrs Ryder. I was late in getting away from my cleaning duties."

"I did not ask for an excuse. I did not ask for any form of reply. So do not venture forth with one you infuriating girl."

"Sorry."

"Enough. There is work to be done."

Mrs Ryder explained that The Master was entertaining some friends this afternoon in his chambers at the museum. These friends were eminent men of some standing and it was quite rare that all their schedules could accommodate such a meeting. The afternoon would take the form of lunch followed by conversation in the Master's chambers which adjoined his office. It was necessary that there be someone to wait on them whilst they were in the chambers, supplying them with what they required. It was customary in these circumstances for a girl in training to be given the task and Mrs Ryder had selected that Marie, newest of all to formal training at the museum, should be given the chance to show herself worthy of such a scholarship.

"I already regret my decision," Mrs Ryder said.

It was a responsibility that had Marie feeling very nervous. Waiting on the Master and his guests without any assistance was as frightening a prospect as she could imagine at this moment. She had no idea how to "wait" on anyone. Pour drinks for them presumably? Pass them drinks from a tray? What drinks and when? How much and where? And she knew full well that she would be as clumsy and as easily confused as the worst waitresses that served in the world. The elation and honour she felt at being invited onto formal training at the museum was vanishing, as this first genuine test would be her undoing. She was certain of that.

She was taken by Mrs Ryder into a small room and instructed to change. Whilst the older lady watched closely Marie removed her shirt and her skirt until she was stood in only her bra and knickers.

"Did your Mother buy those for you, girl?" Mrs Ryder asked, with a look on her face that showed plainly her revulsion at Marie's current undergarments.

"Yes." Marie was embarrassed. She hadn't thought anything was wrong with them. They were just underwear.

"They are quite vile. Remove them and put them directly into the bin."

Marie, somewhat reluctantly, stepped out of her knickers and removed her bra so that she was stood completely naked before this beautiful older woman.

She took hold of the plain items of underwear and did exactly as instructed, throwing them, a little rebelliously, into the bin. She turned to Mrs Ryder and smiled.

"Marie, do not think to give me any attitude. You are just a small creature in this new world, vulnerable, weak and ignorant. You would also be friendless if it were not for me. So regulate your behaviour a little or you will sorely regret not doing so."

The message registered instantly. Marie's very brief, very modest, display of girlish rebellion had been smashed down swiftly.

"I am sorry. My mum didn't buy the underwear. I did. Yesterday. They were expensive."

"Then you wasted your money girl, for you looked as sexually alluring as piece of meat in paper. Now who would want to fuck that, Marie, honestly? If any girl was in want of an education it was you. Let me demonstrate something to you."

Mrs Ryder proceeded to unbutton her blouse and loosen of her skirt. This she did as elegantly and as alluringly as Marie had ever seen it done.

"Although I am only working today on The Master's diary and managing some of the purchasing for the year I still ensure that I am well dressed. More than that, I ensure I am exquisitely dressed underneath, as you can see."

Stepping from her skirt and completely removing her blouse she revealed herself to Marie, a woman of remarkable beauty clothed in the finest of undergarments. She wore a black bra of silk made so delicately and skilfully that it skimmed around her breasts and nipples and lifted and pulled her chest in the lightest, most delicate way. It looked elegant, sophisticated and intensely alluring. It begged for a hand to touch it, or a mouth to glide from silk to flesh in an excited breath.

Below she wore a matching item, black silk knickers cut high on her hips to show off her legs and cut thinly through the middle to allow the slightest exposure of that tender flesh between her legs. The material was so fine that it seemed to drape over the body loosely, yet also pull tight up to it. Around her waist she had a suspender belt and down from this elegantly detailed suspenders that held up her stockings without any imperfection in their form. Marie was quite in awe of such beautiful items and wished desperately that she could be wearing them.

"You see, Marie, it is right for a lady to be well dressed. Firstly, a lady benefits herself hugely by being dressed in this way, for she carries herself elegantly if she is dressed elegantly; she will feel attractive if she is dressed attractively. Secondly, a lady never knows when she might be fortunate enough to have need for such items, and it is most unpleasant to have an opportunity presented to you and to be ill prepared to take it. Trust me on that, I speak from bitter experience."

Marie was quite transfixed. Without quite knowing what she was doing a hand reached out and stroked over Mrs Ryder's breast, touching the silk garment and flesh and relishing the delightful feel they had through her fingers.

Mrs Ryder smiled, a little taken aback, but not wholly surprised by the girl's reaction.

"You realise I shall have to punish you for that, Marie? You are a girl in training, remember."

Marie continued. She had entered into an isolated space where she was not concerned with consequences, but only with the remarkable sensual delight of Mrs Ryder's skin and the beautiful silk she wore over it. She kept on stroking over Mrs Ryder despite the warning of certain punishment to come. Now both hands were upon the woman, stroking her breasts and sliding over her buttocks, Marie was completely naked and there were very visible signs of arousal about her now, with her nipples swollen and warm, her whole body becoming fidgety with desire, her thighs rubbing against each other without her quite knowing what was going on.

"You have had fair warning, Marie. I will not be too harsh on you, for I did invite you to look."

With that Mrs Ryder took hold of Marie and turned her around briskly so that she was facing away from her. Seizing hold of a belt that was hanging within the small changing room, she bent Marie forward and very swiftly applied three rasping strokes upon her bottom.

Marie hopped up with the sudden, rather unexpected pain. Released from Mrs Ryder's grip she fidgeted around more vigorously now, and with much less soft and tender feeling through her. As ever, though, the feelings were no less pleasing to her.

Mrs Ryder put down the belt and stood before Marie again. Marie rubbed her bottom and, for no obvious reason related to the punishment just administered, she also rubbed her chest.

"You may proceed, but I will punish you more if you do," Mrs Ryder said in a way that clearly wished to tempt Marie into her trap.

There was nothing Marie could do to resist. She was totally absorbed by this beautiful woman standing in her underwear in front of her. The brisk punishment on her bottom that had just been issued only amplified the wondrous feelings through her. The threat of more punishment was no threat at all. Marie wanted more of it and wanted it now.

She now started to fondle Mrs Ryder's breasts, sliding a hand underneath the silk fabric to caress the full curve of flesh it concealed. Her fingers slid over firming nipples and made Marie feel melting warmth spread through her smoothly and slowly. She moved in closer and ventured, bravely, to kiss the flesh at the top of her breast very gently, almost respectfully. A hand now traced a line down the woman's flat stomach and then fingers slid imperceptibly under the top of those black knickers to linger and softly brush through the neatly trimmed hair that was so near to that most precious piece of feminine flesh.

Marie sighed out aloud, the feelings in her building up into something she was not in control of. Each touch was a beautiful joy to her senses. The sight of this woman before her, the feel of her flesh and the smell of her perfume, the sound of her breathing – it all was entering Marie and affecting her like an exquisitely moving piece of music, or sip of a luxuriously smooth fine wine. All of her was warm with a lovely glow of sensuality.

Mrs Ryder had allowed her to drink it in quite long enough, however. As before, and without any malice, she grasped the girl, turned her and bent her over, revealing the lovely round, slightly plump, backside, and set about it with the belt, putting four very solid contacts upon it. Marie jumped forward evasively after the first but was well constrained. She was pleased that Mrs Ryder had held her so firmly, for she did not want to miss out on that unique feeling being lashed on the bottom gave her.

She was fully aroused now, totally given over to lust and desire, desperate for further punishment and ultimately craving her own sexual gratification through pain. If Mrs Ryder was willing to spank her then she would try and take this lovely, sharp, burning punishment as far as she could.

Marie pushed her hand back into Mrs Ryder's knickers and, much more directly now, slid her fingers further until one was between those warm lips, excitedly coated in a little feminine moistness. With her thumb she started to agitate the clitoris, finding it easily and working it out of the flesh that held it before rubbing over it firmly. With her other hand Marie pulled the black silk bra low and cupped one of Mrs Ryder's breasts so that it was fully revealed. She then set upon this gorgeous breast with enthusiasm, kissing and licking over it, biting at the pale flesh and sucking on the swollen nipple. Marie was totally lost within her desire for this woman.

Mrs Ryder was clearly not impervious to the Marie's efforts and could be heard sighing loudly from the pleasant sensations being fingered by this girl were inducing in her. But there was never the sense that she was out of her own control, as Marie clearly was, and the careful, sophisticated, classy woman remained alert and self-controlled, albeit half naked and with a beautiful twenty year old girl plunging a hand into her knickers.

Marie now sank to her knees, sliding those silk panties down slightly so that they revealed the beautiful mound and lips of this delicious older woman. Looking at it with unconfined desire Marie was about to commence kissing, licking and sucking at that sweet scented flesh when her hair was grasped close to the scalp by Mrs Ryder and her head yanked back. Seizing the belt once more the woman turned Marie around her leg and, with the girl's breast open and exposed, sent down five crashing blows with the length of leather, each cracking upon the young flesh of Marie's tits with a terrible power.

The thrashing was so swift that Marie had no time to comprehend it. From being just inches from tasting the flesh between the thighs of this woman, lost in the delightful prospect of tasting it, to receiving that brutal fifth strike, had been but a few seconds. Everything needed to catch up – her feeling, senses, comprehension, were all lagging behind with shock at the suddenness of it all. And suddenly, with her chest feeling as if it had been doused and set alight, she realised that she was coming, a violent tremor of her foundations, a shaking of her insides and a pushing at her pussy that she could not stop though she wanted to so much, wanted to prolong this, but couldn't because she was there, damn it, coming on the floor. How good it felt though, that beautiful pain induced orgasm, blasting through her and through the fire of the pain and coming out the other side as a squirt of juices from her pussy.

Mrs Ryder still had hold of her hair and was poised as though she would continue with this little game she was playing with Marie. Marie's rather listless body and gormless expression made it clear that the game was over early. If there was some initial doubt why it was over, the realisation that Marie had squirted some of her orgasm onto Mrs Ryder's shoes made everything abundantly clear.

"Marie, you have come over my shoes. That bloody well won't do."

"I'm sorry. I didn't realise until it had already finished."

"Lick it up this instant."

"What?" Marie said, still a bit uncertain of her bearings such was her post orgasm bewilderment.

"Don't you 'what' back at me, young girl," Mrs Ryder said sharply before sending down a whack with the belt that made firm contact upon the girl's upper arm.

The swiftly administered corporal punishment had the desired effect for Marie immediately lowered herself down and began to lick the thin liquid that had been sprayed upon Mrs Ryder's black leather high heeled boots. Diligently Marie licked away, checking for signs of any more of her come upon the boots, and licking that up also, while Mrs Ryder stood imperiously over her, examining closely the effort she was making.

"Good work, Marie. But we really will need to work hard on your self control. You can't be breaking down in floods of come every time a superior lashes your tits."

"No, Mrs Ryder. I'm sorry."

"Well, my lesson to you took an unexpected digression. However, the point I wished to make is in here somewhere. Look the part to play the part. Now, whilst you wait on The Master and his guests he wishes you to be in corset, stockings, heels, and suspenders. You shall be knickerless however. I am relieved to see you have tended to your mound recently. That is something at least."

And on that final positive note Mrs Ryder pulled from the changing room drawers the items that comprised Marie's uniform for the afternoon's duties. It made for an unusual outfit for serving guests, but not so extraordinary given The Master's particular tastes. It was, however, going to make Marie feel an outrageously self-conscious, to have her full femininity on display for these distinguished men.

The more she thought about it the more she liked the prospect. And the more she liked the prospect the more she felt herself becoming aroused. The remarkable corset she was wearing, and the tall heels, and the way it coerced her body into a shape that made her look and feel so incredible, were the only things that she was aware of in her mind.

Mrs Ryder kindly gave her the final details of the task, showing her the chambers whilst it was empty and pointing out the cabinets where drinks and glasses were kept, advising as to what decanter had what spirit within it. It was not going in. What drinks, and where, and what thing when, was all forgotten as soon as it was spoken. Oh dear, she thought, this was destined to be a failure for sure. This was careening towards a car crash display of embarrassment. Concentrate, she told herself, but she couldn't get beyond that word. Her mind just wandered off to think about how fucking horny she was right now. Damn it.

"Stand there and stay there until they enter. They should not be too much longer. Then do as I have instructed you," Mrs Ryder said before leaving Marie alone in The Master's chambers.

Standing in an elegantly detailed black corset, with black stockings and suspenders on and wearing nothing else except a pair a polished, black leather, high heels, Marie looked an impressive girl. The outfit accentuated her curves perfectly, and drew the eye along them as though the lines of the underwear were made to lead the eye from one fine physical attribute to another. Her sweet young breasts, full and round, were pushed up without being misshapen as is often seen, and her legs were lengthened by the heels and stockings, as though they were being served in stages to the observer, who might dwell on the feet and ankles, move onto the stockinged calf and thigh and then feast on the flesh of the thighs and all that sweet, sticky final course that lay at their junction. She looked astonishingly beautiful and innocent whilst simultaneously being irresistibly sexy and capable of acts of jaw dropping depravity.

She was nervous of what awaited her. A simple task like serving drinks to strangers had undermined any confidence she had felt emerging from the last few weeks and returned her to a previous state where anything new, unexpected or outside of her planning was a disaster. The familiar anxiety rose, making her hands shake.

The Master walked in with three other men. The Master was, as always, very smartly dressed with a neatly pressed suit, shirt and tie. His guests were a bit more casual, but still wore the items associated with gentlemen of standing and good breeding. They were all around the same age as The Master, perhaps one was five or ten years younger to Marie's eye and maybe another was a few years older. They were all very well presented men, distinguished looking, intelligent looking and each, in their own way, fairly handsome, though none of them was quite capable of rivalling The Master's rare good looks.

Their lunch had obviously gone well as spirits seemed to be up. Marie began to tremble. As they entered they all eyed her intently but said nothing, nor gave her any acknowledgment.

"Yes, yes, we know that. It is not simply nostalgia, however, Peter. Not in this instance. It is an objective comparison of girls now and girls when we were young men. They are more insolent, less compliant and very reluctant to take orders. The first dozen girls I trained were models of subservience, in everything. My methods haven't changed. If anything, my methods have become tighter." This was spoken by the tallest of The Master's guests, a slender man with grey hair and spectacles. He addressed one of the men who had just slumped into a leather chesterfield armchair.

"Hogwash, Terence, and you should know better," answered Peter, his cheeks a little ruddy, presumably from the wine they had washed their lunch down with. "They were insolent then as well. You just look on them more favourably because time has smoothed over those rough passages of your recollection. Girls were little bitches then, just as they are now."

"No, it's plain to see and makes perfect sense. Girls are taken on at eighteen or twenty often, yes?"

"Yes. The same as forty years ago."

"Precisely. But the girls of today have undergone a vastly different upbringing to the girls of forty years ago.

They have been spoilt materially but also been made feckless, work-shy and insubordinate. These are faults of character pushed into them by society. Forty years ago, society was still able to instil virtues such as obedience, a work ethic and general vigour of spirit."

"Oh, dear. Hear him now, chaps. He sounds like some dusty old Victorian schoolmaster."

"It's sense. Because of their formative years we are having a harder time producing the exceptionally obedient girls."

All the guests turned to The Master now, who had so far remained silent as he moved about the room. He sat down now and considered his response.

"Terence makes a persuasive argument. But I am not for it, I'm afraid. It feels more to me and my experience that what we work with is something more fundamental within the girl than can be altered by general social conditions, how they have been brought up, or what they watch on television. What we work on within a girl, some girls, is an innate desire to be dominated sexually. That innate quality is too deep within the girl to be altered by anything they encounter. Our influence is not to alter it, but to alter everything around it, to reveal it, and to let them understand it. In so doing we achieve the perfect score in this sport of ours, do we not?"

"Indeed we do."

"And anyway, Terrence," The Master replied. "You speak as if the disobedient, feckless ones were less fun. Surely they provide the best number of opportunities for you by going against your orders? God knows I relish it when a good one of mine gives me cause to lash her."

"He hasn't the energy for lashes or a great deal else, you know. Too much disobedience and he needs a day's rest in bed."

The gentlemen broke the conversation with gales of laughter at the jibe, and the conversation turned to other matters. Marie watched intently awaiting an order.

"Girl, pour me a whisky and soda, and don't be too heavy handed with the latter," said one of the gentleman seated, the one Marie noticed who was a bit rounder bellied than the rest.

She froze momentarily as she tried to get into her head what had been ordered of her. The Master picked up on this hesitation and gave her a powerful look direct in the eye, which was both his consent to go and fulfil the guest's order but also a slight reproach for being so slow to comprehend.

Marie turned to the drinks cabinet and grabbed at a glass. This was going to be a problem, she quickly realised, as there were a lot of different bottles at the back, and lots of different decanters at the front. None of them was she familiar with not being much of a drinker, or her family being much that way inclined either. She lifted up a decanter that had some brown fluid in it and poured half a glass full. She then poured on top of this some fizzy stuff that was beside the decanters. Nervously she walked over to the rotund man and handed the drink over.

His eyes had watched her walk the distance of the room and had been examining her in detail, clearly quite approving.

"A very fine looking girl you have there. Superbly proportioned and with such an innocent expression. Very fine indeed."

He watched her walk back to her starting point, his eyes delighting in the way her bare buttocks moved and swayed as she walked. As he watched he took a sip of his drink. Instantly he spat it out, spraying it half across the room, as though he had suddenly choked on it.

Red faced he apologised to his other guests profusely.

"Terribly sorry. Goodness! Caught me off guard there, she did. No, didn't mean to make a mess. But, damn it if the girl didn't give me a brandy and lemonade when I asked for a whisky and soda. Thing like that takes a man from behind you know. Not what he's expecting."

"Marie, clean that up now and apologise," The Master said, really quite displeased that one of his girls should have made such a mistake.

"I am very sorry, sir. It was a mistake. I'm sorry," she said as she started to clean the mess she had made on the floor.

She was on her hands and knees scrubbing at the mark on the carpet. Her bare bottom and the perfect flesh between her legs was opened and revealed by her position. The man who had sprayed the drink had fixed his eyes upon this beautifully proportioned backside and was enjoying the way it gently moved with Marie's scrubbing.

"Pardon me, gentlemen, but I shall have to partake of some of that. Too good to pass up."

"I hope it is to your liking," said The Master, gesturing for his guest to proceed.

The round bellied man who had sprayed the drink pulled himself up from his chair and cleared his throat. He began to undo his belt and unzip his trousers. Marie realised something was happening behind her but was so caught up in the embarrassment of cleaning the spilled drink that she did not comprehend what was planned for her this moment. When she heard the gentleman's trousers fall to the ground, the belt buckle rattling, she instinctively turned her head to see, standing behind her, the guest naked on his lower half, a good sized hard-on forming in front of a heavy set of balls. Her jaw dropped open with surprise.

"No need, girl. Stay as you are scrubbing the floor. It rather suits my mood."

And so she turned her head back to the stain and continued to work a cloth over the mark, a little slower now, and certainly with a distracted mind. This man, this distinguished gentleman, guest of The Master, was about to take her from behind in the middle of The Master's chambers, while conversation carried on around them. She had no conception of what she should do. Her mind was frozen. He had asked her to keep scrubbing the floor and that was about the only thing she could coordinate her body into doing as she awaited the guest's next move.

He knelt down behind her using a hand upon her bottom to steady his descent while he continued to talk with the other guests, about some current piece of legislation or something similarly unfamiliar to Marie, while he rubbed the side of his fingers against her pussy. The first contact he made with her was like a sudden shock, making her recoil a little bit, catching her unexpectedly, although she knew his broad intentions. It quickly changed from that cold shock to a warm, delicious feeling. He made no effort at movement whatsoever, merely holding his hand in place and allowing the little movement created by Marie's scrubbing to move her flesh against his finger.

She was getting wet at an alarming rate. In a few seconds she realised she had transformed from unaroused and embarrassed to incredibly horny and utterly shameless. It had required nothing more than this man's finger to brush her pussy while these men watched disinterestedly around her. It made her hot and wet and she craved more.

"She's quick to warm up. Bloody hell. Just the job."

The round bellied man removed his finger and guided his firm cock up to the entrance of her dripping hole. She was eager for it inside her and was instinctively pushing back, whilst still cleaning the carpet, trying to get it in so that she could satisfy that desire in her, and feel his dick insider her. He slid in easily, pushing firmly past the first resistance, making Marie moan softly in the slight discomfort of it that was instantly followed by the flush of delight through her whole lower torso. The gentleman was similarly affected, feeling the first resistance, and pushing through it into a well of beautiful sensations transmitted up through his cock and around his body.

"Damn fine girl you have here. Perfect cunt."

The man gripped Marie at the hips and pulled her back onto his stiff dick, building up a steady rhythm that allowed him to continue to engage in conversation with the other men in the room. He was able to pull his erection out until the tip just lingered at the wet lipped entrance before sliding it back in to the hilt of his shaft, big balls bouncing against Marie's clit and mound. She continued to move her hand about the stain upon the floor but it was little more than a sop to her orders, for she was totally lost in the mix of sensations emanating from her sex at that moment. A cocktail of unknown emotions were also flowing into her now, the feeling of being used so disinterestedly, while still under orders to clean the carpet of a stain, and all the time being fucked from behind. And the feeling of having all these men's eyes on her while being so degraded. And to be fucked by an older man who she had seen for the first time only a minute before, taking his stiff cock inside her cunt. All these thoughts, and all the sensations of that hard dick pumping into her pussy, had her swelling with arousal and desperate for more of the same.

The gentleman had become a little removed from the conversation. He had started to focus more attention on Marie and his thrusting at her from behind, and his grip at her hips, was becoming stronger.

"Damn fine cunt. Really is damn fine."

He fucked hard into her now, impatient, feeling the onset of orgasm. Marie was feeling a wildness come over her as well, lost to the animal nature within her, enjoying the prospect of him coming so much. She wanted to have him shoot his come into her mouth so that she could taste it, so that she could feel it run down her chin and drip on her tits. She loved to luxuriate in a man's come like that. She wanted to so much.

She was denied. The man kept on his fucking at a very brisk pace, pulling her back hard onto the full length of his cock. Then, with a flurry of obscenities, he emptied his big balls and poured out his ivory coloured, thick come into her hungry snatch.

"Mmm, fuck that was good," he said, his intense satisfaction obvious in his tone.

He withdrew his shaft and stood up, his legs a little unsteady as he rose. Marie was unsure what she should do, but kept on making the gesture of scrubbing as she had been earlier instructed. She turned her head to look at the man still stood behind her, looking flushed and fatigued. He pointed to his deflating dick and she knew straight away that she was expected to lick him clean and put his dick away in his trousers.

Without the slightest hesitation she spun round and took the cock into her mouth, sucking and licking to take the mix of her own juices and his sperm from the flesh. She did this not as she might have done at other times, energetically, trying to firm that cock back up, but instead she proceeded quietly, gently, instinctively doing her task properly. Although the taste of his come was a sweet pleasure for her, she knew that he wanted to be cleaned, not made hard again.

The man tightened up his belt and Marie tucked his flaccid penis back into the fly. He stepped back and slumped into the chair, spent. Around him the gentleman's conversation continued, and he quickly picked up the thread again and entered.

No orders were given to Marie, and she still knelt on the floor. From between her legs she could feel the man's spunk seeping out of her, forming a small puddle on the floor. Without thinking because she was half lost still in her own arousal, she lowered her hand down to her hole and used her fingers to scoop out the remaining come. This she put up to her mouth and licked from her fingers, completely unaware that all the room's eyes were on her at this time. She then shuffled back slightly and lowered her head down and licked up the pool of sperm that had formed beneath her pussy. It tasted lovely on her lips and tongue and she didn't want to waste a drop.

The gentlemen watched in astonishment, mouths agape as they observed. The conversation had temporarily halted as they were observing this remarkable, only half conscious behaviour from Marie.

She pushed the last drop of come from the side of her mouth past her lips and licked the tip of her finger clean. Looking up she was taken from her peculiar bubble by the attention of the guests. It startled her.

"I'm sorry," she said softly and quickly returned to scrubbing the floor, which, by now, had received quite enough scrubbing.

"Impressive," said the taller of the guests, Terrence, to The Master. "Nice to see that in a girl."

The Master also appeared to be a bit surprised by what she had done so instinctively. "Not a day into her training," he said.

"I shall have to partake of this prodigy," Terrance said.

"I can wholeheartedly recommend it," said the exhausted round bellied man, reclined in his chair, gathering his composure slowly.

Terrance, who was sitting on the leather sofa, gestured at Marie, drawing her attention to him.

"Girl, I want you to get me a glass of brandy..."

"Don't overtax her, Terry," came the mocking voice of the round bellied man.

"A glass of brandy. Then I want you to suck me to firmness and then I want you to ride me gently while I enjoy my drink and some good conversation. Understand?"

"Yes, sir," answered Marie.

Standing, she poured a glass of what she now knew was brandy into a tumbler and then handed it over to the gentleman. He took it without acknowledging her, for he was leading the conversation. Marie then knelt down in front of him, between his parted legs, and undid his trousers. Unbuttoning the boxer shorts that he was wearing beneath she was able to reach her fingers through to take gentle hold of his soft penis. As her hands felt their way into this area she felt a thrill of excitement, not knowing quite what was within. It turned out to be a rather large length, considerable in all its dimensions. The prospect of sucking it hard and gently riding it was even more exciting now she had seen its potential.

Without causing the gentleman a single tremor of disturbance she took the soft cock into her mouth and started sucking. Sliding her hand gently up and down the growing length, rolling her wrist and moving the skin over the already firming meat of the shaft, and licking in upward strokes from the very base, up the underside, to the very tip before passing the fat purple head past her lips where her warm mouth wet the tip and she turned her tongue in long slow circles around his shaft's foreskin collar, she soon had him very hard and very large.

"An adept mouth on her. I can hardly concentrate."

Marie heard the comment and considered halting, in case she was distracting him too much, but decided that she should carry on as instructed.

He was now very hard indeed, his cock twitching with the pressure she had brought to it. Marie had been able to taste the pleasant first drops of pre-come on his tip and knew that it was a good time to start to ride him. Giving his cock one last lick along its length, and twirling her tongue around the engorged head, she stood up, keeping a hand on his cock still, and climbed up so that she was kneeling on the sofa, her legs straddling him, her breasts level with his face. He could not prevent himself from smiling at the graceful way she managed to achieve this position, her body moving with a feline fluidity.

Marie was happy now. All that early anxiety, all that nervousness, had vanished. She was in a place where she was not being viewed or judged. At least, not judged on anything other than her ability to satisfy these men and follow their orders, and she found that a very easy thing to do indeed. Her self-awareness had gone so much that she would not have recognised herself if she had been able to replay the scene at a later time. She had entered into a perfect place mentally where there were no distractions, just her doing something that she was naturally, and unexpectedly, very good at. It was the experience known occasionally by great sportsmen, which they call entering 'the zone'. She was in 'the zone' now, as she guided the gentleman's long dick up into her wet hole.

It slid up into her beautifully, easily, aided by her own arousal, the other man's come still inside her and the wetness of this man's cock from her sucking on it so thoroughly. It was a wondrous, lasting sensation sliding down on it, so long that the delight of the first entrance was prolonged and she was forced to sigh out loud with the pleasure.

"She likes that, Terry," spoke a voice from behind her.

"What's not to like," was Terry's quick response. He, also, was awash with the feelings of pleasure through him that being fully up inside this girl was bringing about in his body.

Marie started to slide up and down his length very gently as instructed, lifting herself off him so that she just held his tip within the grip of her sex and then sliding down very slowly, keeping that tight grip of her muscles around his length so that his foreskin was pulled tight with each downward motion and so that his cock felt her tight grip from its tip down to its base. The slow rhythm was a new sensation for her and the way it made each up and down motion so exquisitely drawn out, the pleasure so lasting, every piece of feeling clear to her, and so remarkably powerful within her, made her wish that she could spend all eternity riding slowly on this cock, drinking in the feelings it gave her sex. She could never grow tired of it.

The gentleman guest continued with the conversation going around the room whilst sipping brandy from his glass. Marie was very careful not to bounce around too much and cause him to spill any of his drink. She could see that he was becoming quite engrossed in what she was doing to him, however, and when he abruptly downed the large amount of brandy he had remaining and tossed his glass away onto the floor she sensed that she was being allowed a freer rein.

The look in his eyes confirmed this. His lust was up. The conversation about global markets could hang. He wanted to fuck this girl. Marie could see it all plainly in his eyes and it made her feel a great rush of happiness.

She started to speed up her rhythm, rising up and down his shaft with considerably more pace and meeting his newly appeared upward thrusts with a downward push so that his whole length, right down to his balls, was up inside her. He was unconfined now, the gentleman suddenly turned to a brute and he yanked at her corset, pulling it loose at the front so that Marie's tits popped out and he could set about sucking and biting at the nipples and licking over the flesh, almost slavering in his eagerness to have her all. His dug his nails into her buttocks and scratched over her skin causing her a sharp burning pain. He began to whisper obscenities at her and this excited Marie greatly, urging her on to fuck him harder.

"Go on, you little slut. Go on. Ride that cock. You dirty, fucking, bitch!"

She was panting aloud with excitement. He was becoming breathless himself. He started pulling her hair as he bit into her breast, marking her, making her shriek, and all the while she continued to pump up and down on his cock like a piston, up and down, harder, faster, all of it slamming up inside her, hurting her. He bit her again on the side of her breast and she screamed. He slapped at her tits with his free hand, whacking them from the side with the full force of his hand, making them red and throbbing, making them burn with a beautiful irresistible pain. If he kept doing that she was going to come like a fucking steam train, she told herself.

"Have all of it up you, bitch," he muttered, his face contorted. "Have the fucking lot. Ohh!"

His eyes rolled then shut. His face went tight as though in pain. He slammed his cock up into her as he pulled her down onto him and then he held her there as he emptied out his full sac into the depths of her sex. She could feel it bursting forth, filling her, twitching as it fired out all thick and rich. She loved the way a cock shooting come inside her felt.

She remained where she was, perched on top of his cock, while he shook out the last final stages of his orgasm and drew his first few controlled breaths. Then, with no regard for the girl who had just serviced him so excellently, he pushed her aside and pointed at his glistening cock with the implicit order that she clean him up.

Marie was oblivious to his disregard of her or the slightly rough physical treatment she received as he pushed her off. She just wanted to be allowed to lick him clean and she set about the task as she had the previous gentleman.

However, the glass that had been discarded by the gentleman was lying by her and, whilst still licking over the man's formidable length, she took the glass and placed it beneath her hole so that the semen that dripped past her lips would be collected. She did it discreetly, only The Master actually noticing. When she had cleaned up the gentleman's cock and tucked it back into his trousers she took up the glass and showed it to him.

"May I drink your come, sir?" she asked softly, worried that this might be considered insolence.

The gentleman was taken by surprise. "Goodness," he said. "I clearly gave you a lot there. Proceed, girl. Drink it as a reward for pleasing me."

And Marie, knelt in front of him, tipped her head back and poured that glass of come onto her lips and into her mouth, purposefully allowing quite a bit of it to run onto her cheeks and down her chin so that she could savour the pleasure of licking it from around her mouth. Little droplets fell onto her exposed tits and she used her finger to collect them up and put them on her tongue. It was a show for the gentleman, but also something she really revelled in, the way it felt on her, warm and thick, and what it represented, the total sexual satisfaction of a man. It made her happy.

The gentleman in question, Terry, addressed The Master.

"I have to say, she's got something about her this one. And fresh in training. I hope it plays out to the end as well as it's started. If it does you'll be well pleased, that's for certain."

"Yes," The Master replied. "But we don't offer up too much praise, Terry. Risk of conceit."

"Of course, of course. My apologies. Damn useless waitress."

The Master and his guest need not have worried about heaping too much praise on Marie, for she was in a world away from them, only thinking of her sexual desire and satisfying the other gentlemen in the room. She was desperate to keep going and blatantly scanned the room looking for someone to take her.

Peter, the gentleman who had been involved in a long debate with The Master for much of the afternoon's proceedings, was clearly not willing to pass up a trial of what appeared to be a quite remarkable girl. He broke off from his conversation and summoned her over. Instructing her to kneel on the armchair and leaning forward so that her elbows rested on the low leather back of the chesterfield, he circled behind her and, without any prelude, inserted a finger into her bum.

It made Marie jump. She wasn't expecting this to be his first act. She liked it immensely, however, and hoped this area might be the focus of his desires.

It was precisely the focus of his desire and he fingered at the sweet little bum hole whilst stroking his own cock hard. He seemed quite intent on just one thing, to fuck her hard in the ass. Nothing seemed of great concern to him. Foreplay, fellatio, cunnilingus, the usual warm up acts were only obstacles to him this moment and it was quite clear to Marie what was coming her way.

Firm now, he slipped his finger from her and placed his cock at her bum's entrance. With a total lack of compassion he pushed at her tight hole forcefully, breaking into her quickly despite the natural reluctance he met. Marie winced with the pain. His cock was quite thick and she had been given hardly any lubrication. It felt just as if a glowing hot piece of metal was being fed into her. It was a searing, astonishing pain. Tears were already welling in her eyes.

Mercilessly the gentleman continued to push into her. Soon, through sheer force of determination on his part it seemed, he had covered the ground and was up to his balls in her bum. The look of pleasure on his face was marred somewhat by the flush on his cheeks for clearly the entry to her anus had brought him a great deal of pain as well. But he obviously took great satisfaction in it as well. He started to pump away at her now, back and forth, the action becoming easier with each movement. There was something in his manner, Marie sensed, that suggested he was building up towards a powerful effort.

He was doing precisely that. A few thrusts more and he felt he had sufficiently widened her, or lubricated his own shaft, to fuck her as hard as he desired. He now set about fucking at her ass hole with a violent rhythm, faster by far than she had ever been fucked. He pounded into her asshole powerfully, almost maniacally, pulling at her hips hard, smashing into her. She was forced to scream out.

"Ahh! Oh, fuck. Oh, fuck. Ahh!"

"Too much for you? Too much to take you filthy slag? Come on, you know you fucking love it hard in your ass."

Marie could not deny that. The feeling was raw and brilliant, something like a flash of lightning trapped inside her, hot agony and brilliant light at once. He was so forceful, too much pain, but god, keep going, please, she begged silently, because the pain is what brings it on so hard that you crumble into dust. Oh god, please keep going this hard for a bit longer.

The gentleman with his cock in her anus was building now towards his climax. Such vigour could hardly have been sustained much longer. He was still at her viciously, thrusting deep and not allowing her any respite from the pain of one hit before he delivered the next. He began to snarl, his teeth exposed, his breathing loud and rapid.

"Oh, yeah! Here it comes. Turn round, bitch. Turn roun!," he shouted.

Marie quickly spun round, his cock slipping out of her relieved bum, and spun around so that she was sat in the chair facing the cock that had so violently fucked her anally. The gentleman wanked at it hard, his face still snarling like a wild dog, spit coming from his mouth. His thick cock erupted, his hand pumping the shaft so hard he must have been hurting himself, and a series of thick dollops of his come shot out of it into Marie's face and mouth and over her tits and into her hair and onto her shoulders until she was covered. She had never seen a man come so much or so hard.

She was covered in sperm. Licking it up off her tits and gulping it down, scooping the thread that dribbled down her chin and licking it from around her mouth she felt her own urgency. The pain of his cock in her anus had ignited her desire to come and now, as she took his still twitching dick into her mouth to lick up the last coating of come, the same dick he had just pulled from her ass, she could do nothing but give in to the flood of pleasure inside her, opening up and squeezing out of her pussy as a powerful body-shaking orgasm. Her cunt lips quivered as she involuntarily fired out thin jets of her accumulated pussy juices and other men's come onto the floor. Oh, it was a beautiful feeling, such a build up of arousal, of animal lust, of cocks inside her, of come up her and over her, of tastes and sounds and smells and the feel of this dick in her mouth and it was just too much. Oh, fuck, it was too much to take at once.

Marie slumped back in the chair, devoid of any strength. Her sex still quivered, contracting, squeezing out tiny droplets of her come. But she was exhausted completely and had no power to move and hardly the sense to understand where she was.

The Master and his guests carried on a while longer in their conversations, impressed but not overly diverted by Marie's display. The Master had Mrs Ryder come in and take Marie aside to recuperate and after another hour's conversation the guests made their way from The Museum and The Master returned to his office to carry on with his work.

Mrs Ryder came into the office.

"Excuse me, Master, but I thought I should let you know she is recovering well. Just a touch drained."

"Thank you," he answered, not looking up from his work.

Mrs Ryder remained in his office until eventually The Master was forced to look up.

"I had wondered how she did, Master?"

"She did fine, thank you Mrs Ryder. I will call through if I need you."

Mrs Ryder walked from the room with a faint smile forming.

CHAPTER 15

Whilst engaged with her duties one day in the library Marie was met by Mrs Ryder. The older lady put her hand softly onto Marie's back and stroked her tenderly.

"How are you, Marie?" she asked.

It was unusual for the Master's personal assistant to speak to her and not be issuing a directive.

"I'm fine, thank you," she replied politely.

Mrs Ryder continued to run her hand over Marie's back. It was a very sensual and feminine touch and it made the young girl feel a tingle of pleasure over her skin.

"Tomorrow night, Marie, the Master is hosting a function. He would like you to assist with the work during the evening and through the night. It will be a busy night so you must inform your landlady that you will be not be back until the following morning."

It sounded a touch peculiar to Marie but, given the propensity within the Museum for irregular behaviour, she found no good reason to object.

"Because it is such a busy evening you will take the rest of the afternoon off and come in at midday tomorrow. I insist you use this time only for rest and for sound sleep. Come directly to my office tomorrow."

"Yes, Mrs Ryder," Marie answered, her thoughts tempted away from the conversation by the woman's touch over her back.

"One more thing, Marie," Mrs Ryder added, her eyes intent on the girl. "There is no need to bathe or otherwise concern yourself with such matters."

On that Mrs Ryder let her hand stroke over Marie's bottom. She then turned and exited the library, leaving Marie to ponder what exactly tomorrow night's function would involve.

Obediently Marie took herself home straight away and let herself into the empty house. She made a drink and then got changed from her work clothes. She read a page of her book but her mind kept wandering back to the conversation with Mrs Ryder. Even more than that she found her mind wandering to that gentle, sensual touch upon her back. It was as if that touch had set her on a one-way path that ended in her achieving the sweet, warm oblivion of sexual gratification. She could not step back once set upon that path. She could only take it to its natural end. She could try and resist but she would only be putting off the inevitable. Increasingly aware of this she settled on acceptance and went upstairs to tread that sublime path of pleasure.

The fact that she was alone in the house, and would be for a few more hours, allowed her an opportunity she had not previously had. Full of curiosity and simmering sexual excitement she removed her clothes and walked into John and Isabelle's bedroom.

It was a wonderfully arousing feeling to be in a place she shouldn't be whilst completely naked. Her curiosity led her immediately to the drawers where she felt Isabelle would keep her underwear. When she found it she felt her heart quicken just a little bit.

Isabelle's underwear was all beautiful, full of special pieces like delicate French knickers of silk and lace and panties and thongs, all of quality and class. The attractive bras were like nothing Marie had really encountered before. She was determined to one day have a drawer filled with such items.

Though the lingerie brought thoughts of Isabelle's wondrous big breasts and perfectly formed pussy to mind Marie knew she needed something a bit dirtier to fire her arousal.

In the corner was a small basket that Marie instantly knew as John and Isabelle's dirty clothes basket. This is what she wanted, that extra connection.

Digging into it deeply she pulled out a pair of John's boxer shorts and held their crotch to her face. They smelt manly and of fresh sweat and also of the way a cock smells when it is getting hard and it is first pulled it out of the clothes that confine it. It was a smell that put Marie back to a memory of her first meeting with John, that taste and smell of manliness and hard cock. Her excitement climbed and a wetness and warmth descended to her sex. She began to squeeze her hand over her breasts.

Next she pulled out a pair of Isabelle's French style knickers, laced and silky and delicately made. She could see in the gusset the thin marks of a woman's natural moistness and was further excited by it. She held it to her nose and breathed in the subtle smell of Isabelle's pussy, clean and sweet, like a warm desert of fruit and syrup. Somehow it was a smell that Marie could not resist, a naughty smell for a girl to enjoy, delicious and irresistible. It brought her close to Isabelle's sex, as if it was there in front of her to lick and kiss and taste to her own endless gratification.

As she held the knickers to her face she closed her eyes and let her hand fall down between her spread legs to stroke at her softly fleeced flesh that was not hot and swollen and wet.

She was taken not to a memory but of a newly imagined fantasy where she and Isabelle were chained in a dark and dirty room with no movement except that Marie's mouth was between Isabelle's thighs so she could lick at the her pussy. As she did this they were being whipped, their hair pulled and their faces and tits slapped by the masked master who was stood over them.

Marie's own sex was allowed to rub over this unknown master's polished leather boot while he abused them.

Three fingers now pushed up into Marie's pussy, working in and out in firm movements. She pulled out and slapped her cunt hard then thrust the fingers back inside her hole. Delightful sensations of sharp pain and swelling arousal mixed over her skin and inside her body making her desperate for more of both.

She put aside Isabelle's panties and searched in the basket again. She felt something that seemed more soiled than the first two items and seized it immediately.

It was a pair of Isabelle's panties in black silk. At the gusset were clear signs of Isabelle's feminine juices in abundance, clearly the evidence of her being in a heightened state of arousal when wearing them. There was also a different stain, one that made those delicate panties feel stiff. It was unmistakably the mark of semen.

The realisation was like a sudden burst of fire inside Marie, fanning embers that quickly flashed into flame that then glowed brightly inside her. She knew this was the means by which she would be satisfied.

With the knickers held to her face she stepped back and looked for something to aid her enjoyment. Straight away she saw the upright, heavy wooden bedposts. They were stout posts, polished hardwood and lathed into attractive and subtle curves.

Stepping over one of these posts she lowered her beautiful naked body until her moist sex made contact with the hard wooden upright. It was a cool feeling at first, but the heat of sexual pleasure was quick to overtake it and work up inside her body. Breathing in the scent of Isabelle's sexual gushing and the unmistakable smell of male come she began to rub her sex over the thick, rounded top of the post. Her juices had already coated it generously and her pussy lips slid over the top of it easily and with an amazingly pleasurable sensation for her. The feeling was intense, so much so that she could feel the post acutely, from her mound that was gathering up some of her copious wetness, to the hood of her clit sliding back, then her clit, beautifully tender against the lubricated hardness, then the length of her labia undulating out over the post and then her wet entrance being pulled open by the thickness of what was between her legs.

She lost herself in the barrage of this delightful succession of feelings and the images she had in her head of Isabelle and John making love and creating the passionate flowing of fluids that she could smell now on these panties.

She pictured Isabelle wrapped in rope the same way she had seen in pictures at the museum where beautiful Japanese girls were bound with coarse rope in uncomfortable positions. Isabelle had rope digging into her breasts and her arms were tied behind her back. She was wearing the same panties that Marie was holding to her face. John was naked, his sculpted body displayed in its entirety. His penis was flaccid, but the length and girth were latent with exquisite promises of pleasures.

They would be in Isabelle's office at work. It would be late and John would have arrived unannounced. He would have stripped her and then wrapped her in the rope, making sure it was tight against her skin. The rough rope would make Isabelle feel a constant low sting of irritation, like the touch of a nettle.

With his considerable strength John then pulled Isabelle by her hair over the desk sending items crashing to the floor, so that she was laid with her head over the edge and her breasts squashed down onto the desk surface. The extra pressure of the rope now heightened her pain. Stepping up to her head John lifted her by her hair and, taking his flaccid length into his hand, fed it into her mouth. Isabelle reacted instantly and enthusiastically, taking it into her mouth and sucking it and licking it with an almost hedonistic abandon.

Marie had her eyes closed as she pictured all of this. The underwear was still held to her face. She picked out that manly smell, almost sweaty, almost sweet, of John's dried spunk and felt the odour stroke over her senses and transform itself into more heat in her pussy and more moisture in her hole. The thick post she rubbed her sex over now started feeling more like a stiff and massive erection and her cunt lips and hole were starting to stretch over its curved top. It was too large, however, to enter inside her, even if she were to try.

Her mind continued to picture her fantasy. As Isabelle sucked and licked John's growing cock he held her head up by her hair. When his cock accidentally slid from her mouth he rubbed it over her face and teased around her lips and tongue that clearly wanted more of him. As he got fully firm he started to fuck her mouth with powerful thrusts that pushed down Isabelle's throat and made her eyes water from the strain. But, despite the forcefulness, she craved more of him when he slid his length from her mouth.

He took from the desk a long wooden ruler and used it to strike Isabelle while he let her suck his dick. He hit her hard on the exposed parts of her bound arms, on her back and on her bottom which was still covered by the black silk panties. The strikes made her whimper but she did not falter in licking John's enormous length. He then held his cock upright against his stomach and has Isabelle lick over his heavy balls.

When he had had enough of Isabelle's eager and skilful mouth he spun her round on the desk. A lamp smashed on the ground and trays and folders and papers spilled over the edge of the desk.

Marie was deep in her fantasy at this stage. In her imagination John was about to push his hard dick, wet from being deep in Issy's mouth, into his wife's pussy. All the while, Marie had her eyes closed, the soiled knickers held to her face, rubbing her wet cunt over the bulbous bed post and fingering her swollen clit as quickly as her fingers would go.

She was so immersed in her fantasy that she did not hear John and Isabelle return home. The couple had entered the house and immediately set upon each other, their lust allowing them to only just get inside before it turned into groping and clothes being pulled off. John pulled at Isabelle's hair and kissed her passionately and hard on the mouth while his hand pulled at her shirt so that buttons fired off. Isabelle was equally unrestrained in her desire to be fucked and was rubbing her hands over his crotch as she tried to help him remover her clothes.

Their tryst spilled upstairs, towards their bedroom. Marie was still unaware right up to the point that the groping couple entered the room, John with his stiffening cock hanging out of his trousers and Isabelle with her breasts out of her bra and her pussy being fingered past her knickers.

For an instant there was terrible shock for all three. A few seconds ticked past with everyone in the room frozen in a state of unconfined sexual desire. Marie had no clothes available to cover herself with, and the door was blocked by the lust mad couple. Her face was colouring quickly, burning like it had never done before in a life full of shame, guilt and embarrassment. But still she could not steady her mind from the shock sufficiently to get her thoughts clear and to make a decision. She could not even get her head straight enough to move her naked body from the bedpost, nor even move the dirty, come-soaked knickers from her face. She was petrified.

Her inertness inadvertently allowed John and Isabelle time to comprehend the circumstances they had found themselves in. Their desperate passion had joined them and their desires were entirely united. Naturally, almost as though they had hoped this might be waiting for them when they came home, they entered the room. Isabelle walked up to Marie and gently stroked her hair, comforting her in an almost maternal way. John stepped behind her and put his hands upon her slender shoulders.

Marie's embarrassment eased. She lowered her hand, taking Isabelle's knickers from her face and dropping them to the floor. Isabelle stood directly in front of Marie with her luscious breasts pushed out over the top of her bra cup, her nipples red and erect. The older woman pulled Marie towards her slightly and kissed her delicately on the mouth, her tongue touching the girl's lips. Isabelle's hand then traces down Marie's neck, over her shoulder and along the pert curve of her young breasts, caressing the tips of her swollen nipples, exciting Marie with the tenderness of her fingers. The sensations in Marie's body that this touch aroused were unparalleled in her experience. It made her whole body feel like it was humming with a perfect musical note.

Instinctively Marie's own hands reached forwards towards Isabelle, caressing the woman's breasts and then sliding up her thighs to her sex, where that perfect warm flesh met her fingers with a silken moisture. That feeling and that touch, the wonderful, delicious feeling of fingering a beautiful woman was like a powerful drug for Marie. It thrilled her, made her feel happiness and warmth and excitement simultaneously.

Behind Marie, John had pressed himself close to her back so that she could feel his cock. It was still not fully erect but clearly aroused and growing. As she continued to play delicately with Isabelle's pussy through her panties she reached behind with her other hand and took hold of John's manhood. She worked her hand up and down the shaft in long, slow and purposeful strokes, occasionally sliding her fingers down to cup his balls. He began to grow harder. Marie knew his size and excitedly felt each pulse of blood increase his length, girth and firmness. With the bulbous tip she directed it towards her parted buttocks, sliding it up and down the space between them, rubbing it directly over her asshole, down to where the bedpost had spread her own pussy juices over her perineum. It made the tip of John's cock wet, and her own bum hole become slippery. She wanted him in her ass and his growing arousal was ready to reciprocate.

He took hold of her buttocks and pulled them wide apart. She held the tip of his erection against the entrance of her rear hole and braced herself in readiness for him to push inside her. His own desire to fuck the beautiful young girl in the ass was rampant at this stage and as soon as she had him in place he began to push keenly into her.

Isabelle, always in tune with Marie, her young protégé, sensed the coming pain that the girl was about to experience. To ease her discomfort she knelt down between Marie's thighs and kissed the soft pussy lips that still perched on the bedpost. Marie's clit was easily accessed and Isabelle sucked and licked and flicked her tongue over it with skill and enthusiasm. Isabelle reached her hands around to pull Marie's buttocks wide apart so that John could better gain his entry, and, with his hands now free, he reached forward to squeeze hard at Marie's tits.

The entry of his cock into her hole was exquisitely painful, stretching her to the limits of her tolerance. But she welcomed it and wanted it, all of it up inside her. Isabelle's gentle tongue upon her clit made the small space between her legs a wonderful, joyous expanse of pleasure.

Marie was now able to reach down and caress Isabelle's fine breasts. Her own were being gripped hard by John. His strong, manly hands were hurting her, making her feel completely overpowered. Her arousal had her feeling the beginnings of her orgasm swirling through her body already. The immensely pleasurable episode of self fulfillment she had enjoyed moments earlier, with Isabelle's come-drenched panties and their rich, dizzying aroma had been an intensely experienced fantasy but this reality was beyond anything her imagination could have ever spun. The realisation that this was no longer in her mind, but was happening in a physical reality, was enough to accelerate her into the first full rush of climax blasting quickly through her body. It was brilliant and bright and invigorating and she wanted so much more before she was going to have had enough.

John continued to pump into her tight ass, working in and out of her smoothly, pulling at her breasts and digging his fingers into them. Marie, still with the bedpost between her legs, began to push herself down onto it, feeling its massive breadth spreading her wider, so wide that she felt like her flesh was close to tearing, but still she pushed down, determined to feel the hugeness of it up inside her.

"You little bitch," John whispered into her ear. "You want two huge lengths inside you."

"I want it all," Marie replied, her words faltering because of the pain she was feeling.

Her response brought on more violent thrusting from John. He pushed in and out of her hard and fast, his long dick going deep inside her hole.

Isabelle stood up from where she had been licking Marie's clit and faced the girl looking her intently in the eye.

"You cheap whore. Fuck my husband behind my back and then fuck him in front of me."

"I want his come."

"I get his come. He's my husband," Isabelle barked back at her.

Marie was now fully around the bed post, its massive width stretching her pussy. She could only take it inside her a few inches because it was so wide. The sensation was agonising. She felt nothing but red hot pain blazing over her labia and scorching her insides. It made the pain of John's big dick in her bum feel like pure, luscious, tender pleasure, despite the vigour he was now using in fucking her.

Isabelle took hold of Marie's hair again and pulled her head back sharply. She slapped the girl firmly on the cheek.

"You like that you fucking slutty bitch?"

"Yes."

"You aren't supposed to like it bitch."

Isabelle then kissed Marie directly and forcefully on the lips, pushing her tongue into the girl's mouth. She then lowered her hand and began slapping very briskly on Marie's exposed, stretched sex, making resounding contact on the girl's clitoris and lips.

The pain was brutal. It was too much. Marie was already stifling screams of agony from what she was being subjected to but this was no too much for her to endure. Surely her body couldn't take this. But something compelled her to keep going one second of pain at a time.

"Ahhh. Fuck. Fuck. Oh, god, fucking hell!" she screamed as she grimaced in pain.

John reached round and clamped one of his large hands upon her mouth to muffle her outburst.

"You really like that, don't you?" Isabelle said venomously and slapped Marie hard on the clit six more times in very quick succession.

John began to groan with the building of his climax. He began to focus only on himself now, his eyes closed, his efforts to inflict pain on Marie less concentrated. His cock speeeded up its thrusting into her ass which was now wet and wide and could be slid into and out of smoothly.

Isabelle sensed that John was very close to coming. She gave Marie one more hard slap on the clit and lips then went round behind her to facilitate John's eruption of spunk which was now just moments away.

She wet her finger in her own pussy and then slipped it inside John's anus and with her other hand delicately caressed John's balls as they slapped against Marie's buttocks. The added stimuli sent him careening over the edge into his orgasm.

"Mother fuck!" he shouted out. "Oh, fuck, come on bitch, take my come!"

Isabelle withdrew her hand from the front and back of John and quickly snatched her husband's cock out of Marie's ass and directed its copious jets of spunk into her mouth and onto her face and over her tits, lashings of ivory coloured come ran down her chin and streaked over her beautiful, big breasts.

John fell back onto the bed completely spent of everything he had. In Isabelle's mad lust for the taste of her man's semen she grabbed at his cock and continued sucking, determined to have every last tasty drop from its softening tip. She rubbed it over her face and tits, luxuriating in the way it felt as it glided over her skin, spreading his come over her.

The stunning woman now turned to Marie who was still working her pussy up and down the bedpost as she watched John and Isabelle on the bed.

Isabelle kissed Marie again full on the lips, her come-covered mouth exciting the younger girl into a wild desire. As Isabelle opened her mouth to tongue the girl she passed a mouthful of John's come, from tongue to tongue, mouth to mouth, and Marie moaned in delight that she had been allowed to taste that man's climax.

She swallowed it and couldn't control herself from trying desperately to lick more off of Isabelle's face and neck and tits.

"You greedy little bitch," Isabelle whispered. "I didn't say you could have it all." She then took hold of Marie's hair again and pulled her head back and bit her hard on the breast so that the girl screamed.

"You like this all too much," Isabelle said and then bit the other breasts as hard.

"Ahhh!" Marie screamed out. "Bitch!" she shouted angrily.

"How dare you!"

Affronted, Isabelle set about Marie with intent, first slapping her on the side of the breasts and then across the face and then hard between the legs on her stretched and exposed sex. She then did it repeatedly, slapping the girl's cunt hard, making its lips glow bright red.

It was an intense sensation for Marie, raw and unadulterated and painful beyond the normal thresholds of physical pain in life. But it was precisely this rocketing, unbounded pain that she was now able to use for her own satisfaction. Though it made her eyes water and made her scream she still wanted the pain to continue because she needed it to achieve estasy. It was this pain that went through her, raw and brutal which annihilated her inhibitions and self-awareness and exposed her completely to the delightful, semi-divine realm that is sometimes fleetingly glimpsed, by the few, during coitus.

Marie had all of this swirling wildly within her, like a force of nature, a cyclone trapped in her belly. She used her hands to grip her own breasts and dug her nails in fiercely, adding another swirling blast of pain to storm that was agonising her flesh. She fucked up and down on the bedpost, its thickness beyond anything she had ever known, the limit, surely, of what her sex could take.

The slapping of Isabelle's hand on her clit, the thick bedpost in her cunt, almost like two or three big cocks pushing into her little hole, the pulling of her hair, her own nails digging into the tender flesh of her tits and the taste of John's come still in her mouth and on her lips all conspired against her desire to prolong the exquisite pleasure she was feeling. She could contain herself no longer.

"Oh, yes!" she screamed. "Fuck, yes!"

"You like that now," Isabelle whispered and then increased the force of her hand slapping Marie's burning pussy.

The climax hit the girl like she had never known, even in her increasingly indulgent sexual education. She came like a burst of bullets was shooting from her, each one leaving a trail of heat that was like a feeling of ecstasy that was filling her up quickly in a web of overlapping sensations that then all suddenly caved in, collapsing from the weight of pleasure, crashing down through her and then gushing out of her climaxing pussy. It was beautiful and painful and euphoric and dizzying and kept on coming and then still kept on coming.

Instinctively she lifted herself up off the bedpost. Her quivering pussy contracted rapidly and it gushed out a stream of cunt juices that ran down her thighs and pooled beneath her as her body shook uncontrollably.

Isabelle, compassionately, ceased her rough treatment of the girl and held her close, supporting her as the last throes of a wonderfully intense and prolonged orgasm passed out of her.

Cradling the young girl, who was totally lost in the bliss of her climax and utterly exhausted by its demands on her, Isabelle rested her on the bed where she curled up contentedly. Isabelle and John left her where she lay and took a shower together where John lovingly fingered his beautiful wife to a sweetly felt orgasm that shook her body as deliciously and splendidly as a gentle breeze shakes the cherry blossom.

CHAPTER 16

The next day Marie allowed herself to rest in bed longer than normal as Mrs Ryder had instructed her to come to work at twelve.

Dutifully Marie told John and Isabelle that she would be working throughout the afternoon and overnight and told them that they should not expect her back until the following morning.

"You're working the Vestal Ball?" Isabelle enquired with a touch of incredulity in her voice.

"I'm not really sure what I am working. Mrs Ryder just asked me to stay on longer than normal tonight."

No more was said on the subject and all three, John, Isabelle and Marie went their separate ways. Marie had been momentarily embarrassed about seeing John and Isabelle after the previous afternoon's impromptu threesome but the couple were so casual and comfortable about sex that Marie felt being embarrassed was rather a childish emotion. She understood that there was no reason to be embarrassed or feel any shame. They were three willing adults all enjoying their sexual desires and indulging their fantasies.

When she entered the Museum she was running a little late. As she rushed through the reception she overheard Daniella, the dark, mature woman who dominated the reception desk in a moody and sultry manner, say out loud something that sounded distinctly like, "undeserving whore" in a very acerbic tone. Marie was sure that she said those exact words but found them so unexpected and unprovoked that she doubted her hearing. She had little time to ponder on it though as she was determined not to be any later than she was currently.

Mrs Ryder stood waiting in her office, arms folded and a stern look on her face. As Marie entered she knew she was very likely to be punished for her tardiness. The expectation of imminent punishment was distinct within her, and it was a complex feeling for her now. The mixture of guilt, remorse, fear and arousal collided and vied for dominance over one another. Currently she rather hoped she would be punished as she felt acutely and powerfully aroused. This in itself unsettled her a bit. How could she feel so horny so much of the time? It was not healthy to be this turned on this often, surely?

"You are late, Marie," Mrs Ryder said sharply. "I told you very precisely twelve o'clock. We are behind schedule right at the start and it is entirely your fault you stupid, slatternly girl."

Mrs Ryder then took hold of Marie by the arm and pulled her out of the office and into the showers and changing rooms.

"Undress and enter the shower," Mrs Ryder instructed the girl, clearly unimpressed that she had been left waiting.

There was another girl already in the communal shower block. She was not a girl that Marie recognised as working at the Museum, or ever remembered having seen visiting the Museum, but a stranger in the shower was not that surprising to Marie, not now after the time she had spent working here. The Museum was a place where the unexpected had to be expected. This other girl was equally unperturbed by having to share the shower and continued to rub soap over her full and smoothly curved body, lathering her large breasts and between her big, round buttocks. She was a very beautiful girl, with big bright eyes and long blonde hair. Marie's attention was instantly drawn to this girl and she was aroused by her.

Marie undressed and entered the shower cautiously moving under the stream of hot water. Both she and the blonde girl were out of view of Mrs Ryder now, concealed by the wall of the shower block.

"Clean yourself thoroughly, Marie. Leave no part of you uncleansed. I want you spotless. In fact, Tamsin dear, would you please assist Marie? I do not trust her to complete the task adequately on her own."

The blonde girl replied in a very cultured voice; "I'd be happy to, Mrs Ryder." She then turned to Marie and smiled.

"Thank you Tamsin," Mrs Ryder returned.

Tamsin had a lustful look in her eye as she approached Marie, who herself felt an immediate sexual attraction to the blonde girl. A thrill of sexual energy coursed through Marie's body as the curvy girl came so close to her that their breasts touched. It felt as though electricity was flowing back and forth between them.

Taking hold of some shower cream Tamsin loaded her hands and, turning Marie to face the jet of water, began to work it over her slender shoulders and smooth back. The blonde girl's breasts were then used to rub the cream in further as she reached forward to gently caress and lather over Marie's pert tits, swollen and firm already from the arousal she was feeling.

Applying more cream Tamsin started to work her hands over Marie's buttocks. Instinctively and enticingly Marie leant forward putting her hands up against the tiled wall and sticking her bum out. Tamsin then slid her hands over the pale, smooth flesh in sensual circles, allowing them to drift into the space between her buttocks where her tight little anus was, sliding over it quickly, fleetingly, in a way Marie knew was meant to tease her. Tamsin's hands then slipped a little further under to glide over Marie's sex, wet and warm.

"You have been quite honoured by the Master," Mrs Ryder said from her position in the changing room. "Only one student of his a year gets to attend the ball and he has decided it should be you. Do not allow this to inflate your ego though, child, as it is his generosity of spirit ahead of your abilities which sees you in this position."

Tamsin applied more cream directly between Marie's buttocks and then worked a finger into the hole slowly, easing past Marie's instinctive contraction and resistance. With her other hand the beautiful, curvaceous blonde girl slid her fingers over Marie's swelling pussy lips. Marie closed her eyes and sighed in pure, heartfelt satisfaction as the water from the hot shower ran like a waterfall over her face.

"There is a long and remarkable history that precedes tonight's ball, and it stretches back well beyond the Master. It is recorded that the French court of the seventeenth century held a similar ball, and that they did so knowing they kept an ancient ritual alive. It is known the world over among the sexually enlightened."

Tamsin had knelt down and was now sliding her tongue into Marie's bum, circling around the tight little hole and darting her stiffened tongue into it making Marie shiver with a sweet arousal. As the new girl delighted Marie's bottom she also treated her pussy, sliding slender fingers up into her sex, using her thumb to slide repeatedly over the top of her clitoris. Marie fought back the urge to moan loudly as she knew Mrs Ryder would not approve. It was hard to contain herself, however, as the wet, warm and wonderful feelings she had rising through her did not encourage self–restraint. She did not want to disobey Mrs. Ryder, and she knew that she ought to have acted more obediently, but this girl was too beautiful, too damn sexy, and too filthy minded for Marie to resist.

"The Master has hosted this event for many years. It is a ritual, a ceremony, more than a ball or event. You will be the centrepiece of this ritual."

The beautiful blonde girl was now pushing three fingers into Marie's pussy, fucking them in and out hard and fast. Marie was so wet that it made a squelching noise as those fingers fucked up into her. Tamsin's tongue also working in and out of Marie's bum, and then circling naughtily and teasingly around the highly sensitive entrance. Marie moaned out loud, consumed by the amazing depth and range of sensations that she was experiencing.

"Are you listening to me, Marie?" Mrs Ryder said sharply.

Controlling herself momentarily Marie answered that she was listening.

"Be firm with her Tamsin," Mrs Ryder continued. "She must be spotless and I know that she is a dirty girl with low standards."

"I'll be firm," Tamsin replied and then pulled her fingers from Marie's pussy and stood up. As she did she forced Marie to turn around and to sink to the floor, gripping her shoulders tightly and then forcing Marie's head so that it was between her spread legs.

Immediately Marie set about licking at that beautifully formed parting between Tamsin's legs. It was soft and warm and as luscious and silky as melted chocolate. It was hairless and beautiful. Marie was feeling that beautiful, perfect sex giving her a delicious pleasure in her mouth and through her other senses. She loved the taste and smell and feel of the girl's pussy around her mouth. It was sweet and arousing and totally irresistible. Licking and sucking on that girl's clitoris and labia Marie was in her own special heaven. With one hand she pushed a soapy finger into Tamsin's bum and with the other hand she started rubbing over her own pussy in hard, rough strokes.

There was a quiver in Tamsin's legs and Marie could see up past her femininely curved stomach and big breasts that there was the unmistakable look of building ecstasy on her face. Marie accelerated her tongue, working it over and into the girl's pussy with a furious effort to give total satisfaction. Tamsin at once pulled at Marie's hair and pushed her face deeper into her quivering flesh. Marie's finger fucked in and out of the girls bum and she then felt that hole begin to contract and she knew that the girl was going to come in her mouth in a matter of seconds.

Tamsin's knees trembled and she let out a sigh, a stifled moan, cursing in ecstasy under her breath. Pulling Marie's face away from her pussy sharply and holding her down the blonde girl burst forth with her orgasm, vivid before the knelt Marie who had induced it, with her hole pulsing and squeezing tight, pink and swollen with arousal, then shooting out a jet of runny come onto Marie's pert tits so that it ran down over her nipples and dripped onto her stomach.

Marie's own hand had not stopped working over her tender sex, each motion adding to the mass of beautiful feelings already in her. She was very close to climax herself, brought perilously close by seeing and feeling this girl squirting juices onto her tits. She felt the sensation of orgasm swirling in her lower belly and she wanted to let it out.

Tamsin knelt down to Marie's level, exhausted by the delightful sensations brought on by cunnilingus from a beautiful girl in the shower. She kissed Marie quite tenderly on the lips, stroking her cheek in a way a lover might do to the one they loved. But then she grabbed sharply at Marie's hair again and pulled her head back and bit Marie on the shoulder and then quickly bit her again but on the breast so that Marie let out a squeal from the sting.

"Be quiet, Marie, you little whiner," Mrs Ryder said loudly.

The blonde girl then started to slap Marie on the breasts, still holding her hair back, the noise of the contact drowned out by the powerful shower.

Marie winced. She continued to work her fingers quickly over her red hot pussy. The feeling of pain in her breast was agony and ecstasy at the same time. It made her sex feel like it must be glowing with the heat.

Tamsin was a beautiful girl, a natural, healthy, beautiful girl with an innocent face and gentleness of movement and manner, but she could have been the Devil's first lieutenant the way that she was administering pain to Marie right now.

Sensing she was close to climax Marie started fucking her fingers up into her ass. Tamsin picked up on this instantly and began to slap at the tender flesh between the girl's legs instead of her tits. She slapped with hard, swift strokes as one might have smacked a bottom if they wanted to truly punish the receiver. It forced Marie to clamp her mouth shut to minimise the screams she could not help but release.

Pushing a finger up into her own ass Marie spread he legs further apart exposing more of her attractive sex for Tamsin to punish. It was a beautiful feeling, pain beating through her like a drum, adrenalin shooting through her with each hit, her heart racing, her mind a mess of pain and delight and sensations all heightened by the illicit way in which she was experiencing them.

Marie shook, her body bucking, her head fighting against Tamsin's grip and her free hand squeezing hard, as hard as she could grip, on her own breast. The blonde girl, dominating her so thrillingly, slid two fingers up into

Marie's sex, fucking them in and out quickly, bringing on the full rush of Marie's orgasm.

It was wonderful, powerful, forbidden, bursting like a joyous scream internalised, like a celebration of hedonistic, extravagant, wasteful, decadent explosions of champagne inside her, corks bursting and foam gushing up and pouring through her, down to her pussy, fizzing inside her, and out of her in a beautiful burst of her own come over Tamsin's fingers.

Marie slumped against the shower wall, breathing deeply. Tamsin stood and then stepped from the shower, leaving Marie to clean herself.

CHAPTER 17

As the evening approached Marie went through the final preparations for her role in the Master's ball. Having showered and cleaned herself according to Mrs Ryder's exacting specifications she was also ordered to submit to a comprehensive waxing of all her most tender parts which brought her a great deal of pain and which also gave her, along with the discomfort, a fleeting tingle of arousal. This feeling was further developed by Mrs Ryder gently massaging a lotion into the newly hairless parts.

"You're a very beautiful girl, Marie," Mrs Ryder said as she slowly worked her hand over the smooth, bald surface of the girl's mound.

"Thank you," Marie replied, a little embarrassed.

"I sense you never thought that you were."

Marie hesitated before answering. "I never did feel beautiful, not until I came to work here. Sometime, now, I think that I maybe am."

"You clearly are."

Mrs Ryder went on with the application of her lotions in a very slow, deliberate, methodical way. Marie was laid on a bench in the changing room and was completely naked, her youthful body unashamedly exposed. The older woman explained the significance of these preparations, about how it was a continuation of ancient ceremonies performed in civlisations that were the foundations of modern civilisations and enlightened sexuality, where Vestal Virgins would be worshipped and service dozens, even hundreds, of men in a prolonged and uninterrupted orgy.

Marie suddenly became excited at what awaited her. She was also nervous and said so to Mrs Ryder.

"Will I be good enough?"

"You will. I have no doubts at all."

Mrs Ryder then stood Marie up and started to wrap some plain white cotton lengths around her until her body was neatly and splendidly bound. This took some time and involved a very careful arrangement of the material. Marie's breasts were held up and wrapped flatteringly, so that their pertness was accentuated and their natural curve displayed. Her shoulders were partly exposed and her slender arms displayed. Her waist and hips were defined in perfect proportions and the simple cloth garment was left to fall down past her already eager and excited sex reaching down to her feet where it bunched and trailed behind her as she walked.

"You look like the perfect Vestal Virgin," Mrs Ryder said with a smile on her face and sincerity in her voice.

Marie saw herself in the changing room mirror and smiled. She was then led to a corridor unfamiliar to her in which was a small cell with iron bars and a heavy lock. Inside was only a wooden stool. She was placed inside by Mrs Ryder and left alone to wait.

The time in the cell seemed unending to Marie who was full of anxiety about exactly what was awaiting her. However, the pampering and traditional garment had made her feel very special and gave her confidence to handle whatever was put before her.

Noises started to become audible in the far off parts of the Museum, then growing nearer, they resolved themselves into sound of revellers approaching. Marie's anxiety escalated. An age seemed to pass with this din getting gradually nearer to her.

The door at the end of the narrow chamber opened and Marie could see a crowd of fancifully dressed people, almost as though they were in costumes but somehow more refined, more real than just dressing up and pretending. The women were adorned like Greek or

Roman nobility, with elegant fabric draped around their bodies in a similar way, though more elaborate, to Marie. Many were not much older than Marie while some were middle aged. All clearly took good care of themselves and had a grace and confidence that made Marie wilt and weaken, feeling distinctly outclassed and inferior.

The men she saw were dressed from the same period in history. Their robes were cut and worn so that their masculinity was emphasised with Marie eye's drawn to the simple fabric that was draped over their manhood which could be clearly recognised from certain angles. The men were all handsome and had bodies that showed they appreciated the importance of physicality to their masculinity. The fleeting glimpse of them made Marie feel a surge of excitement and she could not resist the thought entering her head of these men surrounding her, laying their hands on her, and her laying hands on them.

Mrs Ryder was there too, opening the door and ushering people through. The crowd started to walk along the chamber towards a door at the far end and as they did so they passed Marie in her small cage. All looked over her intently, some commenting to other guests about her beauty or her plainness or whispering to one another about a feature of her body, like her chest or legs. The women seemed envious of her position in the cage and more broadly as the centrepiece of the evening while the men seemed quite frustrated by the bars of the cage that kept her tantalisingly out of reach. Mrs Ryder stood and watched closely how Marie reacted to being such a spectacle for the guests.

A male guest whispered to Marie, "Come here girl. Let me see you up close."

Marie was hesitant. There were many people around the cage looking at her. Mrs Ryder had instructed her to remain seated and silent until she, and only she, instructed her to do otherwise. But Marie did not want to offend any of the Masters guests by ignoring them.

"I said come here girl," the man said much more sharply. "I want to see what you have under those robes."

"I haven't anything under them."

"Then come here and show me. Better still, let me feel for myself."

Another male encouraged her and a beautiful young lady reached her hand in to draw Marie nearer the bars and the eager crowd.

Marie reluctantly stood up looking to see where Mrs Ryder was. The older lady was further off and detained in conversation, quite possibly as a ruse to prevent her interrupting this effort to corrupt Marie. Marie then took a few steps forward.

"Good girl. Now, let me see what you have under that robe," the man said, desire making his voice thick.

His hand reached in and went straight under Marie's robes and took hold of one of her breasts. He rubbed his hand over her chest coarsely, squeezing her nipples and then pulled down at the garment so that both her breasts were exposed.

"She has splendid tits," one lady said. People crowded round the cage and reached in to feel the pale skinned beauty.

The first few hands stroked her breasts then others reached in and seized any part of her that they could reach. She was pulled closer to the crowd and she felt hands sliding up her thighs and rubbing over her soft sex, fingers trying to work up inside her, hands pulling at her tits and pinching her nipples and then more hands putting fingers in her mouth and pulling her hair.

It was happening so quickly. One moment she was being spoken to, the next she was consumed by these people and their hands over her. The first hand through the bars had set the whole crowd ravenously upon her like a starving pack of dogs and the rush of stimulation had sent Marie's perceptions spinning out of control. Her senses were bewildered. A hand, two hands now, were reaching round to finger her bum and before she knew it her own hands were clasped around stiff cocks, one in each, that had been thrust expectantly through the bars. Her head was being pulled down so that her mouth could kiss the bare breasts of a woman who had her tits up to the bars desperate for the beautiful, caged nymph to suck on them.

Marie was awash with pleasure, her whole body and all her senses responding acutely to the hands of these strangers plunging into her wet hole, hands of people she could not even see. Fingers fucked her pussy and in her anus and squeezed her nipples brutally hard. Cocks, big and hard and hot, were in her hands as she wanked them hard and with each quick movement along the shaft she fuelled the flames of her own arousal. She wanted more cocks to play with, more hands to touch her, more fingers to fuck her. She bit and sucked and licked at a big, beautiful pair of breasts that were pushed against the bars and she wanted to just scream out in joy.

A shout came from Mrs Ryder. "Get away from there, girl!" The woman marched over and pushed her way through the crowd of guests who all playfully complained to her for spoiling their fun.

Mrs Ryder was not at all impressed with Marie's conduct. As the young girl stepped back from the bars Mrs Ryder reached through and covered her up, putting her robe back over her pert breasts and straightening it so that her shaven sex was concealed.

"Sit down you stupid girl," she said angrily.

Marie felt suitably chastised by those few words and by Mrs Ryder's rather forceful handling of her. The guests still playfully tried to tempt Marie and stiff cocks were still being pushed through the bars by handsome men. The slender fingers of beautiful women were wrapped around those stiff cocks and were wanking them slowly in a way designed, very effectively, to distract Marie from her duty. Some brave male guests even tried to entice Ms Ryder with the promised of a finger up inside her, or of a hard dick to put in her mouth, but the look she directed at those foolish enough to try and draw her out was more than enough to deter them from venturing further.

"Come back here, girl," a guest said softly. "Come back here and have some more fun with us."

Marie resisted. Just. Her desire had been ignited by that rush of sexual stimulation and her chest and the flesh between her thighs burned hot.

The guests eventually got bored and moved through the chamber to the main hall leaving Marie and Mrs Ryder alone.

"Now we wait," Mrs Ryder said. There might even have been a hint of nervousness in her voice at that moment.

"I'm sorry I messed up," Marie said very faintly.

"You did fine," Mrs Ryder replied. And then the two sat in silence waiting for their moment and listening to the sounds of the revelry in the adjoining hall.

Inside the hall the many guests were enjoying drinks and conversations. People appeared to be having a lot of fun and the drink flowed freely. Yet everywhere there was the suggestion of a deeper and more powerful energy at work. The amiable conversations, the laughter and smiles and enthusiasm to engage with others were clearly just a prelude for the crowd, the warm up for something more intense, something more hedonistic.

In corners of the hall a few guests hinted at what was to come. A broad shouldered man reclined on a sofa and sipped champagne as two beautiful women shared his stiff dick between them, sucking and licking and working their hands up and down his length while they massaged his balls. Elsewhere a young man of lithe, athletic physique had a mature and elegant woman pinned against a wall as he rubbed his hand over her hairless pussy, slipping fingers up inside her. As he did this she searched out his cock from beneath his robes and eagerly pumped her hand up and down it. In another area two men held a conversation while a girl fellated both of them energetically. Throughout the hall there was the simmering excitement that precedes the wanton, unashamed descent into animal desire and orgy.

As though he had been waiting for the perfect moment, and had gauged, from a feeling in the air that it was now, The Master decided to enter the hall.

The guests turned to watch his entry. Conversations were abruptly halted and sexual acts slowed down and were then abandoned. All eyes were on The Master.

He looked regal, wearing robes different from the other guests, worn more impressively and more naturally as though he had known the era they originated from. He walked over to the centre of the hall, parting people around him, raised his arm and commanded people focus everything on him at this moment.

Loudly, his voice strong and authoritative, he called out.

"Bring me my slave!"

Through the main door into the hall came Mrs Ryder with Marie following behind her on a length of rope that was bound around her wrists. She had a blindfold on that prevented her seeing the lascivious attention she was paid by everyone present. She was led to the centre of the room where there was a thin marble pillar that reached up to the top of the high ceilinged hall.

Marie was pushed so that her back was on the cold marble pillar. Her arms were raised above her head and manacled. Her legs were spread and her ankles also shackled. Beneath her blindfold she felt extremely vulnerable. She didn't dare to speculate about what was intended for her but she was shaking with fear with so much out of her control and so many people around her somewhere. She hoped desperately that Mrs Ryder was going to stay with her.

A hand touched her face. She flinched from it in her nervousness. The hand continued stroking over her cheek, the line of her jaw, her neck and then gently over the exposed parts of her chest and shoulders. It was a man's touch but gentle and knowledgeable of a female's weaknesses.

The hand revealed itself as The Master's and Marie was relieved.

"This is my Vestal Virgin. I am master over her. She is my slave in everything. You are my honoured guests. Tonight I offer up this subordinate, my most beautiful and accomplished slave, for you all to enjoy. She is yours to exhaust your desires upon. Use her however you please, let nothing limit you. She is bred for endurance and is capable of taking anything you can imagine and more. Tonight she is yours. Enjoy."

And with that The Master turned and left with a cacophony of applause and cheering following him out.

Marie sensed that he was left the hall. She had been exhilarated to hear his voice and had also been comforted in this large hall of strangers to hear his powerful, consistent voice. But now that he was gone she again was exposed and felt defenceless.

Someone approached and kissed her. It was a soft kiss and definitely from a woman. Their hand traced over Marie's shoulder and up the side of her neck making the chained girl tingle with the first moments of sexual excitement. The kiss was reciprocated and Marie circled her tongue around this woman's and let her lips roll over those of the woman. There was noise and talk and muttering in the background, a din slowly rising, an excitement in the crowd that was building.

Suddenly the woman pulled away from the kiss and ripped at Marie's robes, pulling hard at them so that the knots that held them tight around her breasts tore open and her beautiful, youthful breasts were completely exposed. The crown erupted. Suddenly the woman who had torn her robes had descended onto that full, soft skinned breast and was sucking and biting at the nipples frenetically.

More people came around her. Marie could not tell how many but it seemed she was covered in hands and mouths all upon her own mouth and breasts and neck. Teeth were biting her shoulders and nipples and the tender flesh of her chest. Hands were cupping them, squeezing them, and her hair was being pulled and she was being slapped in the face by others. More hands yanked at her garments, clawing at them like animals trying to tear into its prey. They pulled hard, angry at its resistance, tearing the cloth and wrenching Marie around until the robes were sufficiently torn to expose her beautiful body.

More hands and mouths were upon her. It seemed like every guest was touching her somewhere. The feeling for Marie was beautiful and dizzying, bewildering and terrifying but also astonishing in the way it rushed her arousal through its stages so that now, just moments after being thrown to the lions, her skin was burning hot and her pussy dripping wet.

Fingers were pushing up into her sex. Fingers from different hands all fighting for access to her hole, frigging up inside her roughly and quickly. A mouth was then on her cunt, sucking at the already swollen lips, pulling on the clit with its teeth, biting and licking and then slipping a tongue up inside her and then a finger was going up through her tight little hole. Another person's hand pushed in behind her, parted her buttocks, and was probing at her ass. They were doing whatever they wanted to her. She felt the greatest, most terrifying, exhilaration she had ever known.

Someone started to slap the backs of her legs, on the sensitive skin at the back of her thighs, sending pulses of suffering firing up and down her body. Her other leg couldn't be slapped because someone was fucking it, rubbing their wet pussy over it so that Marie could feel the hot, wet flesh gliding over her. There was so much noise, so much moaning and heavy breathing that she could not tell what noise was what except for the loud, deep grunting of this woman fucking her leg who Marie knew must be getting close to climaxing. The woman was absolutely breathless with ecstasy, rubbing over Marie with an accelerating enthusiasm until she came loudly, wailing, her orgasm expressing itself as a low howl and a burst of come onto Marie's leg.

The woman's cunt was instantly replaced by a tongue licking the woman's juices off Marie's leg then the unseen woman was performing the same cunt-rubbing motion whilst digging her nails into her thigh.

People were pulling hard at Marie's hair and also slapping her tits like they would slap a face, striking her with sharp, unexpected blows that caused the chained girl to wince with the pain. The women seemed to like digging their nails into Marie's pale, smooth skin and the blindfolded slave felt that they must surely have drawn blood from her with their clawing by now. The men brought their own methods of inflicting pain with their abrupt and rough handling of her. Their thick fingers were fucking into her so fast it hurt and there were too many trying to get up there at once. Mouths sucking on her tits were so eager they were hurting her, surely marking her with crude love bites. It all compounded to make her body feel the massive swell of pain and pleasure that so thrilled her.

The tongue that was licking her ass had gone. Now, in its place, a stiff dick jabbed at her tiny hole, still wet and warm from the earlier attention. The erect dick was being guided by a hand, not the man's hand, and others seemed to be getting into help the dick towards its ultimate goal. Slowly it gained ground, entering her and bringing on that dull and pervasive pain that now was like a tender caress to Marie, something to be savoured. As always for Marie, the first ingress to her anus was like torture, a burning poker being slowly pushed through her. But, oh, it was in every way worth it.

Other hard dicks started to come at her. One was being guided up into her cunt. By this stage Marie was throbbing with heat between her legs and she needed a cock up inside her to appease the desire. As a long, hard dick was fed into her perfect little pussy she breathed out a sign of sweet relief, the emptiness of her pussy feeling more of a torment to her than the clawing at her skin.

The two dicks started fucking at her, stretching her and pushing deep into her. She whimpered with each thrust and the pain it brought.

The men fucking couldn't keep up the pace any longer. Other women's hands were cupping their balls, fingering their asses and trying to bring them off like it was a race. The man behind her was first to break.

"You fucking bitch! You dirty, slutty fucking, whoring piece of fucking shit," and then he groaned out in ecstasy as he pumped out masses of his hot come into her ass, his cock twitching violently inside her with each spurt of his seed. Marie could feel it flooding into her. She loved the feeling of a man shooting his load inside her.

The man fucking her pussy soon followed, the attention of the assisting woman and the beauty and helplessness of Marie all amounted to too much strain on his cock to keep his come off any longer. As he thrust his length up as deep as he could push it he whispered to Marie.

"Take all my come. You fucking deserve it with a cunt like that."

The man then emptied out his balls into in a few quick seconds. His muscular body grabbed her as though he would otherwise fall, his semen blasted up into her, deep in her hole, pulsing out of his shaft and filling her.

The appetites of those who were on Marie now become even more wild and they started to get impatient as well. No sooner had these two men pumped their spunk into her cunt and ass than hands and mouths moved in to finger and suck and lick at those holes, people relishing the runny come that was spilling out. No sooner had those tongues tasted the heady mix of Marie's juices and the men's climax than another pair of rock hard cocks were slammed into her, fucking at her furiously.

Eight more men must have fucked her this way, all shooting their sperm up inside her until she felt it running out over her pussy lips and anus and down her legs almost too quickly for the attending females to lick up. The rough treatment she was getting from all sides, but particularly from those men who double penetrated her, made for a diverse and consuming mix of pain, sexual pleasure and excitement. She was now constantly in a state of climax, a sensation she had never known.

The tingling over her body, the heat through her and the quivering of her ass and pussy told her it was an orgasm, but it never stopped. Her bum was burning and her tits were raw from where they had been slapped crimson, and her pussy felt like it had been punished. But her ass, tits and pussy loved the feelings through them and she wanted no end to it.

The feelings that filled her messed her perceptions, and her mind started to enter a different place, started to distance itself from the reality of the situation, though it remained crucially attached to the sensations. It was an almost spiritual experience for Marie, a feeling that this amazing orgy, this storm of sex, was transforming her, taking her into a new world. She was being carried into it so far or so deep that she could never find her way back even if she had wanted to. And, for a moment, she hesitated, as though she had control over the situation, as though she could halt it. But she let go, happy to never return to that place again, happy to give herself over to this new world where you could feel everything. Chained to the pillar, blindfolded and being fucked, she had experienced an epiphany of monumental significance to her.

Two more men shot their come into her, making her shake with her own perpetual orgasm as they did so. Then people stepped back from her, stopped their slapping and biting and sucking and she was unchained from the pillar.

Some men took hold of her and dragged her across the hall some distance. She could not walk because her legs were so weak from the number of men she had just had, and the way it had made her body tremble with pleasure.

She was laid over a cold marble bench or table of some sort. She expected to be chained again but was not. The men unshackled her wrists and ankles. Then, as though the pack could be held off no longer, they descended on her. A girl climbed onto her and rested her wet cunt on Marie's mouth. Overjoyed to have this unexpected treat Marie licked at the lips and sucked at the clit with skill and energy that had the unknown girl moaning at once.

A huge, hard dick was back between her legs again fucking at her pussy with utter urgency. She could also feel her feet being used by women to rub their clits and slide one of her toes up into their wet holes. Each of her hands had had grasped a cock and was wanking away at them with skill. Another man, eyeing Marie's new position, had mounted her breasts, smeared them with the excess of come from her cunt, and had pushed her beautiful tits close together so that he could fuck his dick between them, squeezing her nipples as he did her this way.

Marie was suddenly overpowered by this new treatment. She felt an incredible swell of energy inside her that was completely beyond her control. It was like the sum of all the hot, sweaty arousal she had felt already that night. It was a climax building inside her that had her hurting, desperate to release it and end the pain of holding it, but also wanting to keep it inside her as she loved that feeling of desperation and desire being tormented.

When the man fucking Marie's tits came he shot his jets of semen right into where Marie's mouth was licking the cunt of the woman straddling her. The surprise of that distinctive taste of come on her lips, and on the girl's wonderfully soft, smooth labia, was too much for Marie to withstand and all the power of her climax took flight, ripping through her, twisting her body, shaking her, emptying out of her, making her scream out as her juices pissed out of her cunt in a powerful spray that covered the cock of a man who was fucking her already-come filled slot. The feeling of that release was as wonderful as anything she had ever known.

She was lost for a few seconds. The power of her orgasm had wiped her out of any sense she had control of, but quite quickly she came around and brought the woman who straddled her mouth off in an explosive climax. The woman's pussy was replaced by a man's considerable erection and Marie eagerly sucked it and swallowed its come as other dicks spurted their come over her as her hands worked up and down them quickly, their thick cream running over her fingers or streaking her tits.

The night continued in this way with guests all using Marie for their own satisfaction. She was fucked in the pussy, in the ass, in the mouth. She performed endless hand jobs and foot jobs and tit jobs and she licked the cunts and cocks and tits and ass holes of more people than she could possibly count. Every guest there that night had enjoyed her, many had done so several times, while many guests also enjoyed each other. It was an unrivalled orgy with Marie as its spectacular centrepiece.

When the last guest left Marie was still laid on the marble altar wanting more, hoping there might be someone left who wanted to use her. But they had all finished, their appetites totally satiated. Everyone except Mrs Ryder who took hold of Marie and lifted her up, removed her blindfold, and gently cleaned her up of the excess of that night's overflowing sexual excitement. She then wrapped her in a dressing gown and supported her as they both walked out of the hall to a comfy bed where both had the chance to sleep.

CHAPTER 18

Marie's more structured education was having a very positive effect on her. It consisted of hard work in the shape of cleaning, moving museum pieces and extended stints of clerical work that demanded a lot of her. If her work was ever found to be sub-standard or incomplete she was punished by Mrs Ryder according to the Master's instructions. A small error might only warrant six strikes of the whip across her bare bottom or a ruler on the back of the thighs. Arriving late or forgetting to clean a room meant a harsher punishment. Once, when a door to the storeroom had been left unlocked, Mrs Ryder dragged Marie by her hair to her office, tied her to the desk and beat her exposed breasts, stomach, thighs and mound for fifteen minutes. Marie's skin burned for many days after.

A few times a week she would be called to have a lesson with The Master. He was not easy to predict and Marie was always excited by this potential for new experience.

The anguish she once felt so strongly was nearly all gone from her, the shame of her ravenous and indiscriminate sexual appetite now felt part of her past. Only occasionally did she feel the pang of distaste for her behaviour and this was when she thought of how people she knew would judge her if these private pleasures were publically known.

On one occasion the Master had Marie and the two other girls who were undergoing the same training make love to each other while he and a smart looking man in a suit watched them and discussed future business. At first the girls had been uneasy as they undressed each other but that act, and the presence of the Master, seemed to charge the atmosphere with lust. Before long the three girls were indulging themselves without restraint using every part of their bodies to bring one another to orgasm again and again.

This had been the only unstructured sex where the girls were free to satisfy their own desires. Every other time Marie had to place the Master's needs before her own. She found that this was quite natural for her as her own pleasure relied on knowing she had satisfied him. On some occasions he would have Marie wait on him during his lunch. She would be naked and unsure but he had wine and food and a paper to read and anything else he wanted. Sometimes he would instruct her to blow him before he went back to work. He didn't ask for that as often as Marie wanted him to and she was too timid to offer it and break his relaxation.

Another time Mrs Ryder dressed Marie in the most beautiful stockings, suspenders and peep hole bra. She was then instructed to touch her toes at which point Mrs Ryder clamped Marie's wrists to her ankles. She placed a ball gag into her mouth and then left her precariously balanced in the centre of the Master's large office. When he returned he barely noticed her. Marie was already excited by being in the same room, in this lovely outfit and in this position. He then undressed, something her very rarely did, revealing his still-strong physique, and proceeded to administer the cane liberally over her body before fucking her hard in both holes and coming on her back so that she could feel it running over her marked skin.

Her time away from work was occupied with study. Mrs Ryder had set her a reading list of books covering various subjects from basic etiquette to advanced sexual techniques for pleasing a man. She read them keenly, eager for knowledge, and always thinking of her current Master, though knowing one day she would be handed to Martin.

She was so busy that it took her by surprise to overhear a conversation Mrs Ryder was having that sounded as though there were artefacts missing from the museum. She only half caught what was being said but it immediately brought back a sight she had dismissed as inconsequential.

A few weeks previously, when she had found herself punished for leaving the storeroom door unlocked, Aiden had made his usual attempts to grope her. She had struggled from his grasp successfully. When she had got home that night she found that she did not have her keys. The next day she found, to her surprise, she had left them in the lock and blamed herself for being absent minded. She had not thought Aiden might be involved. But she now saw that it was Aiden who had taken the keys from her pocket. She had also seen him on quite a number of occasions driving his car to the rear entrance of the building, always as the museum was closing. Such was her hatred for him that she never asked what he was doing.

If things were being taken there was circumstantial evidence to implicate Aiden. But, as she thought it over, it was rather a leap given she didn't even know anything had been taken. The girls in training were discouraged from expressing their opinions, or even to speak, unprompted, to a superior. She resolved to watch him and see what was going on.

Marie's suspicion and curiosity continued to dominate her thoughts. She made every effort to see where Aiden was working and also walked past the Master's door at every opportunity in the hope she might hear more details.

Late in the afternoon, as she was preparing to leave, she heard the Master and Mrs Ryder in conversation.

"I prepared them for the lesson as you instructed, Sir," Mrs Ryder said with definite anxiety in her voice.

"I don't doubt it," the Master replied. "Let us apply some reason to what has happened. Two girls are gone. We can say with some confidence that they have not gone unassisted, as they were bound and locked in my office. They had no means of accessing keys. I infer that a third party is involved here. Someone helped them leave."

"Or someone has taken them, Sir."

"Explain."

"Those two girls had no interest, Sir, in leaving training. They were enjoying their studies and looking forward to their lesson. I spend a lot of time with these girls and I don't find it credible that they would run away," Mrs Ryder answered.

"You may be right. I want you to make some discreet enquiries with the staff and with their families. I will speak with a few friends and see if they can assist us with our problem."

The conversation ceased. Marie rushed from the door fearful of being caught.

She was astonished. Leaving for home she thought through what she had heard being discussed and what she knew of the two girls who she had been training with these last weeks.

The streets were dark. The streetlights were on but dim. She turned the corner and was halted by a hooded male stood directly in front of her. He wouldn't let her pass, no matter which way she went. She felt a shock of fear through her and panic started to set in. She turned to go back the way she had come. Her one thought was to get back to the museum and safety. But she turned to find another hooded man standing behind her. His face was hidden in shadow.

A car pulled up at their side. A door opened. The two men inside grabbed her. One had her mouth and chest the other her legs. She screamed but it was muffled and then she was pushed into the back of the car, the two men sitting on her in the back, pinning her down.

A pillowcase was pulled over her head as the car sped off, its wheels screeching. Marie tried to scream, terrified, but the hand was back over her mouth. Other hands were touching her, groping her. One was down her shirt squeezing her tits roughly. Another was up her skirt trying to force up between her clamped thighs. She was hysterical with fear.

The car sped onwards, slamming around corners. Marie tried to squirm against her captors, hoping she might break free, not giving in, but the men that gripped her were strong. They were moving her around and had turned her over. They spoke in a language she didn't understand. The strong hand between her legs gripped her knickers by the gusset and ripped at them. They tore easily. Another hand forced her legs apart against all her desperate resistance.

Marie knew what was coming. Her legs forced wide apart she felt a stiff cock jabbing at her unwilling cunt. A mouth clamped onto one of her tits and started sucking at her nipple, making it hurt terribly. He made a few thrusts and muttered words of some foreign language then rammed his dick into her as hard as he could, his balls suddenly contracting to squeeze his load of come into her tight hole. She felt it burst inside her. She tried not to enjoy the feeling.

With some difficult the two men swapped positions, arguing as they did so. Marie did not attempt to resist anymore. She had calmed down slightly and resigned herself to being abused. There was no chance of escaping at this moment.

She heard the new man unzipping his jeans. With his fingers he played with her pussy lips, using some of her own wetness and the first man's ejaculate to rub her asshole. He manoeuvred himself against her bum hole. Marie could tell that his cock was too big. He took his time, rubbing his tip around her entrance, spreading the come and arousal around, relaxing the tension in her anus. Then, with slow but purposeful thrusts, he worked his long dick into her ass, inch by inch. She felt his balls slap against her buttocks. Her breath was shocked from her by the depth of his penetration.

The other man's free hand groped over her breasts casually.

The man fucking her bum held both her legs so they were wide apart to ease his access. He pumped in and out of her hard, stretching her hole and causing a shooting pain where the top of his dick poked her insides.

Marie managed to free her hand. The two men panicked, but before they could grab hold of it she had thrust it down to her pussy and had started to finger her hole. The men laughed. She didn't care. The feeling in her ass, however crude, was sparking off her amazing acceleration of arousal. She didn't want to resist it. She was horny and wanted to come. She needed to come now this reaction had been started.

The sight of Marie rubbing her fingers vigorously over her wet, come-covered, pussy was too much for the man thrusting at her ass. He started to pump quickly, the urge to explode obviously taking him suddenly, and then, with a loud grunt, he fired his spunk deep inside her.

It was too quick for Marie. As he pulled his cock out of her hole she knew that she could not turn the pain and sordid, debasing, excitement of this act into her own climax. The men had been too unskilled. Instead, in an instinctive act, she swung a fist up and back as hard as she could. She made contact with something like flesh and bone. It was solid contact to the first man's face. He shouted out and she was quickly restrained. From then on there was no hope of escape and she lay quietly for the rest of the journey.

Once the car had pulled up and she had been carried out, she found herself sat on a cold concrete floor in some sort of warehouse. She still had the pillowcase over her head and had been tied by her ankles and wrists. Her captors were talking. Three voices.

The door slammed shut and the foreign language conversation ended. Footsteps neared her then the pillowcase was removed from her head.

Shaking her hair from her eyes Marie looked up. Stood above her was Aiden.

"What the hell do you think you're doing?!" she shouted at him. Looking around her she saw that the two missing girls were also with her. "What is this?"

"First things first, Marie. Have you been injured during your kidnapping?"

"What do you care?" she hissed back.

"I care greatly. But, please, desist with your attitude," he replied calmly.

"They gangbanged me. Is that what you wanted to hear?"

Aiden turned and addressed the three men in their own foreign tongue. His tone was aggressive. They answered meekly and Aiden shouted back. Marching to the corner of the garage her grabbed a length of wood and set about striking the men in a rage. They cowered away from the assault, making no effort to fight back.

Aiden threw the weapon aside and marched back to Marie. "Idiots!" he shouted. "Very simple instruction. Don't spoil the merchandise!"

"Merchandise?" Marie asked, her concern deepening.

"I might as well put your minds at rest, now all three of you are here. None of you will be harmed. You are all perfectly safe. I apologise that my staff have abused you. It won't happen again. My reason for abducting you is simple. You are to be sold to exceptionally wealthy men. Once sold, you will belong to them and I will be wonderfully rich. Until then you will be kept as comfortably as this lock-up permits."

Aiden turned his back on them and walked away to make a phone call on his mobile.

Back at the museum the seriousness of the situation was becoming clear to the Master and Mrs Ryder. Late on the night of Marie's abduction John and Isabelle had called Mrs Ryder to ask how late Marie was likely to be. A few phone calls later and it became apparent that Marie had gone the way of the other girls. It was clear now that the girls had been kidnapped.

John was called in that night to meet with the Master.

"I am reluctant to engage the police at this stage, John, for obvious reasons," the Master said, his expression grave. "A number of paintings have gone missing over the last few weeks. Now these girls. I fear we have a problem within."

"Aiden," John suggested.

"I have, as yet, been unable to contact him. I have nothing to implicate him other than his arrogance, deceitfulness and ambition. Would you attend his home please John? Find out what you can. Here's the post code."

"Of course. I'll go now." And with that John turned and left the office.

"John!" the Master shouted after him. John came back. "It may be appropriate to inform Martin of the development."

Aiden had been on the phone late into the night, speaking several languages with varying degrees of skill. He was brokering deals for the sale of the three girls, playing people off against each other, lying about the level of interest and inflating the prices with every new conversation.

The sums of money being discussed astonished Marie.

"Yes, yes!" he said down the phone loudly as though speaking to someone whose English was poor. "Tomorrow, yes. You understand? Three hundred. Sterling not euro. Understand? Tomorrow or they go. When you are in the country you call me," and then he abruptly hung up. "Fucking Russians. Billionaires and they still try and cheat you out of a few thousand. Bunch of fucking crooks."

He stood up and walked around, stretching his arms out.

"So girls. Tomorrow you will each have a very rich and very foreign owner. I can't vouch for their intentions with you. However, I'm sure, having invested so much they will treat their investment with care. You will be better treated than most of the world's sex slaves, that's for sure." He laughed to himself, a satisfied smile spread across his face.

"Let's all get some sleep so we look nice and attractive in the morning." He threw each girl a blanket and pillow and retreated to the corner where he sat in deep contemplation.

Tired from the trauma of her kidnap Marie welcomed the opportunity to rest her head and warm herself. She knew she would not sleep despite her fatigue.

Tomorrow she was being sold as a sex slave to some unknown man. This was a different world. A world where the law couldn't afford to tread. They could do anything they wanted with her. Though she loved the rapture of submitting to her master's sexual desire, what she now faced terrified her. She lay on the cold floor crying with fear.

At the museum they continued through the night trying to get a lead on where the girls had been taken. It was now dawn and they had exhausted every possible line of enquiry.

Martin arrived and was ushered in by Mrs Ryder. He had driven over the moment he got the call from John.

"What the hell is this?" Martin asked, the anger obvious in his tone. "I want to know how this can happen."

"Calm down, Martin," John said solemnly.

"How it can happen isn't our most pressing concern," the Master said. "Where Marie and the other two girls are is the only thing that matters to us now."

"What are we doing to find them?" Martin was still very agitated.

"Let me update you," the Master said. "We have an insider responsible. It couldn't possibly be anything other. We also have all members of staff accounted for and spoken for, excluding the girls. And one other. Aiden has not answered any of our calls. John has attended his house and there is no reply."

"I forced the back door," John interjected. "There was nothing there of use, though it looked like he had packed some clothes."

"So we need to find Aiden, and quickly," the Master continued. "I have asked a few favours of friends. One I trust is doing all he can to obtain current intelligence for us on where Aiden may be and what he is intending. Aiden has no family and no friends. There is no person to speak with about his activities leading up to this."

Mrs Ryder brought in coffee and the three men stood in silence, staring out of the window where the sun was beginning to enter.

Marie was woken by Aiden talking on the phone again. She had managed to drop off into an uneasy sleep. She looked over at the girls. Both were crying softly.

Aiden walked over to the three sleeping foreign men and kicked them awake. "Get up you lazy bastards. Earn your money for a change. You, Yevgeny, or whatever the fuck we call you, get a bucket of soapy water. You two, get the boxes of clothes."

The men listlessly got up from their sleeping bags and set about their tasks.

"Girls, this is your big day. Your prospective owners are eager to have you and I am eager to have their money. They will be here in an hour, so we must get you looking a bit more presentable."

The bucket of soapy water and box of clothes were brought to Aiden. Addressing the three men, he said; "Clean them. Properly clean them, not clean by your country's standards. Understand? Clean not dirty. Have them put this underwear on. You can touch but you cannot fuck. Understand? No fucking. No dick goes near these girls. You, Frankenstein, do you understand?"

The largest of the men nodded. Aiden left in the car.

As soon as he was gone the three foreign men turned to each other and smiled. They each took hold of one of the girls, gripping them firmly. Marie tried to resist but the large man who held her forced her up against the wall. He was not one of the ones who had taken her the night before. He must have driven.

"You like suck big dick?" he said, staring at her lasciviously.

He ripped her clothes in a sudden frenzied rush to see her naked. The wrenching hurt her. Her breasts were pulled out of her bra and he set upon them greedily, sucking the nipples and licking over them grotesquely.

Marie looked over to the other girls. Each looked terrified and repulsed by the kisses and rough groping of the men whose power they were in.

Marie's captor pushed his hand up under her skirt and inserted a thick finger up inside her hole. It gave her a sharp pain, as her muscles tried to resist. He poked in and out of her crudely then slipped his finger out and put it to his nose, sniffing.

The feminine scent was a like a drug to him, sending him into a heightened excitement. Sinking to his knees her lifted Marie's skirt and pushed his mouth into her pussy. He licked at her like a ravenous dog, working over her with no plan other than to taste as much of her as he could as quickly as he could. He was snorting and snarling, his hand reaching up to squeeze hard on her breasts.

She was disgusted by this man. His excitement was horrible, completely animalistic. But the sensations over her pussy were not altogether unpleasant, and she could feel warmth and moisture beginning. The dirty, calloused hands manipulating her breasts made her wince with a pain that she could not deny was enjoyable. Her pussy was starting to melt, her legs gradually spreading, her arms wide against the wall to support her.

Breathing deeply, lost in his sexual excitement, the man stood up and guided his hard prick to the soft, wet entrance of Marie's cunt and pushed in hard.

A sharp pain shot up Marie. She was wet and aroused but her hole was still very tight and this man's dick was very thick. The position she was in put pressure on her, the wall rough against the sensitive skin on her back. The man was pushing in hard, his cock, thick but not long. He could plunge into her as deeply as he wanted and was doing so, violently. He pushed into her with increasing speed and viciousness, pounding her tender pussy, each entry felt as if she was being struck with a hammer.

The other girls were equally abused. One was on her knees with the small-dicked man fucking energetically into her mouth. He held her head tight and was thrusting his cock into her as deep as he could get it. He was in a paroxysm of pleasure, throwing his head back and breathing hard through clenched teeth.

The other girl was pushed face first against the brick wall. Her breasts had been exposed and were squashed up against the abrasive brick causing her a great deal of pain. Her trousers had been pulled down to expose her buttocks and the long-dicked man was working his stiff cock into her ass. The dry entry was causing both involved quite a lot of pain, though the man was clearly enjoying the access to that young bum.

The rampant pumping at Marie's pussy had brought on a deluge of arousal. She could feel it dripping from her, running over her buttocks. The strain on her hole from this man's unremitting thrusts was building up tension in her that spoke of a final crescendo of come being nearly upon her. She closed her eyes and concentrated on that wonderful feeling and nothing else. That feeling in the deepest parts of her sexuality. She relished the rough treatment she was receiving with its shooting pain and the filthy, snarling, animal energy of this smelly man. It all culminated in a sensation of heat in her that made her feel swollen and tormented and desperate to climax, wanting it to happen and wanting it to never end.

Her captor was sweating with his effort. He muttered something in his native tongue and then buried his face into Marie's shoulder, biting hard into her exposed skin as he shot a thick blast of spunk into her sopping wet cunt. She felt it inside her, the dirty man's sperm filling her up. The sensation of him bursting in her, up against the entrance to her womb, was the trigger for her own final rapture. Everything that had been swelling in her now opened up and poured down through her like warm honey, sweet and smooth, coating every part of her in its glow, then running down out of her pussy to drip onto the floor.

She turned in time to see the man beside her pull his dick from the kneeling girl's mouth and squirt his sperm onto her neck and tits with a long sigh of satisfaction. Beyond them the other girl was in pain. The man upon her thrust hard into her tight ass and pressed her harder against the brick wall. Then he began to shake, his body convulsing, and he shot his hot spunk up inside her anus. He pulled out and his massive gushing of sperm spilled out from the girl's shrinking hole and puddled on the floor beneath.

Their lust satiated, the men lit cigarettes and passed around a bottle of vodka. They indicated in arrogant fashion that the girls should wash themselves. Feeling sullied by the vile male assault the girls endured the icy cold water and cleaned themselves as best they could.

The phone rang in the Master's office, he answered and listened silently for a few moments.

"Thank you," he said, hanging up.

John and Martin were anxious to know if this was some new development.

"That was a friend. We have some information that we may be able to use, but it isn't much. There is talk that three Russian doormen have been hired at short notice by a young man, well spoken and smartly dressed. It is no leap of the imagination to infer this is Aiden referred to. His phone was used last night. He was north of the city."

The Master took a map and spread it over his desk.

"Here," he said, pointing to a field near a main road. "This is where he was last night."

"There's nothing there. Either he has them in the middle of a field or he was travelling out of the city at the time," Martin said, frustrated that they had hit a dead end.

"No. Multiple calls were from that location. He wasn't moving," the Master replied.

"But there's nothing there. It's a road and a load of fields."

John suddenly stood upright. "There's an airfield there. I've been past it and it's had small planes landing there. Not quite there, but near. There is definitely an air strip there in use."

The three looked at each other.

"Let's go," Martin said.

When Aiden returned the girls had cleaned themselves in the cold water and dressed themselves. The threatening gaze of the three men had ensured that they did as they were instructed and kept quiet.

They all wore a bra, knickers and stockings in black. The fit was imprecise and the quality poor. Marie felt strangely more degraded by being in this horrible, ill fitting, cheap set than she had felt when the dirty Russian man had forced himself on her. It was a thought that perturbed her briefly.

"This is lovely," Aiden said in a loud and happy voice. "Don't you all look pretty? Now all we need to do is wait. They should be here very soon."

Aiden, the girls and the three men sat silently. All were clearly uneasy about what was about to happen.

Marie began to think of her future, sold into a life of sex against her will. She would never see Martin or her family again. I've brought this on myself, she thought. I gave in to my basest desires, I learned to enjoy them and feel no shame in my perversions. This is my punishment. How could I have been so stupid? Everything I had planned, thought through, worked hard for, I've thrown away so I can satisfy my disgusting, incessant, lustful body.

The frustration in her made her want to strike out, but being bound, she merely dropped her head and sobbed.

The low, loud rumble of a plane could be heard approaching.

Aiden stood up and brushed himself down. "Look sharp girls. It's time to make some money."

John's Range Rover sped down an empty rural road. The Master sat in the passenger seat and Martin in the back.

On the horizon ahead of them the speck in the sky that was a plane was gently descending.

"Faster John," the Master said. "We have very little time."

"Come in, come in, please. I apologise for the rather utilitarian surroundings. It isn't ideal, I know." Aiden led the newly arrived guests into the building.

The small seven seat plane had brought a tall, surly Russian man, a stoutly built, bald headed minder and a short, weasel faced man who had clearly been instructed to conduct the business briskly.

"It suits our purpose," the short man said, his English good.

"Yes, yes, of course. Low profile is important in these matters." Aiden was nervous. "Well, these are the girls. Feel free to examine them. You will find them of the finest quality, trained at the infamous Museum de Sade."

The weasel faced man translated for his boss. They both stepped forward to look over the bound girls. Handling them roughly the two men looked over every inch of skin. The tall Russian instructed that they be stripped bare. He then scrutinised them minutely, running his hands over their skin, squeezing their breasts, thighs, buttocks, knocking their legs wide and eyeing closely their vaginas. He rubbed his fingers over them each in turn and tested the scent. Stepping back he surveyed all three. He instructed his man with a few sharp words.

The weasel faced man addressed Aiden. "Because they are in acceptable condition we are prepared to pay one hundred and fifty thousand euro each. We will take all three."

Aiden recoiled in surprise. "We have already agreed the price, and it wasn't one fifty. Perhaps I haven't explained the quality of the training these girls have had. They will exceed anything you have ever had."

"We only have your word for that."

"This is this best you can get in the world right now. Are you really going to risk losing the chance to own them?" Aiden was struggling.

"We can have the deal now and we pay cash, or we can leave and you can find another buyer."

Aiden didn't need to think it through. "We have a deal."

"Good decision. We get your money now." The weasel faced man signalled to the plane.

John could see the landed plane ahead. A large man was leaning into it. Hearing the approaching vehicle this man looked up and immediately pulled a handgun from his holster.

"Get down!" John shouted and accelerated at the man, wrenching the wheel round and yanking on the hand brake hard, sliding the side of the vehicle into the man. A shot was fired. The rear window of the Range Rover was blown out. The large man was sent spinning over the ground, senseless.

"Come on! Get out!"

"In the back! Arm yourself with something."

The three men rushed from the vehicle. The Master and Martin grabbed stout pieces of wood. John rushed to the man sprawled half conscious on the ground and took the gun from him.

The door to the hanger opened and Aiden's foreign security rushed out. Martin swung his weapon onto the back of the head of the first to exit, connecting powerfully. The man was propelled forward, stumbling and then collapsing in a heap to the floor.

Fists and wood swung around with little control. Martin was grabbed from behind. He burst free and spun round, ducking a fist aimed at his head and hit the assailant with his length of wood directly on the side of his knee. There was a terrible crack of bone or wood followed by a horrible scream of agony from the floored man.

John charged into the hanger. The Master and Martin wrestled a third man to the ground. Martin pinned him and punched him in the face repeatedly until the man struggled no more.

Martin rushed in after John.

Inside, Aiden had pulled a gun and fired, missing both John and Martin by some way. The Russians broke for the door trying to get themselves and their money, out of this mess. Aiden fired again as John and Martin rushed at him. The shot hit Martin, sending him spinning backwards. John dived into Aiden sending the gun skidding across the floor.

Martin joined John and gripped the wildly writhing Aiden to the floor. Around them the loud engines of a plane powered away from them. From the hectic chaos there was now a sudden, breathless silence surrounding those involved.

Martin had been shot in the forearm. He was bleeding but was enduring the pain without complaint. Aiden's arm was clearly broken, twisted where it shouldn't be, but he remained silent, the pain dampened by the pulse of adrenalin through him.

The Master untied the three girls and wrapped them in blankets. Marie rushed to Martin, tears streaming down her cheeks, and flung her arms around him.

"It's alright, baby. It's alright," Martin whispered to her.

The Master organised everything. Mrs Ryder came to collect the girls. John drove everyone else, including Aiden. The hired men were long gone. So were the Russian buyers. There were no police to be seen. They would be kept out of this.

Back at the museum a doctor was called to tend to Martin and Aiden. Both injuries were soon effectively dealt with. All three girls were examined and given warm clothing and hot drinks to steady them after their ordeal.

"What now?" John asked of the Master when they were alone. "What do we do with Aiden? No police presumably?"

"I have a friend. A very impressive French lady who will assist in this matter I believe. Aiden needs to be punished for his actions and she will ensure the punishment is appropriate to the crime."

The following day Aiden was embarked on a convoluted and uncomfortable journey to a grand chateau in France, in the care of one of the Master's closest friends. There, under the command of Madame Roux, Aiden was set on an indefinite course of punishment at the infamous playground for dominatrices, known to those who used it as the Bastille.

CHAPTER 19

As Martin showered Marie fellated him. He was preparing for his day at work and Marie was obeying an order.

With her mouth around his thick cock, its full length being swallowed to the back of her throat, she felt his legs quiver, heard his breathing change, and then felt the full force of his hot ejaculate pulse into her mouth.

She was as happy as she had ever been.

After her kidnap both she and Martin had convalesced at the private home of the Master. Martin had needed fairly regular attention from the Master's doctor to prevent long term damage to his arm following the shooting. Marie had also helped tend to him and this had gone some way to steady her worn and frayed nerves.

It had given them both time to reflect on the tumultuous few months they had experienced. Marie realised how passionately and deeply she loved Martin and how she wanted nothing more than to serve him.

The Master came to speak with them one day while they were at his home.

"It pleases me beyond words to see you both looking so well," he said with a broad smile. "You will be well enough to return home and embrace its unique comforts before long." Then, with sadness in his voice, he added, "I have thought many things through, as I am sure the two of you have also done, and feel that Marie would be best served by drawing her education at the museum to an early finish. I feel that she knows plenty that she can put into practice and I know she will please her master. I expect, even insist, that you will both be regular visitors to the museum."

"Of course we will," Martin said sombrely.

"Mrs Ryder will make arrangements for you to be taken home whenever you feel it is the right time. You were one of the very best I have ever taught, Marie. I would not have let you go if I had not such faith in Martin to take good care of you."

"Thank you."

Marie had been completely unaware that day with Martin and the Master that they had liaised closely since their first meeting to make preparations for the handover of Marie. Martin had moved out of his shared house into a lovely town house where he and Marie would live together. A degree of financial assistance had been given by the Master, who wanted to ensure Marie's talents were not wasted. So when they left the Master's home they entered a new life together. Marie learned that she would not be permitted to work. Her day was to be dedicated to the satisfaction of her Master. It was a life she entered into with ease and pleasure.

And so she had found herself kneeling before her master, sucking his cock clean of come.

Having ensured she had licked all the come from him she dried him off and then rushed downstairs to ensure everything was in place for his breakfast.

Martin called to her from upstairs. "Marie, come here please."

Surprised, she skipped back upstairs to see what the matter was. When she entered the bedroom she realized, and was filled with embarrassment and shame.

Martin picked up what was lying on the bed. "You left a wet towel on the bed, Marie."

"I'm sorry. It was an accident."

"I really don't care what it was. All I know is that it isn't acceptable. Do you expect me to follow you around and tidy up after you?"

"No. I'm sorry," she said, her eyes downcast.

"It's sloppy and I will not tolerate it. You will of course need to be punished for this. However, I intend to be at work soon which limits my options with you." He stood silent for a moment, clearly thinking through punishments. "Come with me." Taking her by the arm he led her into an upstairs room.

The room had been arranged as an entertainment room. Arm chairs, television, desk and computer and a few items that looked like they could have been on loan from the Museum.

"Remove your clothes," Martin said sternly.

She obeyed. Her pulse quickened as she did so.

Martin then sat her in a chair and tied her ankles to the front two legs and her wrists to the back two legs. It was very uncomfortable for her but the way it exposed her pussy and her breasts gave her a sudden rush of arousal.

Next Martin occupied himself at the television, putting something on for her to watch. A film began playing instantly. On it was a man of astonishing physique and considerable endowment. He was tying a beautiful girl to a workbench. The girl was on all fours and so tightly bound that her arms and legs were turning a shade of purple. She had a ball gag in her mouth and clothes pegs on her nipples. The man mounted her and forced his cock into her hole, struggling to gain entry, the tightness of her vagina causing her to moan through the gaga loudly. The man then picked up a lit candle and let the hot wax drip onto her buttocks as he continued to push his big cock inside her.

Marie watched as though in a trance. She couldn't take her eyes off of the images.

Since she had lived with Martin, watching pornography had been a pleasure for them both. Now Martin was using it as punishment. He was going to leave her watching this fucking and, with her hands bound, she would have no way of making herself come. It would mean hours of agony for her, her pussy tormenting her, desperate for satisfaction all day.

To compound her suffering Martin put a clamp on each of her nipples and two on the lips of her pussy. Then he left.

Already the pain she felt physically was being overtaken by the frustration of her building arousal and her inability to satiate it.

On the screen directly in front of her the scene had progressed. The beautiful woman in the ball gaga was now being whipped across her back by a woman in elaborate and elegant corsetry. The man was pumping into her glistening hole with great power. He then pulled out and shot his come across her back as the corseted woman continued to whip the girl, the lashes leaving bright red marks, the come being sprayed over her skin with each impact.

Marie was desperate. Her body was warm and fidgety, her pussy already wet through. She would have to endure hours of this.

Next she saw a woman with her ankles tied by bundles of cloth to a metal rail in a dirty warehouse. Upside down and completely naked she was surrounded by about a dozen lithe and muscular young men. They all watched and wanked their firm dicks as a stiletto-heeled woman pulled the girl's hair so that the girl's mouth was in contact with the woman's shaved pussy. Gripping her hair the woman varied the contact, occasionally letting the girl have a break for air. While doing this the woman in charge used a large rubber dildo to torment the girl's exposed pussy, rubbing hard over its surface, striking it and then plunging into it mercilessly.

One by one, as the men found themselves about to climax, they chose their spot. Some came on the girl's hanging breasts, some in her face. Others pushed their circling her tongue over its tip she soon had him firming up. Naturally applying the skills she had learned during her training and applying her almost hysterical urge to be fucked she had Martin swelled to his full and impressive size in a few seconds.

He stepped from her and removed the clamps on her nipples. Taking up a leather lash from the corner of the room he began to strike her across her beautiful young breasts.

She yelped in pain then basked in the lovely feeling of it through her.

He struck her again and again, drawing long red marks on her skin, pulling screams from her at each contact. After every few lashes he reached down and coarsely fingered between her legs, rubbing over her wet cunt lips and pulling at the metal clamps on them.

"You're hot and wet like a teenage slut. You disgust me."

"I'm sorry, Master."

"Be quiet."

He yanked the clamps off her labia giving her a sharp shock of unexpected agony then lowered himself into a wide legged position between her spread legs. He clasped her hips and lifted her so that he could give his huge erection full access to her melting flesh. It made her position even more uncomfortable. Pain now pumped through her wrists, ankles, legs and her burning breasts.

He pushed into her hard. His full length slid into her like a weapon.

The feeling was like a rush of drugs through her. It answered her body's insistent pleading for contact, giving her that instant, calming satisfaction, like iced water to the thirsty. It had no sooner achieved that instant of satisfaction than it had moved on to the next stage of big cock into the dominatrix's pussy or ass and blasted their hot spunk inside her. One shot his climax straight into the woman's mouth whereupon she spat it out onto the suspended girl's pussy and worked it over and inside her with the dildo.

So it continued for Marie. Scene after scene of wonderfully depraved sex. Beautiful girls like her, being punished, beaten, fucked, used and abused. Every part of her begged for orgasmic release but no part of her could oblige. The punishment continued for hours.

She heard a car pull up. It must have been midday by then. She had been tortured by the images and her own arousal for about four hours now, maybe longer. Please, she thought in desperation, please be Martin coming home to fuck me.

Her plea was answered. It was Martin in his suit and looking stern.

"I have had to change my entire day around because of your fuck up this morning," he said, emphasising the inconvenience she had caused.

"Anything," she said feebly.

"What do you mean? Make sense," Martin said impatiently.

"Anything. Do anything. Just let me have my hands free." Her hands were all she needed to quickly stroke her pussy to climax and release all that pent up arousal in a pounding orgasm.

"You'd love that wouldn't you? You haven't finished being punished yet, though, have you? Slut."

He undid his trousers and pulled his flaccid cock from his underpants. Straddling the chair he pushed his flesh into her face.

"Suck it."

She took the length of cock into her mouth with unequalled enthusiasm. Running her mouth over it and arousal where she burned with the agony and ecstasy of his thick cock thrusting into her cunt.

Freeing a hand Martin took up the lash and repeatedly struck down onto her tits and arms while he fucked vigorously at her dripping, stretched pussy. Red lines glowed over her skin.

It was too much. She had been so close and so desperate that any contact would have broken her open. Already, despite longing for this to last eternally, she was feeling small tremors of orgasm through her. She was coming, and then after a few breaths she felt it all again, those deep rooted tremors running through her coming again. These small ruptures of exquisite pleasure releasing inside her at regular intervals, like the regular swell and crash of waves on the beach.

The sensation made her throw her head back and close her eyes and scream out loud.

"Oh, Master. Oh, Master. I fucking love you so much my Master."

"Be quiet," he shouted back and lashed her breasts twice as hard.

He was fucking her quickly and powerfully. It was a hard fucking he was giving her, as hard as he had ever put her through. His urgency accelerated and his lashing of her tits and arms was relentless, somehow all coordinated in a perfect rhythm of pumping into her pussy and wielding the leather whip. Marie had her eyes closed and head back, mouth wide open in ecstasy, screaming out in a constant tangle pain and perpetual climax. She was burning with a violent, raging fire through the lips of her cunt and the flesh that lined her inside was dripping like a stream flowing out of her at that point where Martin's cock was invading her so mercilessly. It was terrible. It was as if she could be ripped in two. Everything she had, her whole body, rent in two starting at her pussy and all from the power of her

Master's fucking. All from the power of his fucking and his come.

She screamed as loudly as she had ever screamed. Her body quivered as though in an all-consuming convulsion, every part of her shaking uncontrollably. It felt as if she was splitting apart, the pain in her body too much to withstand, and she then let the fire in her cunt loose like a rocket through the rest of her body, beautiful and burning, explosions that hurt and delighted and calmed and excited all at the same time. As this happened as her pussy contracted involuntarily like a vice around Martin's cock, harder and tighter than she could have ever done willingly, and then the pressure squirted short bursts of her come past his cock and her tense pussy lips, soaking his pumping dick and slapping balls.

That was enough for Martin. He had watched with self restraint, enjoying the effect he was having on his captive slave and feeling very satisfied with the outcome. Now he had to come. His body would permit no more procrastination. It demanded release. Pulling out of her he pumped at his hard cock with his hand and sprayed out a thick, luscious, creamy rush of his spunk directly onto Marie's burning breasts. More and more shot out with Marie opening her mouth wide, hoping that he might shoot some onto her tongue.

Sinking breathlessly in the aftermath, Martin languidly rubbed his dick over Marie's come-covered breasts, spreading his semen like a salve for her burning red lines. He then sank down to his knees in a contented stupor.

Marie looked down at the man between her legs and smiled. She felt a deep happiness that went far beyond anything that she had ever conceived possible.

Already in her head she was scheming. Tomorrow she would disobey him again. He was sure to punish her hard.